PENGUIN BOOKS
PRIYA

Namita Gokhale is a writer, publisher and co-director of the Jaipur Literature Festival. Her books include the novels *Paro: Dreams of Passion*, *A Himalayan Love Story*, *Gods, Graves and Grandmother*, *The Book of Shadows* and *Shakuntala: The Play of Memory*; a short story collection *The Habit of Love*; and the non-fiction works *The Book of Shiva* and *Mountain Echoes: Reminiscences of Kumaoni Women*. She has also retold the Mahabharata for young readers and co-edited *In Search of Sita: Revisiting Mythology*.

PRAISE FOR THE BOOK

'A gripping tale of status, sex and power'—*DNA*

'A rare occurrence in fiction'—*Tehelka*

'The author's observations of the p3ps who colour Priya's life are acutely felt and painfully familiar to everyone who has tried to feel the pulse of Delhi'—*Outlook*

'A satire that takes potshots at today's politicians and well-heeled society'—*Indian Express*

'The hidden story is that of two Indias that are at odds with each other . . . one which is thriving and one which isn't'—*The Hindu*

In Incredible Indyaa

NAMITA GOKHALE

PENGUIN BOOKS

PENGUIN BOOKS
Published by the Penguin Group
Penguin Books India Pvt Ltd, 11 Community Centre, Panchsheel Park,
New Delhi 110 017, India
Penguin Group (USA) Inc., 375 Hudson Street, New York, New York 10014, USA
Penguin Group (Canada), 90 Eglinton Avenue East, Suite 700, Toronto,
Ontario, M4P 2Y3, Canada (a division of Pearson Penguin Canada Inc.)
Penguin Books Ltd, 80 Strand, London WC2R 0RL, England
Penguin Ireland, 25 St Stephen's Green, Dublin 2, Ireland (a division of Penguin Books Ltd)
Penguin Group (Australia), 707 Collins Street, Melbourne, Victoria 3008, Australia
(a division of Pearson Australia Group Pty Ltd)
Penguin Group (NZ), 67 Apollo Drive, Rosedale, Auckland 0632,
New Zealand (a division of Pearson New Zealand Ltd)
Penguin Group (South Africa) (Pty) Ltd, 24 Sturdee Avenue, Rosebank,
Johannesburg 2196, South Africa

Penguin Books Ltd, Registered Offices: 80 Strand, London WC2R 0RL, England

First published in Viking by Penguin Books India 2011
Published in Penguin Books 2013

10 9 8 7 6 5 4 3 2 1

This is a work of fiction. Names, characters, places and incidents are either the product of the author's imagination or are used fictitiously and any resemblance to any actual person, living or dead, events or locales is entirely coincidental.

ISBN 9780143415503

For sale in the Indian Subcontinent only

Typeset in Aldine401 BT by SÜRYA, New Delhi
Printed at Chaman Offset Printers, Delhi

To JE for challenging me to return to the territory of my first novel.

And to Paro, for remaining so triumphantly alive after all these years.

INFACT, I THINK ALL OF YOU SHOULD BE SHOT DEAD!

The Oberoi Hotel, New Delhi, 1982

So there we were, the five of us, quite companionable again, at the Café Chinois one evening, Suresh sipping his coffee like a bellows, Bucky and Paro devouring large cognacs, and Lenin spooning in mouthfuls of cassata ice-cream in between large gulps of whisky. Lenin had been baiting Bucky all evening, but Bucky had consistently refused to respond to any provocation.

Lenin was being elegantly withering, in a very erudite fashion, about the re-emergence of the feudal classes in modern India. 'The trouble with India, as I am sure you will agree,' he stammered condescendingly, 'is that as a breed you are all half-Anglicized, and half-denationalized. And completely irrelevant, if not treacherous, to any advanced society we may dream about or plan for. In fact, I think all of you should be shot dead!'

'I say, old boy, isn't that carrying it a little too far?' Bucky Bhandpur replied abstractedly, as one might to a pesky schoolboy. This infuriated Lenin even more, and he began addressing Bucky as 'Your Excellency', or 'Your Royal Highness', or 'Maharajkumar Sahib'. On his way to the toilet he even executed a low curtsy to Bhandpur, and reserved an even more elaborate 'Farshi Salaam' for Paro. She seemed tickled as a teenager at the idea of playing them off against each other, and tried subtly to push Bhandpur into a more aggressive stance. But he was far too seasoned a player to rise to such obvious bait.

THE PARTY HAD SPILLED ON TO THE TERRACE OF THE OBEROI HOTEL. Outside, a plump yellow moon roosted on the hump of an old tomb lining the greens of the Delhi Golf Club. I remembered how we used to come here, to the Café Chinois, with Paro and her posh friends, all those years ago.

Today's do was in the Mountbatten suite. It was to not celebrate but austerely 'announce' a new SEZ, a Special Economic Zone, for Food Processing and Allied Industries in Haryana. Three thousand acres of subsidized farmland sounds a bit excessive to set up a few canneries and French fries factories, but apparently it's just what Indian agriculture needs. Senior bureaucrats, junior politicians, assorted businessmen, flashy networkers, all got their power fix for the day as they gorged on kebabs and canapés and busily bowed and scraped and snubbed each other.

Everybody in Delhi knows everybody—everybody who matters, that is. As a jumped-up middle-class girl from Mumbai I still can't figure out these equations. Seek out the current lot of 'useful' people, scorn the hangers-on and despise those who might need you. That's the formula for Delhi social networking. It's in the air, this greed to be *somebody*, along with the benzene and the diesel fumes and the suspended particulate matter, and the dust from Rajasthan.

An attractive man wearing an insincere smile and a badly constructed toupee strutted across the terrace towards me. He sported a red tie, and a red silk handkerchief fanned out from the pocket of his double-breasted jacket. His flushed forehead was beaded with sweat. 'Hello,' he said, 'I'm Jimmy Batata, the Tomato Ketchup King of India.'

'Why not the Tomato Ketchup Emperor of India?' I enquired, my eyebrows arching up in amusement.

He found that funny. 'Well said, well said!' he exclaimed enthusiastically. 'Beauty and brains . . . indeed you are the mistress of both, Madame!' Saccharin or aspartame? Artificially sweetened chamchagiri, I thought to myself. But I would have been a little offended if he hadn't bowed and scraped in *some* manner. And I would have shown it, with a little disdain.

I'm somebody now. My husband Suresh Kaushal is the Minister of State for Food Processing, Animal Husbandry, Fisheries and Canneries. Maybe it's not an ATM ministry, like telecom or power, but agriculture is important to modern India, and Food Processing is crucial to agriculture. That's what Suresh says.

I began life as B.R.'s secretary. It's hard for a middle-class girl to suddenly find herself top of the heap. But I'm coping. Like the rest.

Suresh appeared and put his arm around me. 'Mr Batata's company plans to introduce genetically modified tomatoes to India,' he explained. 'They will have built-in multivitamins. It will change the life of India's farmers.'

For better or for worse, I wondered cynically, but not aloud. I am a politician's wife—I must act the part, and be supportive. Carefully readjusting the folds of my sari pallav, I bestowed upon Jimmy Batata a haughty smile. It's a curve of upper lip I practise sometimes, in the morning when I brush my teeth. A minister's-wife smile, modulated to establish who I am, where I stand. There is a trick to it—an easy trick. The smile must never reach your eyes, just hold itself in a tilt of lip.

Batata persisted with his conversation. 'Did you realize,' he said messianically—'do you know, Madame, that only Batata Red Sun tomato sauce is used in Hindi films instead of blood? It is a Bollywood special-effects tradition. Hero is dying, or villain or policeman or terrorist, farmer, moneylender—it is our ketchup only!' He clutched his red handkerchief in convincing demonstration.

Blood ketchup. The thought made me sick.

Mrs Jimmy Batata joined us. She was very large, her skin shone as brightly as the gold-dust fabric of her sari, and she was carrying a cheerful cherry coloured Dior bag. 'Did you know,' she said, 'tomato ketchup makes an excellent hair conditioner?'

I looked up at the dark sky and the jaundiced moon. A mischievous monsoon breeze was ruffling the potted bougainvillea. Snatches of conversation floated around me. A mobile trilled out a Bollywood tune. Distant fireworks announced a wedding procession.

'Let's face it—cricket is the new cash crop. Of course he denies being part of the IPL bidding consortium . . .'

'The EU Free Trade agreement . . .'

'Yes, tariff figures can be misleading, and commodity nomenclature is plain problematic . . .'

'In five years time, by 2010, India will be the largest arms importer in the world. And there are people who say this isn't progress!'

'Did you figure the Chief Minister of Karnataka has had an official makeover? He's moved from safari suits to Italian designer gear! Wants to change his son-of-the-soil image . . .'

'My son is graduating this summer from Wharton . . .'

'Our son is with Goldman Sachs in NY.'

'I must say, you can never know the meaning of hunger until you've been on a macrobiotic diet.'

'My new handbag . . .'

'I told him—"You must remember, India is the paradox of paradoxes . . ."'

A waiter rushed to light a heavyweight's cigar. A paper napkin rose with the breeze, and sailed into a bimbette's face, making her scream.

A pretty woman with a lined forehead was standing by the railing, looking out at the dimly-lit golf course below her. Suddenly she burst into quiet sobs. I saw her wipe her tears with the pallav of her cotton ganga-jamuna sari. I wanted to console her but didn't know what to say.

The waiters began circulating the soup—almond, not tomato—and the buffet dinner was laid out punctually by ten.

'Very classy,' Suresh commented approvingly as we left. 'The future is in SEZs.'

—

I had a flashback moment. I was twelve years old, in that other India of the late sixties, of socialist austerity and a ration economy. My mother was cooking dinner. The pressure cooker was hissing on the kerosene stove. (We had applied for a gas connection, but it took the intervention of a well-connected uncle and two years of waiting to finally get it.) One of our neighbours, whose balcony adjoined ours, had bought a new transistor radio. Mukesh drowned out the hiss of the cooker. 'Mera joota hai Japaani, yeh patloon Inglistani . . .'

I was day-dreaming, imagining Raj Kapoor's blue eyes looking into mine, when my mother's sister waddled in, importantly, swinging her imported handbag. Her son, who worked in the navy, had sent a bottle of Kraft cheese for us. I had never eaten processed cheese before. Paneer yes, but never cheese. Mother thought it a waste of money.

I knew of children in school who ate chips and cheese and drank Campa-Cola, but they were out of my league. My friends ate parathas or vada–pao and knew their place in life.

'We have brought for you imported cheese,' my aunt announced. We, not I, even though she had come alone. 'Didi, I want some bread. We will show you how to eat imported cheese.'

'No bread–shead in this house,' my mother declared unabashedly. The sisters warmed some stale chapatis and smeared them with Kraft cheese. One each for me, my mother, my aunt. Two for my brother, when he returned; he was a boy, the man of the house.

'This is how they eat in phoren countries,' my aunt explained knowingly.

'And also beef . . .' my mother added spitefully. 'That navy son of yours. I'm sure he's eating beef along with this Kraft cheese!'

That India. Those days.

—

It's a symptom of growing older when the past keeps replaying itself in your head, like a spool in a tape recorder when recorders still had spools.

It was Paro who showed me how the other side lived. Paro and BR, my boss, the sewing-machine magnate. Paro was BR's wife. She was an Amazon, an addiction. She was also selfish, cruel and consistently unkind. But something in Paro—her self-possession, her sheer gall, sparked a matching resistance in me. She taught me that life's rules can be bent by those who dare.

Paro—sexy, beautiful, destructive. All that I am not, then and now. Me—I'm just an ordinary housewife. A woman who has climbed up the ladder, step by determined step, with her husband's unexpected luck helping things along. I was Priya Sharma when Paro first met me, BR's lovelorn secretary; awkward, hungry for experience, eager for love.

Twenty-five years, now, since Paro died. Unbelievable, as I look back, how we have all changed. This new India, half dream, half nightmare, from which we might collectively awake. Paro would never have believed that our lives might continue after her, but they have. Loukas Leoros, that 'lonely stalker of reality', mourned her death by directing a darkly funny film on heterosexual marriage, winning him an Oscar nomination. He tied the knot with his assistant Tony soon after, and they appear happy together, happier by all accounts than he and Paro were. How nice it must be to switch one's partner's sex and find contentment.

The men in her life! Bucky Bhandpur, cricketer and philanderer, in his second innings now, always in the news with a ravishing celeb wrapped around him. He didn't need her then, he doesn't miss her now.

We who survived Paro. Lenin, devoted admirer, had later agitated for the landless in Madhya Pradesh. I haven't seen him in years. And BR—her first husband, my first boss. Dare I spell it out? Should I scribble over these lines? BR—my first lover. Wherever is he? I think of him often, dream of him sometimes. *If only* . . . I think to myself sometimes. *If only*.

IT'S THE 15TH OF AUGUST, INDEPENDENCE DAY. THE INDIAN FLAG flutters against the rusty sandstone ramparts of the Red Fort, the bands of orange, white and green dancing in the monsoon breeze. My sari pallav is billowing too, like a yacht in sail, and my hair, pulled back in a discreet ponytail, escapes the rubber band only to get stuck around my eyes, the Gucci shades no help at all.

'Saffron for sacrifice in need.' We sang that during morning assembly in school. The white had been for 'purity in every thought and deed'. And green? What did green stand for? I try, but can't remember, distracted by the Prime Minister's sometimes inaudible speech.

My husband leans across his chair and reaches for my hand. I observe him dispassionately. He is short and solemn, and the carefully styled silver in his hair makes him appear almost distinguished. Time has been kind to Suresh. It is difficult to imagine that he's the same plump, owlish lawyer 'of sober and decent habits' whose photograph my mother had brandished like a war-trophy when at last she received an offer of marriage for me, her only daughter, via her sister in Meerut.

Maybe Suresh is right—everything in our lives is fated by Saturn and Jupiter, sometimes Venus. Only the whims of destiny can explain how my stolid lawyer husband has risen to such dizzying heights of power. And Food Processing is only the first step. Perhaps in the next cabinet reshuffle, kismet could get even kinder.

Shahnawaz Sheikh, the doddering Minister for Minority Affairs, has fallen asleep in the seat beside me. His famously wide mouth, a caricaturist's delight, is open, as he snores to an unpredictable rhythm. A fly enters his mouth and heads for his throat. He chokes, begins to turn purple. I thump him on the back but this seems to make things worse. Rita Ray turns back from the seat in front and punches and pummels and throttles him until the fly escapes and returns to freedom.

The PM's speech is drawing to a close. He has been droning on, from his podium behind the bullet proof glass, about a new vision of a caring India. 'Our strength lies in the people,' he declares, 'in their unity in diversity. In the words of Pandit Nehru, spoken from these ramparts five score and ten years ago . . .' The men and women and schoolchildren herded and corralled below the ramparts are listening patiently. It has begun raining but that doesn't seem to bother them.

'Jai Hind!' the PM concludes at last. The notes of the national anthem swell and fill up the moisture-soaked morning. The people stand to attention. They unfurl their umbrellas, mostly black, some multicoloured, and prepare to leave the historic grounds and return to their daily lives.

We stand up too, in the VIP enclosure. There is a lump in my throat as the anthem soars towards the high notes at the end: *Jaya He! Jaya He! Jaya Jaya Jaya Jaya He!!!* We wait for the PM to leave. Everyone looks bored and impatient. The weather is hot and humid and sultry, and now that the annual chore is behind them, everybody is in a rush to return to the sanity of their air-conditioned lives and the reception in Rashtrapati Bhavan in the evening.

The Home Minister smooths his hair with a vain flick of his hand. It's an obsessive signature gesture. He's rumoured to have over five hundred pairs of shoes and as many colour coordinated safari suits. He blow-dries his tinted hair before every press encounter and changes outfits four times a day, sometimes five. Some say deciding which to wear is the only decision he takes in a day. As usual, only Rita Ray seems sprightly. She oozes the sophisticated self-confidence of a pedigreed third-generation politician with the right leftist family credentials. A large red bindi blazes like the Japanese flag upon her smooth pale forehead. Rita has just been appointed Minister of State for Power and Alternative Energy. The private power distribution companies are trembling with fear at the havoc she will surely wreak on their sweetheart deals and mega projections. It's been a month of horrific power cuts under her dispensation, though not of course in Lutyens' Delhi. 'All power corrupts,' Rita Ray exclaims with a wink, 'and absolute power corrupts absolutely. The light has gone out of our lives, and now the air-conditioning too!' It's not so funny really, but she can never resist taking a dig at Nehru, treating it as a duty, and the way she does it, it sounds somehow hilarious.

—

We get into the car, Suresh and I. It's the standard white Ambassador, with a whirring red bulb on top, and 'Power Brake' lettered on what the driver refers to as its 'backside'. Suresh insists on sticking to the antiquated Ambassador, resisting the other sleeker models available from the ministers' pool. The bodyguard on duty leaps into the front seat, hand on holster. There is silence as we drive home; Suresh meditates on the ways of destiny, as he often does, and I contemplate the past and the present.

'Western ascendancy is over,' he says, suddenly giving vent to some silent train of thought passaging his mind. 'After the recession, the future belongs to us. To India. And China. The green light on liberalization has brought us where we are today!' I try to focus on India that is Bharat, unfurling its potential economic glory before an astonished world. I fail. My mind is not on the green light on liberalization, but on the wedding we have to attend tomorrow.

Paro's son Aniruddha is getting married. Born of her rebellious affair with Bucky Bhandpur, Ani is the second-handsomest cricket hero in India. The reigning heart-throb of the game is of course stocky Gaurav Negi, the small-town boy from Haldwani with streaked shoulder-length hair. Ani's fiancée, supermodel Sujata Sethia (Suzi to the press) is the daughter of arms dealer Manoviraj Sethia. Bhandpur Junior's marriage to pouty Suzi is to be the shaadi of the season, an alliance between an arms dealer and a cricket dynast. Suzi dated Gaurav Negi before she settled for Ani's breeding and old money. Gaurav Negi has outgrown his 'humble' background, but his brother still runs a tea-stall somewhere, and his mother dyes her hair with henna and speaks no English. At the end of the day the elite stick together, they resist outsiders until they are so rich or important as to become irresistible. I know, I've watched.

The wedding is a 'No Press Event'—the tested way to ensure absolute media frenzy. Junior has stardust in his genes. His dimpled smile drives girls mad. There have been suicide attempts by grieving IPL fans because his days of philandering are officially over. It's sweet of Bucky to invite us, considering we've been out of touch for years. I've kept up with them though, via the magazine supplements and 24-hour television. Thinking about the wedding, I'm overtaken by anxiety; it's the forgotten feeling of inadequacy I always associate with Paro. What should I wear? What about the wedding gift?

'What about the wedding gift?' I ask Suresh, interrupting his further views on liberalization and the free economy.

'That's *your* department, Memsahib,' he chides. 'Give him a suit length. Or a silver photo frame. Or something . . .'

'A suit length?' I retort sharply. 'I've read that Ani only wears Armani. And every nobody will be giving them silver photo frames. Suzi is brand ambassador for . . . for . . .,' I fumble.

Suresh gives me a patient look, which only works me up the more. I've admired the handsome Raja of Bhandpur ever since the fateful night when we first met him with Paro. As Vice-President of the all-powerful Indian Cricket Board, Bucky has reincarnated with grace and style to the Indian Premier League buzz. A legendary sports administrator, he's set up the Premier Sports Academy in Gurgaon—the government gave him the land as a grant, since cricket is an educational/charitable activity. (Or is it social service?) Junior's success has cast a further backwash of glamour on Bucky. Between father and son, they endorse all sorts of products—fast cars, diet colas, health insurance. And a rebranded coconut oil.

Ani's bride-to-be Suzi is a silver spooner graduated to platinum. Her dad Manoviraj Sethia brokered the recent Russian submarine deal. Sethia's payoffs always manage to hit the goal; he has tackled all the right people in Russia and India, it's as much a sport, passion and profession to him as cricket to Bucky Bhandpur. What can I give that he has not already gifted? Now, if my husband was the Minister of Defence, or Telecom, or even Power—I could give the girl a set of 24-carat gold bowls then! But I'll stay within my aukat. A sterling silver tray, maybe, exquisitely designed, with both their names inscribed on it in italics.

We halt at the red lights at the Purana Qila crossing, where vultures used to squat on the domes of Mughal tombs until pollution and pesticides killed them off. A beggar woman is peddling the national flag to celebrate Independence Day. Her nose is pressed flat against the window, her eyes fixed on Suresh. The rings on his podgy fingers, each to appease a particular planet, flash as the man of destiny waves her away with impatient outrage. Red coral to propitiate Mars, blue sapphire to appease Saturn. A diamond for good measure, and to strengthen Venus. He's hedged his bets, got all the planets covered.

I let him, and then the driver, glower at the woman and send her away. I'd hate to do it myself.

—

It's always calming to return home: 18 Dara Shikoh Marg, in the green and quiet heart of a dusty, impatient nation. I guess it's a government bungalow like any other, but I'm still intimidated by its size. The gates clang shut behind us, the saluting guards revert to their customary slouches. Inside, a chill double load of air-conditioning copes with the high ceiling. Suresh watches the news with such intent focus that it is almost an out-of-body experience. Gently, with a practice born of years, I transport him towards the dining room. The Garhwali cook, Ram Singh, is on leave. He takes his national holidays seriously. His Bihari helper, Ramdhan, has assembled the dal, roti and two vegetables that have sustained us through thirty years of marriage. There's a glass of lassi, with Splenda instead of sugar, and the gajar-shalgam pickle my husband is addicted to.

We eat in silence. Through the low hum of the air conditioning I can hear the cawing of crows in the garden. Then, as usual,

Suresh strokes his stomach, mildly, with an air of satisfaction. He coaxes an appreciative burp, like an amen. 'It was a simple meal, but wholesome,' he says, 'thank you, Priya, for being such a caring wife.'

This is part of the ritual too. When we first met, the burping would unsettle me, I found it vulgar; now it is a routine, reassuring conclusion to our meals together. I try to catch his eye with a smile. He is busy with the remote, switching channels on the flat-screen television mounted over the mantelpiece, until the flickering pixels resolve into the familiar face of the Prime Minister, still talking about a new vision of a caring India.

In the evening, the President's At Home. There's something about those weathered old stones, and the size and the scale and grandeur of Rashtrapati Bhavan, that takes ones breath away. It was drizzling slightly, so the venue had been moved to the Ashoka Hall. 'Due to inclement weather,' as a gallant ADC explained.

The President looked more wizened than ever, like a kindly walnut. Madam wore an exquisite double ikat handloom sari. It was all a rush and a blur, with everybody seeming to know everyone else. Except me. I felt like a fly on the wall, observing the politicians and generals and admirals and ambassadors talk and laugh and joke with the assured ease of People Who Matter.

'Don't feel intimidated,' I instructed myself. 'These are just people, no different from anybody else.' I took a deep breath and looked up. The elegant imperial chandeliers had cheap white-light ecobulbs screwed on them. 'And this is just a place like anywhere else.'

I sampled the samosas and sandwiches. A fly circled vigilantly over the platter of assorted pastries, like a drone aircraft. The electronic insect-repellant machines mounted upon the venerable wood-panelled walls crackled every now and then, feasting on incarcerated insects. An important politician trod on my toe.

As we were leaving, there was a whir of wings and a plop of wet on my hair and shoulders. A pigeon had shat on me. Suresh extracted a gray-bordered handkerchief from his pocket and helped me wipe the mess away. 'Don't worry,' he said consolingly. 'It's considered very lucky if a bird does that to somebody.'

—

Both the boys are away. Kush is attending a 'Training Leaders of Tomorrow' course sponsored by the MacDougal Foundation. His twin Luv is bumming around somewhere in New Mexico. It's only me at home, and Suresh, spread out thin over this enormous official residence.

A lazy afternoon, and me padding barefoot through the house in a comfortable cotton petticoat and t-shirt, admiring the high ceilings, the columned drawing room, the breezy verandah. I grew up in a 1 BHK flat in Bombay—it wasn't Mumbai then, although Andheri was of course more Bumbai than Bombay. The One Bedroom Hall Kitchen label was a genteel exaggeration—there wasn't even a kitchen, truthfully, just a bedroom and a hall and the makeshift stove in our tiny balcony. My mother, my brother Atul and I; the flat was large enough for all of us, stretching to accommodate the occasional visiting relative.

I actually pinch myself sometimes to check that it's real, this house and me in it. I can't get enough of the sprawling lawns, with their neat flowerbeds and mysterious hedges. The British built the imperial city of New Delhi to rule over us Indians. There are those who want to put high-rises here. It's practical, of course, but I'll go along with the netas and the babus who will never let it happen. The world may need more houses, but I love this old colonial bungalow. Two and a half acres in the heart of New Delhi, with two and a half malis to tend it. One gardener for one acre, that's the thumb rule with the NDMC.

The Delhi obsession for a private shorthand drives me mad. I've learnt to decrypt it, though, and the acronyms roll smoothly off my tongue now—NDMC, MCD, DDA, CPWD, CP, GK, NDSE, and the rest. I've grown accustomed to conversations like 'The

HM told his MoS to tell his PA to write a DO note to tell the MCD to liaise with the CPWD about the RTI.' Think of it as the DAS—the Delhi Acronym Syndrome. In this city, you can't survive if you don't know the code.

With most people, it's life's disappointments that leave them bitter and broken. It's different with me—the dizzying climb, the 'appointment', if you please, has left me a little undone, like a bit of knitting where the stitches have slipped off the needle and unfurled themselves. I propped Suresh up, in the early days, I supported his ambitions as we huffed along the treadmill of Delhi society. Now I can't believe I'm up here, near the top of the heap, my husband a neta, a rising political figure, a minister in the government. I should be brimming with confidence, not consumed by this precarious unease. You could say that I'm a victim of social vertigo, teetering on the edge of imagined rejections.

Why don't I have more friends? My own fault, possibly, for not being able to reach out to people. I was so wrapped up in motherhood that I gave up on the rest. And then, suddenly, this large Lutyens bungalow and the shrinking space inside.

But I have my diaries. These lined notebooks, the secret thoughts and confidences that I entrust them, keep me going. The words laid out in my neat, spiky handwriting are my anchor, locked in my steel Godrej almirah, piled over the years under a heap of discarded silk saris where no one can find them.

—

I retain a middle-class passion for steel cupboards. Home is where the steel cupboard is—that's my philosophy. They stand guard in the spare bathroom, with built-in extra-security digital safes. That's where I stash away money saved from the housekeeping, and the wads of spare cash that Suresh sometimes entrusts to my care. All the 'official' and 'unofficial' gifts, fruit bowls, shawls, silver plates, silver-plated plates, things like that, are loaded into my steel cupboards.

I searched for a wedding present for Junior Bhandpur. Silver statuettes of Krishna the charioteer discussing the nature of duty with Arjun are a stock gift to politicians. There were two in filigree work and one in solid silver. Expensive enough; and cultural heritage is usually a safe bet. I bundled the larger filigree piece in bubble wrap and then silver paper, secured with a gold ribbon. And, finally, my husband's official gold-embossed ministerial visiting card, with all our names on it: 'Love From Uncle Suresh, Aunty Priya, Luv and Kush.'

Got a missed call from Luv, and a message. 'BK SN' it said. 'FLT DTLS FLW.' My son's cryptic textese infuriates me—why can't people simply spell things out?

'GR8' I replied. Luv hadn't phoned or mailed for some days now. His phone had been switched off too. I'd been worrying about Luv, I guess mothers never stop.

Twins are meant to be alike, peas in a pod, but my sons Luv and Kush are the exceptions to prove the rule. It puzzles me, this difference in the way they are, and it troubles me too. Luv is the older by a few minutes, and he is taller and fairer and—let's face it—kinder. They do look similar, but Kush is shorter and stockier, and for some reason had begun to go bald just into his twenties. He shaved his head so it wouldn't be so noticeable. Or so he believed.

Kush quit his investment banker career in NY some months back and returned home. 'I want to scope out the political scene,' he announced to his father. 'I think my country needs me.' He commandeered the guestroom annexe in the front lawn and turned it into a studio apartment. The spare key is always with Ramdhan. I am discouraged from violating his space.

'It's about boundaries,' he told me, his brown eyes turning opaque as he spoke. 'I can't handle a spillover of maternal feelings any more. Please take this in the right spirit.'

And I did. I do. It's Luv who is my unabashed favourite. Why should I pretend otherwise? Kush is the apple of Suresh's eye, so it's fine, in balance. Kush has been shadowing his father, getting into position to 'enter politics'. Some people may call it dynasty, but Kush calls it 'family succession'.

'Face it,' he said to me after he returned from NY, 'if Papa were still a lawyer, chances are I would inherit his practice. If he was a doctor or a dentist, I might have considered a career in medicine. If he was a famous film star—' (at which point I raised my eyebrows and tried not to smile at this absurd idea) '—if Papa was a famous film star I would possibly be a Bollywood hero. So if he is destined to rule the country, it's only logical to think that I am too.'

His elder twin, Luv, had told me only days before this that he was destined to be an artist. There are no artists in our family, so that was a new gene acting itself out. He believed in challenging his creativity, he said, which was another excuse for pretty much doing as he pleased. He was still untraceable, but would doubtless turn up soon, to disarrange our lives.

—

Bano, the 'beauty lady', comes home on call to wax and wash and blow dry. Her inspired gossip updates me on the goings-on in Delhi, as it did while she shone me up for Junior Bhandpur's wedding. Bano had layered my face with a crushed rose pack. My eyes were blinkered with sliced potatoes, to take care of the dark shadows. I sensed her fussing around, buffing my nails, massaging my feet, while she fed me a steady drip of information on the activities of the great Delhi Durbar. I felt inadequate, even apologetic, for having so little to trade in terms of interest and scandal in my personal life.

'Do you know, Priya didi, that Rita Ray madam is wearing wig? Bechari! Big black hair all over her body, everywhere except on her baldy head! So sad, no?'

I was silent from under the fragrant but itchy face pack. 'I charge her fifteen hundred rupees only for waxing her stomach,'

Bano continued in her sing-song English. 'Double-charge, more than other clients, but it grow back also double fast. Four times faster than my French lady. Not like your smooth malai-type body, didi!'

I smiled under the mask. I could feel it cracking up. 'Other day, my lady client's son wants full-body waxing. Metro-sexual look, he say. I say, no baba, no hetro-metro, I am old-fashioned beauty lady, for ladies only.'

A note of righteousness entered her voice. 'In Delhi, we all have to fill our belly. It is survival city, we have to put up with all kind of peoples!'

Bano peeled off the mask and exclaimed at how my skin was glowing. She left, as always, amidst a flurry of insincere compliments, surreptitiously counting my habitually ungenerous tip. I wondered what she has to say about me!

—

The wedding was at the Amrana Fort, on the Jaipur highway. The card specified the dress code. 'Boy's Side: Batting in White. Girl's Side: Men and Memsahibs in Blue.' I decided on an expensive white Upada silk, which the boutique owner had described as 'subtle'. Young girls these days seem to have given up on the sari. There's a comfort in wearing six yards of unstitched fabric that's difficult to explain. The trick lies in the pleats. When you get the first fold right, the rest follow. Draping the pallav a little off-shoulder, I checked my reflection in the looking glass. It looked much too understated, so I slapped on some bronzer on my cheeks, coated my eyelids with glittery green shadow and smiled at the mirror. Maybe I'm looking better as I grow older, I thought. Or just more used to the way I look.

WE LEFT TOGETHER FOR AMRANA, SURESH AND I, IN OUR WHITE Ambassador car, with a light flashing on top and our power statement, the PSO—Personal Security Officer—perched importantly on the front seat. The gift-wrapped chariot was in the boot, with our overnight bags. Traffic choked the unfinished highway through Gurgaon. Everywhere, new cars and new money, old potholes and tall skeletons of steel and glass. Delhi is changing so much every day, growing and cannibalizing its outskirts. A crowd of carefully-ragged teenagers spilled out of a multiplex and moved to the adjacent Barista with the outrageous confidence of the very young and the very affluent. They made me nervous. I remembered a distant aunt who lived in Gurgaon. I had visited her as a child, a lifetime ago. A buffalo was tethered in her backyard and we were gifted a handi of fresh ghee when we left. Perhaps she's still alive. She'd be a multi-crorepati now, if she's had the good sense to sell off her land to some BPO or shopping mall. Perhaps she's had a face lift and is driven around in a BMW.

In the shadow of a bent-over hoarding, a sunburnt family was cooking a meal on the broken kerb. The couple were arguing bitterly as the children watched and a brass pot bubbled over a smoky three-brick street hearth. The man raised his hand to hit the woman, then took her plaited hair and pulled at it violently. She spat in his face. The children turned to stare at the traffic. The signal changed and we edged on.

Even the VIP red light couldn't push us through the chaos any faster. It kept the beggars away, though; they understand not to pursue cars with flashing lights on them and save their entreaties for lesser folk.

Suresh was more relaxed than he had been for a long time. He put his arm around me, quite cautiously, as though I might rebuff him. I saw the driver watching in the mirror—might it give him ideas? The road got better soon, and a mild drizzle made the lights outside look mellow and gentle. I told the driver to put on some music, a nice ghazal, if he could find one. We were going so slowly he didn't need to stop the car while he fumbled with the stack of CDs in the dashboard.

'Ae Mohabbat, Tere Anjam Pe Rona Ayaa . . .' Begum Akhtar's scratchy molten voice enveloped us in romance and regret.

'Can't we listen to something more catchy?' Suresh asked. I shook my head, and pressed closer to him, against his arm, lost to the world outside. I was drowning in the music and it took me some time to register that the car had stopped. The PSO opened the door, leaned out, then quickly pulled it shut again. The driver stepped out very cautiously and then he was back inside, too. 'Lock your door, Priya,' Suresh said urgently, 'we seem to have run over somebody.'

A crowd had gathered. There were no houses for miles around, only silence and darkness and low hills, and I couldn't imagine where they might have materialized from. They seemed, all of them, to have beards of the stubbly unshaven sort. They were carrying staves and rods and sticks. Then I saw some sheep, grey blobs in the dusk, escorting the men, looking up enquiringly at their angry faces.

'I saw blood on the tyres!' the PSO exclaimed. 'Let me contact the control room!'

Wireless static hit against the soft strains of Begum Akhtar's voice. 'Hullo Patrol room?!! Hullo Patrol Room!?' The PSO was squeaking, his habitual bravado gone.

'Turn the damn music off!' Suresh shouted, a note of panic in his voice. 'Don't you have any sense?!' It wasn't clear whom this was addressed to.

The bearded men had now surrounded the car. They seemed to be very upset. 'Have we killed someone?' I asked.

'I'll fix them,' the security officer declared, his hand on his holster. Opening the door a crack, he stepped out like a bad thief, exiting sideways. The driver leaned over to lock the door after him.

'Can't the fools see that this is a VIP car?' Suresh asked. 'Can't they see the flashing lights?'

No one had an answer to this.

The security man rushed back in and locked the door again.

'A goat has died, or a dog, perhaps,' he reported, 'crushed under the front left tyre. But they insist that a child has been run over.'

'Drive on,' Suresh said imperiously, but with a quaver in his voice.

I opened the door. 'Let's find out!' I said, suddenly unwilling to be part of this scene from a bad film or novel. I was surprised to hear myself say: 'If a child has been run over we must take it to the nearest hospital.' The evening was settling into night as I stepped out, dark clouds lowering in the monsoon sky. From the corner of my eye I glimpsed a movement. A child emerged from under the car, at the speed of light, and rushed towards the circle of angry men. In an instant, their faces changed, were washed with tenderness. I dashed back inside the car. 'Hurry up,' I told the driver. 'Quickly. Let's get going!'

We sped off. Just as we were leaving, a police patrol car pulled up. We didn't stop. The PSO told them of what had happened in confused bursts; the static in the walkie-talkie was acting up.

I pressed the glass down and turned back to look. The child was nestling against the protective cordon of the crowd. The policemen were taking notes, the men were shouting and waving their staves. There was a textured look to it, like a moment frozen in a grainy black-and-white photograph.

The driver picked up speed again. The music had returned too, and Begum Akhtar's voice filled up the white-towelled interior of the car: 'Jaane Kya Baat Hai, Kis Baat Pe Rona Ayaa . . .' As we neared the next town, we found a gaily lit halting point that had been set up for the Kanwaria pilgrims, on their Shrawan pilgrimages. It's the same story every monsoon—young boys from villages off to see the city lights, with religion providing the occasion. Disco devotionals blared into the night, silencing Begum Akhtar's sweet melancholy. Hundreds of single-minded young men, dressed in an east-west mix of t-shirts and sneakers and faded orange lungis and dhotis and kachhas, carrying containers of sacred water from the Ganga to their villages. Was this tourism? Was this religion? And what if we ran over any of them? We'd be lynched, I was sure of that.

A young man in a Che Guevara t-shirt and dusty dhoti slapped the car appreciatively. He peered in from the window and whistled at me. He was brandishing a cell phone; perhaps he was taking a photograph. The security officer reached for his holster, but the young pilgrim had disappeared back into the crowd.

'Drive very slowly please!' Suresh said to the driver, entreating rather than scolding. 'Dilli ki dadagiri yahin rah jayegi. Your flashing lights and sirens will get you nowhere if that lot decides to take you on.'

The driver looked chastised. He switched the music off and we drove sombrely through the highway, pondering the real India and our close shave with it.

'Can you imagine Paro's son getting married and all that?' I said chattily. I had to break the solemn silence that seemed to have descended upon us. 'If only she were alive to see this day!'

'Those whom the Gods love die young,' Suresh responded, nodding his head sagely with the carefully cultivated solemnity which has covered him like a new skin.

'The Gods did not love Paro!' I replied impetuously. 'She was a difficult, selfish woman. The Devil would enjoy her company.' I said this partly to irritate my husband, to unsettle him. Increasingly, he has that effect on me.

He didn't like that, Suresh didn't. 'You were always jealous of her, Priya,' he said. 'She was so beautiful, and she was a great lady. You sound so vindictive sometimes.'

His remark hurt me, it was too close to the bone. 'She may have been a great lady,' I retorted, controlling the agitation this conversation had unleashed. 'But she was not a good person. She was foolish and inconsiderate and managed to hurt all those who loved her.'

Suresh looked at me, a little surprised by the outburst.

Would she never let me go?

The fort was outlined in flickering fairy lights against the dark monsoon sky. Tall, turbaned men holding earthen lamps stood stationed beside a row of sneering camels. Eleven PYTs in white and blue saris were posted at the entrance—I counted. Suresh shook hands with each of them in turn. But it was clear the Pretty Young Things were on the lookout for the 'chief' chief guests; they did not recognize mere Ministers of State—or need to.

Bucky Bhandpur, in a white linen suit, received us at the main gate. His slightly protruding teeth somehow only added to his taut elegance. He was, after all, a Rajput, from a minor thikana, and blue blood shows through in these things. Once a royal always a royal. Even Indira Gandhi couldn't end that when she cancelled their privy purses in 1971! Bucky squeezed my hand affectionately and gave Suresh an enthusiastic *yaari*-type hug. The father of the bride, Manoviraj Sethia, was next in line to greet the guests. He seemed distracted, and his eyes were fixed on the front gate. Who was due?

Celebrity faces glow with the self-possession that comes from being observed and stared at. They are constantly on parade. I ogled them unabashedly, with the shaky confidence of being almost, if not quite, one of them. It was a heady mix of khadi-clad politicians, suited businessmen and arms dealers, carelessly shabby journalists, diplomats, expats, and glamorous women with boob-jobs. The film stars and cricket stars were like fixed islands in their midst, models and society ladies waving and undulating around them. The royals, or ex-royals, as Suresh correctly refers to them, stood out with their khandaani airs.

Suddenly, both Bucky Bhandpur and Manoviraj Sethia rushed to the reception area. The 'chief' chief guest had arrived! Craning my neck, I glimpsed a tall, lean man in a buttoned-up bundgala suit, wearing a monocle over his right eye. He had a limp, or perhaps a club foot, for he dragged his right leg as he walked. Maybe he wore the monocle to deflect attention from his leg, I thought.

Behind him, walking slowly to stay in step, was the handsomest cricketer in India, Gaurav Negi. Bucky and his sambandhi Manoviraj Sethia were both deferentially keeping pace as well. The penny dropped—this had to be Dhruv Desai, President of the Indian Cricket Board.

The sight of Gaurav Negi provoked an electric thrill among the celebrity guests—a moment of hushed silence and then an extra buzz of animated chatter. A stylish woman in a purple backless choli lunged through the crowd of socialites and flung herself at Negi. She let out an elegant whoop and landed him a kiss full on the lips. Dhruv Desai looked annoyed at the interruption, while Bhandpur and Sethia stood very straight and observed the scene with polite detachment, as though this was normal behaviour for women guests at Indian weddings. Negi tried to step back, and collided into a waiter carrying a tray. A glass of wine leapt into the air and emptied itself over Desai, Negi, and the woman in the backless choli. It was a classic slapstick moment, and I would have laughed out loud, had I not looked by accident into Dhruv Desai's eyes.

Desai's eyes were blank with rage. He lashed out with his cane, striking the waiter on his shoulders with swift, savage strokes. Other waiters had materialized with napkins and jars of water. 'It's good luck!' Bucky said with forced gaiety. Sethia was scrubbing the backless choli with enthusiasm. The moment passed, and I slid away, somehow unnerved.

Members of the Sethia clan led us up successive levels of the fort. The bride and groom weren't in sight, so I handed over the unwieldy gift to an officious looking relative. When I turned back, I had lost Suresh. Rita Ray, the power minister, spent a few minutes making condescending 'what a pretty sari' conversation. I was staring at her hair to see if it was really a wig, as Bano the beauty lady had claimed, when I saw her eyes set into a fixed glaze. Rita was staring over my shoulder at somebody. It was Queenie Kwatra, the reigning Mumbai QB, epitome of glamour. They air kissed and murmured affectionate salutations. 'And what do *you* do?' Queen Bee asked me, with a convincing show of interest, before her eyes switched off too, and they both moved on to greet a yet more important guest in the food chain. Such is life.

As a mere homemaker, I am accustomed to the peculiar disdain with which my species is treated. 'And what do you do?' successful and powerful women ask me, if they manage to finish the sentence, the condescension sprinkled like black peppercorns in their voices.

'Oh nothing really. I worked in a bookshop, once . . .' I reply, playing along. A strained mask falls over their faces. Powerful women don't ascend the stratosphere for nothing. The fact that I'm a housewife—a non-person outside the pale of the human rights ordinances—shines through the bookshop façade.

Sometimes, it's easier. 'Oh, so you are Suresh Kaushal's wife, are you?' they probe, these MDs of banks and CEOs of technology firms.

'Yes,' I reply truthfully. Then they decide to be nice to me, to the poor housewife, for I have my foot in the pecking order after all and, maybe, the ear of my husband. They talk of Delhi and Bangalore traffic and of children and of pollution and try hard to demonstrate their goodwill. As you can tell, I don't enjoy these encounters. That's why I prefer to keep to myself.

An arms dealer's wife was attempting polite conversation. Wife or mistress? Her plump, smooth arms were encircled with diamond encrusted tagdis. A midnight-blue chiffon sari, studded with Swarovski crystals, was draped snugly around her swelling breasts. Her sari blouse was just a strategic cluster of Swarovski glitter, more illusion than garment. Shocking! Or was that envy?

'Howveryoo?' she chirped, in authentic Delhi dialect. 'Can I get you a glass of champagne? Myself Pooonam!' She pointed to herself as she spoke. 'With three Os, not two. And you are Mrs Suresh Kaushal?'

I wasn't sure if that was a statement or a question. Pooonam shook her head this way and that as she spoke. Her blonde-streaked chignon, covered with crystal danglers, swayed like a chandelier in a breeze. She had, I guessed, been sent to stalk me, to charm and 'cultivate' me, in case my up-and-coming politician husband ever moved to a more useful portfolio. She looked delectable, though a little stale, like a soufflé that's begun to settle.

'Yes, I'm Priya Kaushal,' I replied, and then we stared at each other, both at a loss for words. She was struggling to step ahead with the conversation, I could see that.

'Your sari is so simple,' she ventured at last. 'It is so . . . Swadeshi. A plain cotton with a simple zari border . . . Is it because your husband is a politician?' There was a note of genuine wonderment in her voice.

I looked at her plump pretty face and her silly hairdo and her extravagant sari and didn't know quite how to respond. There was something vulnerable about her, a sort of girlish high-school charm, under the glamour. 'It's an Upada silk, actually,' I ventured. 'It only looks like cotton because the count is so fine . . .'

Here I was, apologizing and explaining to strangers. Why? 'Don't be so pathetic, Priya Kaushal,' I told myself firmly, and moved into the conversational fray.

'Are you Mrs Khosla?' I asked. She was somehow associated with one of the arms dealers, I was sure of that.

'Oh, I'm Pooonam UmaChand,' she replied in a proud defensive tone. 'I'm a Director in Manoviraj Sethia's company. In Universal Hand Tools and Weapons Ltd. And what do *you* do?'

So she was his mistress. I ignored the question. 'And those stunning arm-clasps—do you wear them because you are an arms dealer?'

I thought she might be offended by the silly joke; it had been my defence against her cotton sari remark. But Pooonam UmaChand burst into peals of genuine laughter. 'Hov funnnneeee!' she gasped. 'What a great sense of humour you have. Oh dear!' and another bout of giggles. 'I must tell that one to Manoviraj. I think we will be friends for life, Priyaaa!'

Her giggles disarmed me. People don't laugh much in Delhi, not in the circles I seem to move in, anyway. We chatted companionably for a while. 'I'm sooo tired,' my new friend sighed. 'We are all partied out. Especially us girlz! Four days of continuous mazaaa. We slept after breakfast today. Even Ani and Suzi!'

'Where are they?' I asked eagerly. Junior and his bride were nowhere in sight.

Pooonam giggled again. 'Ouff, they'll turn up. The newlyweds will crawl out from their bedsheets when they are through . . .' she whispered suggestively, as though she had, too. She was playing with the loose strands of her streaked hair as she spoke; her chignon was beginning to come undone. Had she dressed in too much of a hurry?

A sudden movement in the crowd and there they were, the bride and groom. They looked like young gods or immortals. I was so proud to have known this young man as a little boy. A line of guests had assembled to greet them and I waited for my turn.

'Your mother Paro was my friend, beta,' I told Junior, after I had nudged my way through the press of people. 'You wouldn't remember. I'm Priya . . . Priya Kaushal.'

A look of boyish delight flooded his grey-green eyes. Paro's eyes. 'Priya Aunty!' he exclaimed. 'Of course I remember. You were the bestest kindest aunty ever.' The dazzling Suzi gave me a dazed nod. She was, as Pooonam had suggested, clearly partied out. Then I was jostled away by an impatient power couple. But Junior's words stayed with me. I was content, for that moment, to be a kindest aunty and not a glamorous celebrity.

Suresh had disappeared, as had my new friend Pooonam UmaChand. I made my way to the ladies room to repair my lipstick. Two feminine voices were engaged in an intense conversation from across the carved-wood toilet cubicles.

'That Pooonam UmaChand is a real cheez, yaar,' a voice trilled from the corner loo. 'Manoviraj's ex-wife just can't stand her. Sunita Sethia kicked up a huge fuss about her being invited here. But then Pooonam has Manoviraj and his Hand Tool company by the you-know-what! Did you see her trying to play hostess right under Sunita's nose?'

'My husband calls her the Exocet—a top-range guided missile. Aim and shoot! Pooonam's trying to suck up to Sethia's daughters now,' the other voice replied.

I grimaced mechanically at my reflection, to check if my lipstick was applied evenly. I had been warned.

When I returned to the suddenly-less-crowded party, I found the PSO searching for Suresh. 'Sahib is missing . . . got lost,' he said. 'This is a big security problem. I must find him.'

'Look in the gents' toilet,' I said. A passing waiter thrust yet another glass of champagne on me.

Where could he be?

I downed the champagne in a quick nervous gulp. My head was buzzing, not an unpleasant feeling. I had been hovering uncertainly on the outskirts of the party, but now Shriela Shetty, the gossip diva, took me under her wing. Shriela wields an acid pen and her column, 'Pssst', takes the piss out of just about everyone. Maybe I'm too insignificant for scandal fodder, so she's kind to me.

'I am here as a friend, Priya,' she smiled, 'not as a media person.' She examined the glass of champagne in her hands, then gulped it down as though it were a truth serum. 'Do you want to know why Suzi Sethia dumped Gaurav Negi to marry Junior Bhandpur?' she asked, a werewolf sort of expression moving into her sculpted features.

Of course I did not, I said. Shriela began testing her speculations on me. Social snobbery apart, it was a pragmatic arranged marriage to protect the Sethia-Bhandpur sports cartel. Bucky Bhandpur owed Manoviraj Sethia an enormous sum of money and the marriage was a safeguard, a sort of IOU. Besides, Dhruv Desai's daughter was in love with Negi. Some people said that it was Dhruv Desai who was in love with Negi and had the younger man's name tattooed across his posterior. Each of these conjectures was prefaced by a disclaimer: 'I don't know why people get upset with my column . . .' Shriela would smile, flashing a set of flawless teeth.

Shriela began again on newly minted gossip, how the Minister for Civil Aviation was always abroad, in the company of . . . But she could no longer hold my attention. Ved Anand was standing before me, in the flesh. The evergreen hero of Bollywood, the one and only Ved Saheb. When I was young, my heart had belonged, briefly but intensely, to the filmstar Rajkumar Khanna. Ved

Anand was a generation ahead, the greatest and truest romantic of Hindi films. Even in my dreams he was out of my league. I was happy just to stare at him, at his youthfully crinkled eyes, his creased and gallant smile. He was just as happy to be stared at. A crush of fans, assistants, hangers-on, were all fussing over him, bursting into ingratiating laughter in anticipation of his every wisecrack. I basked in the halo of his unfading charm, wishing my mother was alive to view me in such filmi glory.

Then, a roll of drums and a pretty girl in a golden lehnga walked into the spotlight. 'Hi and Hello everybody—I'm Suzi's sister Suki,' she announced. 'Ani's saali, though not his aadhi gharwali.' Catcalls from the distinguished audience. 'On behalf of the Families—Bhandpur and Sethia—I want to announce a special Family Entertainment, humbly presented for our Esteemed Guests!'

Bucky Bhandpur and Manoviraj Sethia, the two samdhis, both dressed now in cricket gear, boogied into the spotlight and took a bow. Then they launched into a song and dance number from *Lagaan*. 'Chale Chalo! Chale Chalo!' they sang. Or perhaps they lip-synched it, I really couldn't tell. The women of the family joined them, glittering in designer lehngas, earthen pots balanced on their heads. Or perhaps they were strapped on. Everyone was having a great time. A GR8 time. We are like that only.

'In the old days, films were entertainment,' Ved Saheb remarked. 'But now everything is entertainment. Everything. Politics is entertainment. Cricket is entertainment. IPL is *mega* entertainment. Not only marriage, even divorce is entertainment.'

I looked at him with awe. 'You are so right!' I exclaimed. 'I never thought of it like that before . . .'

'Even war is entertainment now,' he continued. 'We filmstars are being edged out of business, except when we are having affairs!'

Suki had seized the mike again, and was presenting a hot Bollywood dance number to the latest cheeky lyrics, to do with a mofussil-sounding pain relieving balm. Of the kind her grandmother would have stopped using when she sped up the society ladder. There was a fog machine and a hidden orchestra, and every so often Suki would thrash her head from side to side and lift up the hem of her glimmering golden skirt to display her long legs. I wondered if she was on drugs. She concluded her vigorous performance to enthusiastic applause. 'Ladies and Gentlemen, Bhaiyon aur Beheno, now for the Food of Love! Dinner is served!' she announced, to a concluding roll of drums.

It was a wedding feast of staggering proportions. The tables groaned with khaana, Italian and Thai and Mexican, crabs, oysters and salmon, tacos and spring rolls, noodles and sushi, pasta and paella, shahi paneer and shepherd's pie—typical Delhi fare that no sane person would assemble on the same plate at home. This international menu was laid out in alphabetical order. I walked my way through aaloo, anchovies, artichokes, arvi and asparagus, all the way to zucchini and zabaglione. It was unsettling to see so much food on display. Women in Delhi never seem to eat anything, yet they are usually obese and talk compulsively about their weight. I was getting there. I had to be careful.

Bucky had not forgotten his ancestry and there was a separate section of traditional Rajput food set up by the swimming pool. This was where Shriela and I now gravitated, following Ved Saheb and his acolytes. It was full Rajasthani fare, lal meat, and dal baati churma, things like that, served in gleaming bowls and shining silver thalis.

Into my second fried mawa kachauri, I observed my husband emerge from the side entrance. Suresh was walking with an unfamiliar macho strut, both jaunty and cautious, and something in his gait alerted me. He was followed by the glamorous Pooonam, she of the three os, Pooonam who had only just professed her friendship and admiration for me. What were they doing together?

I turned around to check if Shriela had noticed, but her normally mischievous eyes were hooded and blank.

I didn't confront him. Of course two people can walk out of a corner together, can't they, without suspicious wives jumping to lurid conclusions? Suresh came and sat beside me. 'I've been searching for you everywhere, jaan,' he said. 'I was worrying about where you were.' I don't think he noticed that I didn't believe him.

The Rajput power-group gave Suresh an enthusiastic welcome. I got him some basundhi and jalebis and some for myself, and we settled down to enjoy the remains of the feast.

Bucky had changed back from cricket gear into his white linen suit. He introduced us to a devastatingly handsome man with a cleft chin and a dramatic wing of grey hair. 'This is Janab Imran Aziz, the new Pakistani High Commissioner,' he said. 'His Excellency is an ex-test cricketer. He knows more about the game than anyone in India . . . or the neighbouring country.'

'And a yoga expert tooo,' a shrill sweet voice piped in, and there was Pooonam by my side again. The stray hairs in her blonde streaked birds-nest chignon were back in place and she looked very pleased with herself. She took a piece of jalebi from my plate and dipped it in the basundhi.

'Sorry to steal your jalebi,' she giggled. 'I couldn't resist the temptation.'

And what else, I wondered. All sorts of ghastly images surfaced in my mind.

'You may of course have heard this before,' Aziz Imran said, in the deepest, most thrilling voice I had ever heard. 'It was a wise man once said that cricket is an Indian game, invented in England. Or a Pakistani game, if you hear it across the border . . .' My head was still buzzing from the champagne. Now it buzzed some more. As a young woman, I'd had the inevitable crush on the incredibly glamorous Pakistan cricketer Imran Ahmed. It now spilled over to his personable namesake. I was smitten, so smitten that I almost forgot about Pooonam and her innuendos.

All of us in India are obsessed by our neighbouring country. Our Neighbourer, as Suresh refers to it. A strange refrain sprang up in my head: 'Love thy neighbour. Love. Love.' I feared I was drunk. I waved at a passing waiter for another glass of champagne.

'You may have heard this before,' Suresh said, quite unexpectedly. 'What another wise man said. Most countries have armies. But in Pakistan, your army has a country!'

The High Commissioner gave my husband a polite smile and disappeared graciously. Pooonam doubled over with laughter, displaying her globular boobs to spectacular advantage. I found that disgusting. I was fascinated.

The men were talking business now, the stock market scandal, the nuclear deal with America, the decline of the dollar. Odds and ends of conversation darted around me like fireflies.

'. . . but in the end there are just eight hundred people who matter in this country, yaar,' somebody remarked. His tone of voice indicated that he was one of them.

'Not eight hundred . . . maybe one thousand? Maan gaye, not more than that, even if India has a billion plus.'

'That's the trouble with India—we are an elitist democracy, bhai!'

I looked at them, bathed in the golden light of the illuminations and the fireworks, framed by the darkness around. The eight hundred people who mattered in my country. And I was one of them. Almost.

THAT NIGHT, AT AMRANA FORT, I SHARED A SHAKY FOUR-POSTER BED with my husband. We sleep in separate bedrooms in Dara Shikoh Marg. Here, I lay in my corner (always to the left), wondering if he would reach out to me, wondering if I really wanted him to.

Sharing is a habit we have forgotten. We tugged and pulled territorially at the covers all night. By the morning I was lying next to him, snuggled up close. The hair on his chest is greyer than I remember, but the smell of him hasn't changed. How long since we made love to each other? Long enough that I can't remember.

I slept, and dreamt I was enjoying a romantic candlelight dinner on a lonely moon-swept beach with Aziz Imran. Or was it Imran Aziz? . . . Their faces blurred into one as the waves broke and crashed on those distant dream sands.

The air conditioner was humming ineffectually. I could feel a hot flush coming on. It rose in waves; from my feet, my palms, within each hair of my scalp. I pushed away the Jaipur quilt. Suresh rolled over and pulled all of it to his side of the bed. Male instinct.

A glass of chilled water normally does the trick, but nothing helped. The restless fire was circulating through my body, pulling and ebbing. I tiptoed barefoot into the narrow balcony fronting the room and tried to breathe slowly. Very slowly. It was cool and quiet and I felt calmed.

A peacock stood on the parapet, calling and moaning in a harsh voice. A champa tree in an antique pot stirred in the dawn breeze and left a shower of dewdrops on my face. Dawn is different from dusk, and yet they are the same thing, really. Villages and fields lay before me like a patchwork quilt, the orange glow of the morning awakening them all. I thought about Janab Aziz Imran and my lonely fantasy about him. Now if I'd been Paro, things might have developed further! 'It's menopause,' I told myself sternly. 'Watch out for those hormones, Priya—you know the symptoms.'

Why had Suresh been so rude to the High Commissioner? Maybe his mother was to blame. She had been from Lahore, and their family had known the scars of partition; Pakistan was forever the enemy.

Love thy enemy . . .

The hot flush receded, my skin stopped scalding. Menopause may be a whisper or a joke, but not for those who are living it. Women's magazines skim the Change, except for ultra-advanced older citizens' skincare supplements peddling enzymes and creams made of fresh placentas. During my first pregnancy, before I miscarried, I had bought a book titled *EveryWoman*. It's proved a trusty guide to my body. After turning fifty I've read up conscientiously on the Change: *The process of the ovaries shutting down is a phenomenon involving the entire reproductive functioning from brain to skin*. In the face of extreme anxiety, mood swings and unprovoked irritability, *EveryWoman* provides a label for my sadly departing femininity.

The peacock had followed me almost into the room, its rich plumage sweeping the dust behind it. Suresh began on his morning sounds, the series of grunts, burps and low groans that are his rev-up to face the day. 'Hurry up Priya,' he said, 'I have work waiting in Delhi.' There was a menacing note in his voice. We rushed through our breakfast and out to our car, where he read files and talked on the phone and looked distractedly out of the tinted windows as though he were searching for something but didn't know what.

It's not a long drive from Amrana fort to Delhi, less than two hours. The only conversation we had was about Food Processing. The Food Processing Industries Association had organized a felicitation ceremony for my husband. Suresh read out the speech he planned to make there. 'You are a Housewife—I want to see if it interests you, Priya,' he said.

It went, I think, something like this: 'The Food Industry is the Sunrise Sector of the Indian Economy. Poised to attain Global Heights, it is a Boon for Busy Housewives, Working Couples, Executives, Holiday Travellers, and Foreign Investors.' He continued in a solemn voice about 'Technology Upgradation, Modernization, Integrated Cold Chain Facilities, Mega Food Parks, and Modernization of Abattoirs, etc.'

I didn't ask him about the etc, but listened with growing impatience to his grandiose dreams about the National Milk and Cheese Alliance and the National Meat and Poultry Processing Board. 'Processed Food is Hygienic, Healthy and Nutritious. It complements today's Fast Food lifestyle. Together, we shall at last unleash the Dedicated Age of Advanced Food Technology—DAAFT,' Suresh concluded, all in a rush, giving me a tender look, or through me perhaps to his imagined enraptured audience.

Something snapped inside me, the 'Housewife', like a taut too-tight bra-strap. 'Mr Minister,' I heard myself say, 'you must surely be aware that this laudable Fast Food Lifestyle hasn't trickled down to the bottom of the heap yet? May I bring to your notice that villagers in Orissa, in Kalahandi and places like that, feel privileged to eat just an occasional snack of roots and mango kernels?'

It was not just the Change. I was sick of his political flatulence.

Suresh turned over and studied me carefully. His half-rimmed spectacles were perched mid-way on his nose. His eyes were tired, but also surprised and worried. 'Are you all right, Priya?' he asked me, almost tenderly. 'Is there something the matter? Of course I know of the imbalances in the patterns of our agricultural development. But I'm Minister of State for Food Production, and that's my brief. Trust me, I'm not being insensitive.'

'I've just not been feeling so well recently,' I responded lamely, retreating. My husband returned to his files and I slipped into a wistful departing-hormone daydream featuring a masked ball in Venice and me in a strapless velvet gown.

—

Luv will be returning home soon. He studied for his BFA at the Delhi College of Art for a year, before impulsively decamping to join an expensive art college in New Mexico, funded through a special bursary by Good-Mart, an American retail group. It was a one-off scholarship; maybe they hoped Suresh might return favours so they could catch up with Bhambani retail, and all the rest who are busy trying to change our shopping habits and put the local bania and kirana shop out of business.

'This is a new generation, Priya!' Suresh propounds, when I worry overmuch about the twins. 'Don't judge Gen Next by how you were! This is the new Republic of Youngistan. Remember 54/24—fifty-four per cent of India's population is under age twenty-four. The future of India lies with its youth, with your sons and millions of others like them!'

'*Our* sons,' I correct him, whenever he starts on this script. Suresh gets confused sometimes about whether he's addressing an audience or just me. 'And our sons are not a statistic, Suresh. Or a votebank. And as their mother, it's my job to worry about them.'

It's Luv that I really worry about, not Kush. I remember him staring at me with trusting eyes as the doctors rushed him to the incubator. Kush tumbled out next and let out a loud baby war cry. He was a chubby baby, exceptionally cute and charming, but my heart had already rushed to the weaker twin. I never let my partiality show, and was equally patient and impatient with them both, through all those years of Luv's maths examination debacles and Kush's confrontations with Hindi and Sanskrit teachers.

—

I spent the afternoon sorting out Luv's bedroom. I'm not welcome there, forbidden from cleaning it. I rationalized with myself that dusting and clearing is not to be confused with cleaning. Of course I wasn't snooping—I wouldn't dare! Mothers don't snoop, they rummage to check the minutiae of their children's private lives.

His room yielded no clues. No photographs of girlfriends. No letters, diaries, dirty magazines—all unbelievably tidy, as though Luv had deliberately swept away all clues to whatever he was up to before he left.

A stack of unframed paintings stood against the wall. I studied them, one by one. Naked breasts and buttocks floating around in unconnected ways And that oval shape with a slit in the middle—was that a . . .? His signature was splattered across the backing. 'Luv'. Just that, with the dates. And the baffling titles: 'Painting with CatS'; 'Self Spliced to SplinterS'. What was going on in his head?

I discovered a notebook in a drawer. It was like a funky adolescent scrapbook, with a glued-on collage on the cover. The title page read 'I, Luv Picasso' and had scraps of torn-up Picasso prints stuck into intricate mosaics, with speech bubbles and think balloons inked around them. On closer examination, I discovered that our resident artist had scissored and vandalized an expensive coffee-table book that I particularly treasured.

The opening page had a one-eyed Cyclops with a cubist guitar pasted over the mouth and a carefully calligraphed speech blurb: 'What is a face, really? That which is in front? Inside? Behind? And the rest?—P.P.' Then a thought bubble, with smaller ones leading to it: 'Double Faced Bitch.'

I couldn't make much sense of it. 'What is a face, really?' I found a blank canvas and contemplated it. Emptiness. I haven't painted for years, but something happened to me then. I took a scrunched-up tube of vermilion, pierced it with the safety pin that held my sari pleats together, and squelched it over the canvas in concentric circles, as though I were frying a jalebi. Then I squiggled through it with the safety pin until it formed a drizzly sort of pattern. It looked quite nice, really. I propped my painting against the wall and left it to dry.

'This is Art,' I told myself, as though a speech blurb was floating from my mouth. A thought balloon followed: 'You can always squeeze more colour out of a dried-up old tube of paint!' Luv had inherited his artistic DNA from me. Clearly. ☺

—

Off to the airport early morning. Ghafoor was driving me. He's from the stable of chauffeurs in the ministry pool. A kattar Muslim, devout to a fault, he reads the namaaz five times a day, halting the car at will to roll out his prayer mat and invoke Allah and Mecca-Medina. We are a secular nation, and none dare reproach him. He's not the most sought after of drivers and has therefore, perhaps, been assigned to me.

But I like Ghafoor. He is courteous and kind and does not have the problem of body odour that some younger drivers have. He smells of chameli ka tel and his socks don't stink up the car.

Ghafoor's sparse hair is streaked with varying shades of henna, as evocative in its way as one of Luv's layered paintings. His eyes, lined usually with a fine layer of kohl, carry a mystic sense of detachment. I feel safe with Ghafoor bhai. Maybe it's the Bombay influence—Bombay, before it was Mumbai. The city used to belong to everyone, and Allah's chosen were visible everywhere, as the rest of us. In Delhi one tends to see them only in Purani Dilli and Nizamuddin, unless they are one of us, if you know what I mean.

I was whisked through airport security into the VIP waiting room with the anaesthetic ease that accompanies my movements as a minister's wife. But the plane, being Air India, was running late. Then, suddenly, he was there, standing before me, my son Luv, thinner and loopier than I remembered. A small steel safety pin pierced his left brow, another, miniature version hung from the bottom of his lower lip. I rushed to hug him, and he returned awkwardly to my arms before disentangling himself. 'Mom!' he grinned. 'It's good to be home—and for a change Kush isn't around to hog all the attention!'

All through the drive home, I was examining him hungrily, taking in his long lank hair, his lean frame. I was eager to please, afraid to provoke him. I wondered if the safety pins hurt and if he took them off at night.

'Don't look at me like that!' he snapped. 'You know it makes me nervous, Mom.'

Through the chaotic morning traffic, Luv stared at the streets outside as though he were seeing them for the first time. 'Delhi's weird,' he pronounced at last, 'and the airport is enough to depress anybody.' He hasn't been away that long, I thought. We returned home to quiet, tree-lined Dara Shikoh Marg. As the gates closed behind us, the security guard executed a languid salute and returned to scratching his balls. Luv let out a loud sigh. 'Back to detention days,' he whispered, mock-tragically, to himself. 'Brightest in dungeons, Liberty thou art!' He seemed quite pleased at the prospect.

Suresh was not home. Luv wasn't bothered by his father's absence. In fact, by the time Ramdhan brought him a cup of hot tea and biscuits, he seemed to have distinctly cheered up. 'It's cool to be home, Mom,' he smiled. 'It really is. You mustn't take notice of all the garbage I talk.'

I smiled back idiotically in response. My first born has that effect on me. He is, like Kush, smarter and brighter than Suresh or me, though maybe we might match them if there was anything around to wake us up. This generation is just more focussed and determined than we ever were. Better looking too!

In the afternoon, father and son spent what Suresh likes to grandly call 'quality time' together. My husband emerged from his fathering session looking sanctimonious. Luv was half-dozing on the settee, looking bored but complacent. He winked at me as I walked into the room. 'Take my advice, Dad—' he exclaimed cheekily to Suresh's departing figure, 'get a life.'

'If only . . .' I told myself. 'Me too, please!'

Suresh was leaving for a day for Chennai, to lay the foundation stone for something or the other. We hadn't talked to each other all through the morning; that was increasingly the pattern of our lives. Now he planted a kiss on my cheek as he left. 'Everything all right, Priya?' he stated, rather than asked, and departed without waiting for a reply. Only for you, I thought to myself.

'I have to go to Mumbai for a day,' I called after him. 'Bhaiyya has invited me there—I'm to be the chief guest for an awards ceremony.'

'Make sure Madam is looked after in Mumbai,' he barked, in the direction of his Assistant Private Secretary. 'And take Luv with you, Priya.'

He left in a flurry of excitement and importance I would never have imagined possible for the stolid lawyer I had married in that other lifetime when we were young. It demonstrated only that anything is possible; in fact, as I sometimes feel, the more unlikely a thing is, the greater the chances of it happening.

I was still not used to Luv's new look, to the very odd safety pins. That night, he came to my bedroom with his face scrubbed clean and his long hair tied up in a ponytail. My heart skipped a beat. This was my baby—mine once again, even if the safety pins were in his face rather than in his diapers.

My sons speak to me in English, sometimes Hinglish. 'Kya baat hai, beta?' I ventured tenderly, in what is, after all, our mother tongue. Luv remained silent and unresponsive, and I switched back to English. 'Is there a problem, son?'

'Of course there is!' Luv wailed. 'Why else would I leave my life there and return to all these bakwaas things I had left behind? Oh Maa, I need you! I missed you so much—' And he burst into sobs, my tough independent son.

'Oh Maa, I need you.' Indian mothers sacrifice their entire lives, in films and in real life, only in the hope of someday hearing these precise words. I concealed my joy and gratification behind a mask of motherly concern. 'No beta, no tears, men don't cry!' I exclaimed, stroking the hair I had once brushed and combed and oiled.

That seemed to accelerate the tear trigger. After a range of 'Oh Maa, oh Maa' sobs, Luv stopped weeping and switched to a subdued sheepish smile.

'Umm . . . Maybe you should know that I was engaged to be married. Was. It's all over now. We've broken up. I'm ready to start life afresh.'

'So he isn't gay.' The thought flashed through my mind like a strobe light. The visible lack of suspects in my sons' sexual lives had often puzzled me, there was an unspoken fear I lived with, too afraid to name it.

'Who? When? Where?' I asked trying from experience to curb my raging curiosity. Ask no questions, and it is possible you may get replies from your children.

'Well—it—she—was a girl called Monalisa. Monalisa Das Mann. She was—is—a Bengali Sikh from the States. Classic ABCD. Doesn't know her butter chicken from her hilsa, and wants to return to her roots.'

I disliked her already, this girl called Monalisa. 'What's an

ABCD?' I asked, though I knew the answer. It was the sort of question Luv wouldn't object to. By demonstrating my ignorance rather than my curiosity, I might elicit more answers. That's always been my strategy with the boys.

'An American Born Confused Desi,' he replied patiently. 'Monalisa's parents are academics. Her mother specializes in Virginia Woolf and Commonwealth literature—her father teaches a course on D.H. Lawrence and another on Dislocation and Hybridity. All po co and loco.'

I was losing the thread. 'Have you met her parents? I hope she isn't pregnant. Does anybody know?'

An amused smile broke through the tragic pose. 'Know? Does anybody know?' he said, mimicking my tone with cruel accuracy. 'Yes, Mom, everybody knows. Or *will* know. Monalisa is busy writing a misery memoir . . . a tell all non-fiction narrative about our breakup. Now she says it's healed her. She wants us to get together again.'

'Is she a nice girl?' I asked.

Luv winced. 'Don't tread on me, Maa, with your middle-class definitions. No, Monalisa Das Mann isn't *nice*. She's insatiably sexy, intolerably bright, weirdly wicked. But no, Monalisa cannot be classified as a nice Indian girl. That's why I fell in love with her!'

'So let me find you one,' I said. 'A nice Indian girl . . .'

A mask descended upon his face. 'Read my lips,' he said, the muscles of his face settling and resettling in a way that might have been comic if I wasn't so concerned. 'I'm still hurting. I need time. I need to stay at home for a month, maybe a year. Turn vegetarian, eat dal chawal, learn classical music—maybe the sitar.'

'And take the safety pins off your face,' I ventured. Luv ignored that.

'Or I could learn vocal music,' he enthused, 'instead of the sitar! Join a gharana, loop up with tradition. That would be cool. I need to know India again, to connect with my inner self. Not by scrabbling for political power, like my esteemed twin Kush—but something more spiritual. Maybe I should join yoga classes. Or a Vipassana course. Could you find me a guru?'

'The guru will find you,' I replied loftily. Indian spirituality is like a game of table tennis, one just has to know how to return the ball. And Luv certainly has no aptitude for politics, he's too nice for it. 'I'm going to Mumbai tomorrow,' I continued. 'Maybe you could come with me. Your Papa isn't in Delhi either—it would be a nice change for both of us.'

'I'll think about it,' he replied. 'And I don't want to call him Papa anymore. What's the right word in Hindi, Maa? Papa ji? or Daddy ji? Maybe Babu ji? or Pita ji? Ya, that's it! Pita ji!' This was accompanied by a maniacal laugh. Then he was gone, fled from the room, my son, my little boy.

Luv returned, holding my painting in his hand. 'Who did this?' he asked, in a tone I couldn't decipher.

'I did,' I confessed, a little uncertain—was that the right answer?

He embraced me with one hand, waving the painting up and down with the other. 'My mother is an artist!' he cheered. 'I knew it all along! I'll get it framed and hang it in my room, Mataji.'

That made my day. How we doting mothers just need a few kind words!

Kush called too, from the US. He seemed in exceptionally good spirits. 'I just spoke to Papa in Chennai,' he said, 'so I thought I better talk to you as well, Mummie. I've bought you some really nice skin care cream from here. Don't let my evil twin take over my kingdom while I'm away.'

WE WERE BOOKED ON THE 9 O'CLOCK FLIGHT TO MUMBAI. I CALLED Suresh on his mobile before I left home, but there was no answer. I checked the number of his hotel with his PA and dialled again from the landline. The reception kept me on hold for a very long time, during which I listened patiently to a jhinchak piano version of a Bollywood remix medley.

Finally, a woman picked up the phone. 'Hello,' she said, in a sultry sort of voice.

'May I speak to Mr Suresh Kaushal, please?' I asked politely. There was a sort of echo in the phone connection, and I could hear my question repeated loud even as I said it. 'May I speak to Mr Suresh Kaushal please?' Maybe the speakerphone was on.

'Oh, Suresh is in the shower!' the voice drawled. 'Who should I say called?'

'This is his wife,' I replied.

'This is his wife,' the line echoed again, in a high voice that sounded oddly self-conscious. A suppressed giggle on the other end, and then the woman who had answered the phone put it down again.

Over the years I have trained myself not to fly into jealous rages. A happy secure marriage is founded on trust. I must trust Suresh, it's a reasoned approach, not a form of denial. But the phone call set me thinking. It's not that I'm stupid, only that, like other Indian women of my generation, I've been trained to always shut my eyes—in prayer, in marriage, during the afternoon Horror Show. Think of our epics. In the Mahabharata, Queen Gandhari blindfolded herself, she shut her eyes and stopped looking at the world because her husband was blind. It's in our culture.

I could confront him. Ask who she was. Suresh would present a convincing defence and leave me looking feeling, foolish. After all, it wasn't as if I could walk out on him, leave him—such manic, unconceivable thoughts! Being an Indian wife, being a woman past fifty, I calmed myself down and refused to think about who might have taken the call in my husband's hotel bedroom while he was in the shower.

It's a short flight to Mumbai, just an hour and fifty minutes from Delhi, but a lifetime away for me. I was a Bombay girl when I got married. It has a new name now. And in thirty years it has grown so much that I scarcely recognize it, while I've morphed into one of those Dilliwalas that Mumbaikars are both in awe and slightly suspicious of.

I had been invited by the RSSMS, a Marwari Social Service Institute. Something to do with a rapidly expanding Pharma Company of which my brother Atul is a Director. His boss Mr Mittal has ventured into a 'Swadeshi Foodmart' retail chain, possibly prompting them to decide that I was the person best suited to hand out their '8 GR8 Indian Women' awards. It was only family loyalty that had made me overlook my dislike for Atul's obnoxious wife Dolly and reluctantly accept his summons to be the VVIP chief guest.

Luv and I landed at Chhatrapati Shivaji airport at midday. I draped my pallav elegantly around my shoulders as we alighted. I had dressed carefully: chiffon sari, pearl necklace, a nice handbag. I was pleased with the effect, but my artistic son was forthright in his condemnation. 'You look so dated, Mom!' he exclaimed, with a candour I did not find disarming. 'So last century. Like an old hull enroute to the ship-breaking yard at Alang to be dismantled! What's the image? Who are you trying to project?'

'Oh, I'm just being me,' I said casually, though I was actually furious with Luv for his thoughtlessness, too near the truth if only I could admit it.

'What is a face really? ....That which is in front? Inside? Behind? And the rest?' he persisted. The young think they have a monopoly on being cruel. Luv wasn't actually looking that great himself, what with his strategically inserted safety pins and his dirty unwashed hair and the torn jeans that cost a fortune. But the rules of the game forbade me from voicing this. It wasn't cool.

'Picasso said that, not you!' I retorted. That startled him—would he suspect that I had been snooping through his papers?

My brother Atul had made his way inside the security cordon to receive us. Breaking security protocol is another way of showing off. Dolly and Atul are always desperately trying to demonstrate their status and self-worth against the unexpected barometer of my husband's dizzying rise up the greasy pole of national politics. That's what I think, anyway. And it's pathetic.

It's unsettling to observe them together, Atul and Luv. There is something of my brother in my sons, in the slightly receding chin, the slouch of the shoulders. I hope the resemblance ends there; Atul has never figured in my pantheon of heroes. Would he have been better if he had gone through a safety pin phase?

I am still a Bombay girl at heart. The smell of the city, remembered and forgotten—the sharp reek of Bombay Duck, the stench of drying Bombil fish, the sudden sea breeze—connected me to the young woman I once was. We were in the middle of the monsoon season but magically it wasn't raining and all of Mumbai seemed to have hung their washing out to dry. Every window in the city threw out flexed aluminium spokes to salute my arrival, the waving vests and underwear and multicoloured saris flagging their affectionate welcome.

The air conditioning neutralized the smell of fish. The car smelt only of my brother's aftershave, slathered on in industrial quantity. My son's unexpected resemblance to my brother began to get on my nerves. I caught a sudden glimpse of my face in the rear view mirror, the neck grey, scraggly, wrinkled as chicken-skin, grotesque. This was not me—Priya Kaushal—as I remembered her to be. Kush's expensive ultra skin-care cream was spot on. I rearranged my chiffon sari pallav and concentrated on looking important and imperious. That's the thing about growing older—you notice it happening to other people and then, one day, it hits you that you are one of them.

I was booked at the Taj Mahal hotel, in the old building. We took the Parel road. My son was behaving like a tourist. 'Look Maa!' he exclaimed, tugging at my sari. 'It's so cool! We're passing Dharavi—the largest slum in Asia . . . Shit, man, that's where the action is! I want to check out Dharavi—maybe this afternoon?'

That sort of talk gets my goat. 'Dharavi isn't Disneyland, Luv,' I snapped. 'You don't go there to send out post-cards on poverty! Remember, your papa's a politician.'

'But it's so totally awesome,' he replied. 'I mean, it's about the human spirit, about endeavour. All those slumdogs carrying on with their lives anyhow. I know all about it—I've seen this cool docu on it, on Discovery. And then I know this guy in New Mexico whose brother made a documentary film about it ... Garbage recycling, illicit liquor, informal industries—in fact, did you know that they even do cough syrup and whiteners to get high? It's all there, a real glimpse into the real India. Weird!'

Atul had been trying to get a word in. 'Dharavi is really growing very fast indeed,' my brother declared righteously, as though the credit for this accrued somehow to him. 'And there is a reputable tourist company that is running safe and reliable "Reality Tours". They take you around in an AC coach and the profit is ploughed back. Five per cent returns to poor!'

I shut out his bleating and looked outside. An abandoned textile mill had a red flag hanging limply from the roof. A sign carved on the cement façade said 'Swadeshi Cotton Mills; Mumbai 1953'. That was the year I was born. I was as old as that building. It was as old as me.

'Dharavi is on take-off now,' my brother continued. 'It is full of promise. Three thousand crore rupees turnover ... Great redevelopment plans ... Our Chairman says ...'

'Maa, I'm confused. All this nine per cent growth rate and all that buzz! Where's it really happening?' Luv asked me. We had both completely ignored Atul, but he seemed not to have noticed.

V.T. loomed ahead. Victoria Terminus Station in all its restored glory. It looked magically young again, every stone shining as though it had suffered a facial. And then we were at the Taj Mahal hotel, the old wing gracious and well maintained, the 'new' tower wing still looking like a tacky Air India advert. The Gateway of India standing guard, with its usual crowds of people and churning ferry boats.

If Paro could see me now! I glided up the black marble steps into the humming lobby, in my designer glasses and my discreet chiffon sari, the pearls on my neck soothing the sag. I was somebody now, not the mousy secretary she had once scorned.

The Taj Mahal Hotel is a mystical temple to success. Its over-decorated lobby was bathed in a cool soft light that muted the throbbing clash of colours. Atul's chairman, a smiling Mr Mittal, was waiting there, flanked by two young women brandishing garlands of marigold flowers. These were presented to me and Luv. Mr Mittal handed me a bouquet of pink roses for good measure and then they left. I felt important, even if the pink roses clashed with the yellow garlands.

'Dolly will call you later in the evening, Priya Didi,' Atul declared virtuously. It was only recently that he had begun calling me Didi—I am a year younger, so the seniority lay clearly not in age but social hierarchy. I waltzed through the corridors into the polished lift.

There was a mosquito buzzing around the room, the only irritant in a world of grace and serendipity. I ordered a pot of Darjeeling tea and luxuriated in the moment. 'You have arrived, Priya Kaushal,' I told myself, as I preened before the misted-over antique mirror. In the dim light, with the curtains drawn, I looked rather good. Luv had made one of his mysterious disappearances, muttering about elusive friends in Colaba. On an impulse I picked up the leather bound telephone directory nestling besides Gideon's Bible and an abbreviated Bhagavad Gita. 'Sita Sewing Machines'. There was no entry under the head. I persisted, squinting through my reading glasses under the bedside lamp until I discovered the name I was looking for, the Marine Drive address. Then I rang the number.

'Hullo Hullo Hullo Hullo' on the other side of the line, from what sounded like a Nepali cook or bearer.

'May I speak to BR Sir, please?' I requested, nervously reverting to the role of secretary, factotum and part-time lover. There was a moment of silence and then I heard the beloved fruity voice which still had the power to make me swoon.

'Who is this please, calling on a landline in the age of cellular communication?' he asked.

'It's me, Sir. Priya, Priya Kaushal. I'm calling from Mumbai . . .' I murmured apologetically. Why was I still calling him Sir?

'Priya, my love, how delicious to hear your voice, what a delectable surprise!' he said. 'And when do I have the honour and the privilege of seeing you in person? It's been so long! Much too long.'

My stomach was feeling funny, it was quickening and contracting in pleasurable spasms. I couldn't think of what to say. It had been more than twenty-five years.

'How about this evening?' BR persisted. 'Where are you staying, Priya?'

'In the Taj, the old Taj,' I replied, sounding more assertive than a humble office assistant now.

'Delightful. I shall meet you in the lobby at the very dot of seven,' he said, and put the phone down.

I wasn't sure I had wanted things to turn out this way. I wasn't sure what I was expecting. And now I was nervous and elated. Confused. How old was I? Age is defence against nothing, it cures you of nothing, not even youth.

The 'awards function' I had come to grace was scheduled for the next morning. I shook off my brother, calling him and cancelling the dreary predictable evening that stretched ahead. The past awaited me in the lobby at seven. I was there at a quarter to. BR arrived on the dot. Nothing about him had changed, except that he was leaning on an ivory cane. He stood before me, and our eyes met. Time stood very still for a while.

His smile was both knowing and tender. 'Priya my darling,' he murmured. 'We meet again.'

No point recounting what we did next, the conversation and the two martinis and the bottle of wine and the dim sum feast. Or the familiar lavender notes of his cologne or how he stroked my arm in the lift as he saw me back into my room. I forgot that I was an Indian wife and mother. I did not think of Luv and when he might return to his room from Colaba or wherever he was. All I can remember is that we were in my room, in a clinch, and then

I was naked and he was too, and the ivory cane leaned against the mattress as I surrendered to love and sex and re-seduction.

It was raining outside, a furious monsoon downpour, and the curtains had not been drawn. A flash of lightning illumined BR's face; he was looking up at the ceiling, as though searching for something. I could imagine the Arabian Sea outside, the waves rising and falling as the rain beat down and the thunderous sky lit up and was dark again.

BR sighed. 'Here we are, Priya,' he said, 'older but no wiser.' There was no rapture in his voice, but a note of regret—a reformed smoker who has lit up again. Then his practised seducer's etiquette took over. 'Was it good for you?' he enquired, stroking my shoulders and pumping my breasts in a distracted sort of way.

'It was wonderful,' I murmured. 'I mean, really wonderful.' I meant it. As usual, as forever, BR held the keys.

We lay entwined in each other's arms. I could feel every cell in my body, every pore in my skin, celebrating. Another streak of lightning lit up the room—and I saw a flash of white, the ivory cane propped against the bed, his face, in shadow, and the curve of my arm as I embraced him.

'Independence day!' I told myself, aloud, though very softly. BR seemed not to have heard me. Perhaps I had only thought it, not said it at all.

The room bell trilled. I froze up, though BR continued to stare at the ceiling, as his fingers absently stroked my naked back. I leapt out of bed, dropping the cane, which rolled under the bed. 'Who is it?' I asked in panic, through the shut door. Was it, could it be, Luv?

'Room service, Madame,' a suave voice replied, 'your order, Madame.'

'It's the wrong room, please!' I shouted, the panic not far from the surface of my voice. 'Wrong room . . . can you hear me? We didn't order anything!'

BR got up and sat by the edge of the bed. Another flash of

lightning, and his face again, like a photograph in an album, to be remembered and cherished. The sound of the rain knocking on the Taj roof, rat a tat tat.

'I forgot the Do Not Disturb sign,' BR pronounced at last. 'I knew I had forgotten something. I'm getting forgetful in my old age . . .'

What did that mean?

'And where is my cane, Priya? You seem somehow to have misplaced it.' There was a querulous, petulant note in his voice, an old woman's voice.

BR winced as I switched on the bedside lamp. I bent down to retrieve the cane. It had rolled deep under the bed. I was naked, on all fours. My once-firm bum, now raddled with orange-peel cellulite, stuck out like a vanquished emblem of desire. The soft pile carpet stroked my skin as I tried anxiously to position an arm under the bed. There were two scrunched-up plastic bags breathing gently under the bed, and a . . . condom? Two condoms and an empty can of Coke.

The cane remained just out of reach. Finally, I got a shoehorn from the old-fashioned cupboard in the dressing area and used it, successfully, to manoeuvre the cane out. Then I returned to the bed and switched the light off.

There was a patch of light from the bathroom, an irregular cube which framed the sounds of BR's toilette. I could hear him shuffling back into his trousers, brushing his teeth in the bathroom. Was he using my brush?

I switched on the bedside lamp again, and settled myself seductively against the pillows, arraying my hair in a casual halo. He didn't take much notice.

'These fragments I shall shore up against my ruin,' he declaimed. 'That's T.S. Eliot, my dear, in case you didn't know. I must go now. I will call you again tomorrow, Priya my love.'

And he was gone.

We checked out of the hotel the next morning. I was coming down with a cold and feeling awful. Atul was lurking about the lobby, brows knit in an anxious frown. His thin face, disquietingly like my plumper one, mirrored extreme stress. 'Priya didi, Mr Mittal will be waiting,' he said, the short sentence dipping from wheedling to reproach. I was rushed towards the waiting car, security man in tow. Luv followed in another car, escorted by two men in starched white khadi kurtas and dark glasses.

The awards ceremony was in an air-conditioned hall in a distant suburb. We passed new condominiums and housing colonies with faraway names like Malibu Heights, U.S. Housing, Dallas, Buckingham, Pallas Athene. I was rushed to the stage, where the '8 GR8 Indian Women', a lawyer, a social worker, a classical dancer, a fashion designer, and so on, were presented with silver-plated orbs on a cut-glass base. They posed and re-posed for photographs as a girl with a sing-song voice and an earnest ghati accent read out endlessly detailed bio-datas and citations. My job was only to graciously bend forward and hand over the inscribed orbs to each of the 'Status Achievers' on behalf of the RSSMS Awards Committee. I had practised a short speech which I delivered without mishap.

Atul's boss Mr Mittal read out a marathon vote of thanks at breakneck speed. Commending the glories of our five-thousand-year-old civilization, and the greatness and dignity of Indian womanhood, and asserting that India was not Europe or America, Mr Mittal thanked the Rani Sati Samiti Memorial Society, and Respected Madame Srimati Priya Kaushal, for upholding and propagating the values of Hindu culture. The Sati word should have alerted me. I should have realized that the RSSMS was saffron in its political hue and registered my protest. But my cold was building up, and somewhere, still in a parallel reality, I was reliving of the touch of BR's hands, remembering the flashes of lightning that had lit up the hotel room the previous night.

We set off for the airport, with a final glimpse of Juhu Beach before we left.

'Bombay Meri Jaan,' I murmured dreamily, struggling with the seatbelt in the aircraft.

Luv heard me, and his safety pin leapt up into an indulgent smile. 'You look happy today, Mataji,' he said. 'Stay there!'

As the airhostesses fussed around us, Luv switched off his phone, looking perturbed. 'It's Monalisa, she's landed up in Delhi now. I don't need to open up that front again, I require closure.'

Perhaps there is something about being alone with one's mother in business class, on a bumpy flight, drinking foul airline coffee, that elicits confession. Luv turned to me from his window seat and started spilling out his secrets.

'You know, Maa, I respect you for being a very normal sort of woman,' he said. 'It's weird, but you are extraordinary because you are so ordinary.'

Was that a compliment? It didn't sound like one, but I smiled encouragingly anyway, to keep him talking.

'Monalisa is the opposite. She's too hyper, much too intelligent, too well read. It's all that Virginia Woolf stuff she was brought up on. She really is extraordinary, I suppose. Monalisa's older than me, and better educated. And we are great in bed together, total chemistry . . .'

The opposite of too intelligent is stupid. Besides, the prude in me was getting embarrassed. Indian moms don't talk sex with their sons, even if they have been with an old lover the night before. But I continued smiling.

'Is she pretty, your Monalisa?' I asked.

'She's a looker. Very pretty, very intense—big and small at the same time. You know what I mean? Great tubes! So what's wrong? That's what I ask myself, Maa! What's wrong? Maybe she's just too bright for me.'

We hit an airpocket. I struggled with my seat belt as the airhostess delivered an unintelligible announcement in garbled Hindi and confused English.

'Monalisa may smoke and drink and hang out with the guys, but somewhere she's been conditioned to seek an Indian Bridegroom. Provider, protector, sex supplier. First it was all freedom, then the parents moved into the picture, and it's the same old story, and the plot isn't new either. "You have slept with our daughter, now you must marry her!" That's what her father said. It's Emotional Atyachaar, and no irony that Dad teaches a course on D.H. Lawrence.'

'Phir what happened?' I asked intently. This was serious.

'Monalisa's radical, Eng Lit father started talking about honour—he actually used the word izzat! "Why didn't Monalisa marry any of her previous boyfriends?" I asked her parents.'

'"But they weren't Indian men, beta!" Honest! That's what her feminist-sheminist mother said. And her father got really upset, he even tried phoning Pitaji. He didn't get through—all the PAs and secretaries saw to that. And then I sort of surrendered, and agreed to marry Monalisa. Her parents got uber excited. I think they had dreams of Band Baja Ghodi and Disco Bhangra and all that! Or some Bengali fancy-dress tamasha.'

'And it didn't strike you to call your mother, to inform her? You didn't think of taking your father's permission?' I exclaimed, outraged. A one-sided engagement is a fundamental attack on Indian Family Values. Unlike adultery, it is a declaration of war.

Luv asked the airhostess for another coffee. I had one too, with extra sugar. A petite, determined girl called Monalisa was trying to crack up my family. She would have to deal with me first.

'I ducked,' Luv continued resolutely. 'I made a cowardly exit. I told her father that my family wouldn't let me marry Monalisa. I said that I was already engaged, that you had decided when I was very young that I would marry your best friend's daughter. American Desis exist in this confused timewarp. Her professor parents watch Hindi films all the time. That's where they get their ideas of reality. They completely believed my childhood engagement story, it's so out-of-Bollywood that it rang true with them.'

I stared at him in disbelief.

'But Monalisa hasn't given up yet. She's in Delhi now, hot on my heels. So you have to support the script, Mataji, about my childhood sweetheart and all that.'

He wriggled off to the toilet, and was no longer in confessional mode when he returned. Dozing with his head against the window, his face framed by the fleecy clouds, he looked angelic and vulnerable.

The airplane circled around Delhi for ages, and then we were back in the proud capital of India that is Bharat. The city is bursting at the seams, spilling over with Dilliwalas squeezing into buses, crowding into auto rickshaws, searching for scraps of footpath to walk upon. Driving back from the airport, it was all dhool and dust and grime, and roads dug up everywhere for the never-ending Metro construction. Famished street children, coated in wraithlike dust, haunted this extended excavation site.

Drop eye contact—that's the rule with beggars. Lock up your heart. Never look them in the eye. Don't ever reach for your handbag, even if only for your lipstick—it sends the wrong signals. Never yield; if you put a coin into one outstretched hand, another hundred will swarm towards you in hope. That's what I've learnt, anyway.

At the traffic crossing, by the dug-up road, under the shadow of a new flyover, I was accosted by a young girl with such wistful dreaming eyes that it was impossible to look away. There was a polished red apple in my handbag, I had slipped it in from the fruit platter in the hotel, just in case. I handed it to the beggar child, and her mouth split into a speckled smile that shook me up. I surprised myself by reaching again for my bag and handing her a hundred-rupee note.

The little girl launched into a series of perfectly executed summersaults to show her appreciation. Two young boys, both holding crutches, began a wailing sing-song beggars' litany. A eunuch appeared on the scene as well, knocking on the car window, the hands miming seduction, anger and threat. The lights changed. The children abandoned their crutches and began playing hopscotch on the dug-up pavement. The hijra hurled an abuse as the car sped away.

'I guess that's how you middle classes negotiate poverty; through a rolled-up car window,' Luv said to no one in particular. He was being infuriating again.

As we approached the wide roads and tree-lined avenues of New Delhi, Luv brought the sati subject up. 'Don't you think there was something inappropriate about your speaking at a Rani Sati function, Maa?' he asked.

'Of course not!' I replied. 'No one told me that RSSMS stands for Rani Sati Samiti Memorial Society. And anyway, Indian women don't burn themselves on their husband's funeral pyres anymore. The British legally abolished Sati in 1829.'

'Please Mom, don't throw dates at me,' Luv snapped. 'We are talking real life, not Wikipedia!'

I HAD ALREADY SUCCUMBED TO A COLD WHEN I FOUND MONALISA DAS Mann, Luv's ex-fiancee, waiting for us at 18 Dara Shikoh Marg. She was perched on a sofa in the living room, a small girl with creamy skin and implacable eyes, dressed all in black, a maroon silk scarf draped like a dupatta around her neck. There were three stubbed-out cigarettes in the brass bowl that wasn't an ashtray. Should I phone Ramadoss, I wondered!

'Hi Mrs Kaushal—I'm Monalisa,' she announced, as she stood on tiptoe to give me a peck on my cheek. 'I've been waiting to meet you.' A dewy brush of soft skin. Somehow it felt as though she were sniffing me.

Luv looked shaken up. All the cockiness had drained out of him. He was staring at me in panic, his eyes pleading for help. 'MOM PLEASE!' he mouthed silently, before turning to Monalisa with exaggerated delight.

Somebody had to do something. I rushed to Suresh for advice. A TV crew was recording an interview in his office. My husband was in conversation with a strikingly pretty girl. He was replying rather glumly, unmoved by her charm. They seemed to be winding up as I entered. I waited till the interview was over and Suresh began struggling to get the lapel mike off his starched white kurta.

The girl turned to me. She had the most liquid, trusting eyes I have ever seen. News anchors are trained to look mean and sceptical. What was she doing on television with eyes like that?

'I have to wash my hands,' the girl said to me. 'Please could you show me where to go?'

An idea was formulating in my mind. 'Come with me, dear,' I replied. Draping my arms around her in a conspicuous, proprietary sort of way, I led her to the washroom, past Luv and Monalisa. Then I escorted her back to the rest of the TV crew. She must have found my behaviour puzzling, but said nothing.

'What a charming young lady you are!' I exclaimed. 'What's your name, beta?'

'I'm Paromita,' she replied, handing me a visiting card while she turned those soft eyes on me full force.

The day had already yielded enough surprises. 'Paromita . . .' I responded thoughtfully. 'Paromita'.

I returned to the living room, maternal resolution resounding in every footstep. 'That was Luv's childhood fiancée,' I declared. 'My future daughter-in-law. Sorry I couldn't introduce you, Miss Das Mann, but I didn't want to upset her. You see, Luv has already told me all about your friendship with him.'

Her eyes challenged mine. 'Luv and I love each other,' she said slowly, forcefully as though spelling things out for a deaf mute. 'Luv loves me. In the real world, the modern world, young people decide whom to marry. For themselves! At least that's how we are, back in the US—we don't let our parents make the decisions.'

'I'm sure Luv will respect his parent's wishes. He respects our ancient Indian culture,' I replied sternly. 'Of course you must visit us again, but do telephone before coming. The security guards may not let you in, otherwise.' I bent down to give her a peck on the cheek, which felt strange, as most people I know are taller than me. It was me smelling her now.

Luv looked at her and at me and shrugged his shoulders in a helpless way that seemed to exonerate him on all fronts.

Monalisa looked me straight in the eyes. Very pretty eyes, I noticed, black with green flecks in them.

'What you are doing is not right, Mrs Kaushal,' she said. 'I'm sorry I'm putting it so bluntly, but I'm a truthful person. Like it or leave it.'

Leave it, I decided.

'Goodbye, Mrs Kaushal' she said. 'We shall meet again'

My son led her out. He returned looking troubled. Then he cheered up. 'You are a star, Mom,' he exclaimed. 'Straight out of Bollywood! A veteran actor—or should I say liar? And who's that delectable daughter-in-law babe you brought in? She's utterly gorgeous! I may have fallen in love with her already.'

A lie in the interest of one's family is not an untruth, but one's dharma. As an Indian mother, I am aware which side of the truth my duties fall. I didn't tell Luv that, and it was all too complicated to explain to Suresh. There was no need for him to know, he had troubles enough already.

Poor Suresh had been at the receiving end of a media witchhunt. The *Clarion* had headlined shocking statistics from an 'Internal Audit' about food adulteration in the Public Distribution System. According to this (and I didn't find it difficult to believe) cat droppings, horse shit, lead powder, arsenic and more were being doled out to India's poor and needy through the PDS. Over 500,000 fair price shops which supplied more than 170 million families had set up a cosy mutual-interest supply and purchase group of poison passed off as food.

I had taken care to stock an organic brand of dal and chana, and I told Suresh this as he glumly surveyed the lunch. 'No lead or arsenic here,' I said cheerfully. 'It's not from the PDS.'

It was an untactful remark and I had to pay for it. Suresh went red in the face, and there were tears of anger and frustration in his eyes. 'Don't be so stupid, Priya,' he said. 'Nothing is what it seems. Of course there are rats jumping around the government godowns, and we haven't created special toilet facilities for them. But that's just the front scandal. The real facts stink even more! The response section of the *Indian Times* wanted the Press Officer to commit funds for a dedicated news delivery scheme. But we had already signed up with the News Today Group for a special supplement. So the buggers decided to give me hell. Free Press—Ha!'

Suresh never uses words like bugger. This was serious.

Even as Suresh was protesting the paid news syndrome, the Private Secretary scored a major victory as he pointed out that the actual culprit was the Ministry of Consumer Affairs and Public Distribution, not Food Processing at all. His Private Secretary and Personal Assistant are at constant war with each other, so the P.A. was sternly reproved by the P.S. for not clarifying this to the P.O. in the first place. The Press Officer rode the battle by fixing a lead interview in the *News Today* Sunday Special.

Once the blame had been laid at the door of the other Ministry, Suresh seemed actually quite upbeat about the whole affair. I found him admiring the cartoon by Ravi Menon in the *Clarion* magazine section. 'A good likeness,' he pondered. 'It makes me look thoughtful.'

'But it's only as a joke!' I replied sharply. He looked hurt.

I really must learn to control my sense of humour, I told myself, it never seems to amuse him.

—

There had been an honour killing in Haryana, and a sati episode as well. Both in the same family. Two sisters called Radha and Roop Kumari, from the Haryana village of Patrela, had hijacked the news channels with their connected tragedies. The younger one fell in love with a boy from the same gotra, and was shot dead, apparently by mistake, in a 'family celebration'. Her sister's husband, her jijaji, was also injured in the firing and died on the way to the hospital. Later, the surviving sister 'committed' sati. There was footage showing the girl being pushed into her husband's funeral pyre by her mother-in-law. As the flames gathered around her, garlands of marigold flowers were flung into the the fire by her own family and assorted neighbours.

Radha was dead, with two bullets in the stomach and one between her eyes—so neat, it could only have been at extreme close range. Her sister Roop Kumari was in the burns ward in Safdarjang hospital. The local MP condoled the 'death by accident' and condemned the sati as barbaric. But he added a calculated political conundrum: 'India is a society in transition,' he said to the cameras, fingering his tie as he spoke, 'and honour is a subjective thing. We must respect the age-old practices that define a society.'

The image of the teary-eyed young girl in her red sari stumbling into a heap of smoking wood to embrace her husband's burning corpse had been broadcast across every network in India. It was eerie, but she even had the same first name as that other, more famous sati, Roop Kanwar from Deorala, who had followed her husband to the afterlife in another village nearly twenty years ago.

We watched the news in silence, Suresh and I. It was clear both sisters had been done away with by their families, both in the name of honour and culture. Radha's death was being projected as an accident, even as village headmen twirled their moustaches and spoke of tradition. As for the sati, the local police intervened reluctantly and only at the very last moment, to extract a charred Roop Kumari from the fire. Although her mother-in-law Jamuna Bai had been arrested—and no one else—garlands, coconuts and red-and-gold chunris that celebrated Roop Kumari's martyrdom were selling at a premium along the Haryana Rajasthan highway.

Feminists and social activists had plunged into passionate public debate about 'Hindu fundamentalism'. The rightist loonies were equally excited about this miracle of faith. Papers and news channels hurled relevant sections of the Indian Penal Code knowledgeably at the public while the state governments of

Rajasthan and Haryana each claimed that the border village of Patrela fell in the jurisdiction of the other.

The right-wing rabble-rouser Naveen Jogara had rushed to the immolation site to pay homage to the Sati Rani, to the delight of all the competing news channels and their devout crews. The only problem was that Roop Kumari was still alive—barely—in the burns ward. She was not yet a martyr, only a potential one. And a potential criminal too: under the Commission of Sati (Prevention) Act, she was still liable to be tried for self-immolation and 'abetting culpable homicide'. Her own!

—

Luv has been sitting at home watching television. I suspect he's trying to avoid Monalisa. 'What kind of absurd religion is this, Maa?' (in an accusatory voice). 'How do you give social sanction to murder? What sort of politics endorses it? Face it—civilization has simply passed you by.'

'At least we are a free country with a free press,' I replied weakly, trying to come up with something positive.

'Everyone free to trample everyone else's freedom—Jesus Christ! You all live in the middle ages still!'

'It's "us", not "you". You can't become and un-become Indians as convenient. And what does Jesus Christ have to do with this?' I was quite proud of standing up to my son.

'I want to secede from your India. Many in my generation do. Maybe I should just return to the States,' Luv declared, the safety pin under his lip trembling in agitation.

'It's not *my* India!' I protested, back in my usual defensive role. 'Are you accusing me of endorsing sati?'

'That's what you did in Mumbai,' Luv retorted. 'The India your generation is leaving behind can't be our India!'

All this was happening at the dining table over a wholesome family dinner of dal, gobhi ki sabzi and bhindi fry. Fortunately Suresh hadn't picked up the sati reference. The television screen flickered on the wall, repeating the same breaking news headlines over and over again. And suddenly the lovely girl with the liquid eyes appeared, mike in hand. 'The people of Patrela are praying for a miracle . . .' she said, 'even as Roop Kumari battles for her life in the burns ward of Safdarjang Hospital!'

'That's Paromita!' I exclaimed, but the camera had moved on.

Luv sat up to catch a glimpse of the 'utterly gorgeous' TV reporter, and irritated at seeing not her but yet another shot of the burning pyre in Patrela, said: 'Barbarians!' And this finally provoked Suresh to speak.

Suresh's father was from Rajasthan. My husband carries a residual loyalty to the Idea of the Indian Woman, the Sacred Sati Savitri. 'What you must understand, son,' he said sagely, 'what you must understand is that India is like a serpent with its hood in the next century and its tail still in medieval times. Indian Womanhood is always associated with self-sacrifice. In no other nation, no culture, no continent, no religion—' he was getting carried away now—'do women live—exist—only for their families. Your Mother—' here he turned tenderly to me—'your mother is a True Indian Woman, the personification of a Bhartiya Nari. If I died, I very much doubt if she would want to continue living! Would you, Priya?'

My jaw dropped. What could I possibly say? Tell him it would be like reincarnation without dying? But no, I am an Indian woman. I stared at him speechlessly as he continued, a dreamy look playing upon his plump, superficially distinguished face.

'We must respect the feelings of Mother India, and her noble sentiments,' Suresh concluded, holding on to my hand as he spoke.

Luv had been feverishly scanning the channels, trying to locate Paromita again, but now there was a fresh headline riding the news. 'I'm going out with some friends,' our son announced, casting aside the remote. 'I'll be returning home late. If at all.'

And we were left alone together, man and woman, husband and

wife, mother and father. Suresh reached out for my hand. 'These young people,' he said, in a voice that was almost tender, 'how can they understand the deep depths of an Indian Woman's heart?'

I gave him the best un-reincarnated Indian Womanhood smile I could muster. It seemed to do the trick, for it pushed my husband to relocate his romantic impulses. I found myself in bed with him, wearing only my petticoat. Suresh had taken off his clothes too, except for his socks. It disconcerted me, somehow, all that pale flesh, and the white paws.

That night my husband made love, not just to me, but to Indian Womanhood. His movements were solemn and jerky when he began, like in a slow-motion film, and I was impatient rather than overjoyed. Suresh was eager to please, but that has never been his forte. He is a fumbler, lacking the velvet touch of my former boss. Yet, under the sheets, under the petticoat, I was suddenly hungry and full of desire. But my husband was paying homage to a Bhartiya Nari, and he was respectfully brief about it. Later, as his face loomed before me like an inflated balloon, his eyes met mine, and I saw love in them.

'I want to ask you something, Priya,' he said hesitantly. 'And I want you to reply with complete honesty.' Beneath the sheets, below the petticoat, something had stirred. I looked at him, at his large round eyes, his mouth, his lips as they mouthed those words.

'We have had an arranged marriage, Priya,' my husband continued. 'We have lived together in wedlock for three decades now. Not only have you shared my success, you have been responsible for it.'

I stared at him, a part of me distant, yet needy for his touch.

'If we were to meet, today, now, for the first time, would you say that you loved me? Would you love me? *Could* you love me?'

I am an Indian Woman. I cannot lie, but even more than that, I cannot tell the truth.

'Of course I love you, Suresh,' I said, as tenderly as I could, reaching out to stroke the distinguished streak of grey by his temples. But there were bits of me that had awakened, that were throbbing, screaming to be heard.

Suresh had tears in his eyes. 'It means a lot to me, Priya, what you just said,' he whispered. 'I love you too.'

I was shamed by his words. He turned over to switch the bedside lamp on, then he switched it off again. 'I want to tell you something,' he said, his voice laden with tenderness. 'If something should happen to me, if I were to suddenly die, I would want you to continue living, to be happy.'

I have thought over what he said, what he meant, what it means. It's puzzling to be a True Indian Woman, a Bhartiya Nari.

—

Got an sms from Pooonam, whom I'd met at the Bhandpur wedding. 'Gal palz get together sooon? Love smooch hugga bugga! Pooonam'

'Very sooon!' I replied. I really needed to make more friends.

—

The bad news came soon after. I came down with a massive full-blown cold. Also, I hit the headlines. Not the front pages, exactly, but a gossip item in the Deep Throat column of the *Indian Times*. 'Minister of State for Food Processing and Animal Husbandry Suresh Kaushal has been in the news recently, for all the wrong reasons. First his ministry was exposed for corruption under PDS. And now his wife Priya Kaushal has been sighted with their artist son endorsing sati in Amchi Modern Mumbai! Fundamentalists under the skin, perhaps?'

Suresh would be furious. It was an assault on his secular credentials.

I tiptoed into Luv's room to check if he was awake; he might know how to react. His bed had not been slept in. Had his resolve faltered? Was he trysting with Monalisa? I kept it all from Suresh, Luv's absence and the provocative item in the newspaper. Experience has taught me that things blow over if only one allows them to.

Roop Kumari died that afternoon. There had been rioting outside the Safdarjang Hospital. Teargas and marigold garlands, coconuts and incense and burning buses. Jogara was thundering on about the Bhartiya Nari and 'the Noble Indian Womanhood'. Strips of cotton from the bleached curtains of the burns ward were being sold as sacred relics at prices ranging from ten rupees to a lakh. I saw a gallery owner and her London-based installation artist lover at the auction, too—live on national television.

Luv was watching the riots on TV over a paratha brunch when he encountered the news item in the *Indian Times*.

'Oh no!' he screeched, very real panic reflecting in his young eyes. 'The tish will hit the ceiling now. The Rani Sati Samiti Memorial Society! Ha ha ha! I vote we don't tell Papa about this. Or Kush!'

We didn't tell his Papa about it. Instead we watched the media hysteria, while Hindu faith flexed and questioned itself. The Rani Sati Memorial Society surfaced again. A popular talk show had a public intellectual wearing thick glasses refer contemptuously to how a minister's wife, and members of the so-called political elite, defended sati, celebrated it, even. Fortunately I wasn't yet important enough for him to remember my name.

'I can't understand the Indian media . . . what's wrong with them?' I exclaimed.

'It's their job to mediate, that's why they are called the media,' Luv replied matter-of-factly. 'It's a free press, as you were pointing out the other day.'

Kush called from the US and he wasn't so tolerant. 'What's wrong with you, Ma?' he demanded. 'You and your idiot artist son seem bent on destroying my father's political legacy. The Google alerts are making me weep. The Overseas Indian News Agency has picked it up too—"Politician's wife endorses Sati." We—your husband, my father, and I—belong to a secular party. S.E.C.U.L.A.R. Get it?'

Of course Kush had spoken to his Papa as well. As had the Press Officer, and the PS and the PA, both busy demonstrating how each was busier than the other. Shriela Shetty carried an item in her dreaded column. 'Pssst . . . Is Ms Priya Suresh Kaushal asking us to be good women and commit sati?' she wrote. 'The wife of lawyer turned politico . . .' and so on.

I decided to blame it all on my brother. 'Atul Bhaiyya didn't tell me anything, just that there was an 8GR8 Women award. He tries to show off about being related to you, to gain points with his boss. I'll never speak to him again, or to that Dolly . . . never ever,' (and here I coaxed a tear from under my eyeliner) 'you mustn't blame me or Luv for this.' It worked, at least on a holding basis. Suresh shut his eyes and breathed very slowly as his lawyer's mind went into constructing a defence.

I was glad Kush wasn't around and could only be difficult long distance. Luv was being unexpectedly supportive and even offered to escort me to an art show to 'divert' me, so that I could 'chill' and let the 'tish' settle.

—

Pooonam UmaChand, Manoviraj Sethia's friend, mistress, business partner or whatever, was telephoning me. 'I've been hearing naughty things about you,' she said. 'You need to meet my astrologer soonest.'

One is cautious about astrologers. They can be fraudulent and manipulative, insinuating themselves into Delhi lives, trading the influence and gossip they collect. I'm not gullible, at least not as gullible as some of the people around.

'You must have a session with her,' Pooonam insisted. 'Nnutasha is a new-age numerologist. She is a healer, a mystic, a saint. Reiki, chakra, chanting, gemology . . . she knows everything. Nnutasha is ama-a-zing!' Here Pooonam launched into an incomprehensible story about her cousin or her best friend who was dying and penniless and was then retrieved from this unfortunate situation by the addition of an extra alphabet into her name at Nnutasha's suggestion. 'You absolutely *have* to meet Nnutasha, Priya!' Pooonam said with conviction. 'It will change the course of your life.'

I didn't want to change the course of my life. Okay, so there'd been some problems. Ground reality could always be improved upon. But Suresh and I had both worked long and hard to get where we were. I remembered the dreary train journey to BR's posh office in South Bombay, I could recall every stop and station along the way. Andheri, Dadar, Churchgate, V.T . . . It had been a long journey to 18 Dara Shikoh Marg.

I didn't say these things to Pooonam, only hemmed and hawed and promised to meet up soon.

—

That exhibition. It sounds like a cliché, but any child could have scrawled those pictures. The prices got me to re-examine the zeroes. Luv had made the right move—artists seemed to be raking in more moolah than even lawyers! (But not politicians.)

Llilly Vaish, Elvie to her friends, had curated the show. She was a lawyer before she discovered Art. I had suspected Suresh of having a crush on her, then. Elvie arrived, swinging her trademark Viutton bag. She introduced the glamorous society-lady artist who appeared to have painted her face with more skill and care than her canvases.

'So, Mrs Kaushal, did you like the works?' Elvie asked ingratiatingly, as the cameras crowded around us. 'You have such a true instinct for art . . .'

'These are lovely,' I replied insincerely. 'So colourful.'

'Oh, I'm sooo glad to have heard your views!' Elvie gushed, giving me an ecstatic hug. 'And we must show lovely Luv's talents soon.' She landed me a squelchy kiss on my cheek. That was when I realized something was very wrong. My cold had subsided but I still couldn't smell anything—nothing at all. The bouquet of expensive perfume and body odour and Delhi diesel that should have enveloped me with her embrace was absent. To use Luv's very favourite word, it felt weird. Like an absent sense or a misplaced instinct.

The gate-crashers had swooped upon the snack trays. The fashionistas and opportunistas and Ms Moneybags were parading and circling the hall. The art critics were looking depressed.

A tall young woman in a black khadi kurta and white khadi pyjamas was standing beside us. Her almond eyes, dabbed and streaked with kohl, were curtained by a long, deliberately straggly fringe. She turned to Luv and held the microphone before him. The camera-crew began fiddling with their cameras. 'Could you explicate on why you liked the work, exactly?' she asked.

It was Paromita. The angelic news anchor who had come to my rescue, my imaginary daughter-in-law—my Monalisa antidote. I looked at her with respect. It is not every young woman who can use words like 'explicate' in conversation, especially with strangers.

A coy look settled into my son's eyes. 'Well . . . I feel . . .' he said, smirking more than was necessary '. . . you know . . .' She smiled back encouragingly. Suddenly he took off.

'It's optic and tactile, although a bit sentimental . . . and the brushwork is uncertain, ill defined, if you get what I mean . . .' he said. 'I mean, I like it very much but . . .'

I didn't see what he meant, but the two young people were staring into each other's eyes as though they were using their optical apparatus for the first time, as though they had never before had a chance to observe eyelashes or pupils or even eyebrows. Love was clearly in the air. Lavaria, we had called it, when I was young.

'What do you mean, tactile?' Paromita asked. Now *she* was coy.

'I mean that, like a child, I want to reach across and touch it, stroke and explore it,' Luv replied.

Oh yes. The long fringe had parted to reveal her shining eyes now. I held my breath—any sensible mother-in-law would want her on the menu.

'We must never forget that the purpose of Art is to create enthusiasm!' Luv concluded, looking slightly embarrassed by his own vehemence.

'I'm Paromita,' she said. 'In case you've forgotten. I came to your house the other day . . . to interview your dad?' She had a way of concluding a sentence by modulating it into a question. We left the gallery together, Luv and I and the lovely Paromita, and found ourselves at the adjacent Alternative Art Ramp. The exhibition there was titled 'Tribal Dreamz' .

'You must meet the artist,' Paromita declared enthusiastically. 'A poet and craftsman equally in connect with rural tradition and contemporaneous idiom!' I winced. Her talent for long words and sentences was both charming and disconcerting.

The AAR had just a few stragglers, in handloom weaves and indigo dyes, the fuzziness of their styles and silhouettes as much statement as conviction. My nostrils were sort of tickling and I couldn't smell anything, but I'm sure BO was more in fashion with this crowd than cologne.

Luv was still staring ecstatically at the momentarily silent Paromita, when an untidy man with shining eyes and a gray beard clutched me by the arm.

'P-Priya Didi . . .' he stammered. 'I'm Lenin—d-don't you remember me? Aapka Lenin?'

How could I not remember him? Paro's boyfriend, my honorary rakhi brother, Lenin had been our first introduction to the heady heights of political power. Lenin's father was a minister in the cabinet, all those years ago, when Paro first fell in love with him. When Paro died, it was Lenin who had accompanied me to her funeral pyre to say that last farewell. How could I forget him?

'Are you Priya's son?' Lenin asked, scrutinizing Luv. 'You look so like your mother. I'm your old uncle, I've kn-known your parents for a lifetime.'

'And this is my daughter Paromita,' Lenin continued, a look of paternal pride filling up his familiar-unfamiliar face.

Paromita was Lenin's daughter! 'Luv, meet Avinendra uncle—whom you have heard so much about!' I said, rushing into counter-introductions. 'It turns out he is Paromita's father.'

'But your mother knows me as Lenin,' he beamed, 'an obsolescent politician, not the adolescent pop singer.' And as I heard him speak again, I smiled—of course Paromita was his daughter, she had his easy way with big, odd words.

'It's like the six degrees of separation,' Luv replied, switching suddenly to what I classify as his fake-firang voice. 'It's weird. In America, people have private lives. In this country, everybody seems to know everybody else, even though you have a billion plus people floating around.'

Luv had said you, not us. Again.

We did a round of the paintings. They had happy scenes of birds and animals and foliage, of hunters and lovers and gods—a nicer jungle than this dusty urban one. Lenin introduced us to the painter, Rangarh Shyam. 'From the Gond school of tribal art,' he explained. 'Bringing innocent folk dreams to your corrupt capital.' The painter was taut and watchful, like a crouching leopard or panther, ready to take on any unfamiliar urban confrontations.

We stopped before a series of portraits where the painter had stepped out of his naive folk style. These were powerful line drawings of tribal women, standing, squatting, gossiping, holding their children. Lenin seemed extremely moved by one of them. It was of a young woman with a flower in her hair. He took the painter aside and whispered into his ear, and Rangarh Shyam immediately placed a red sticker on the side of the frame. Lenin had bought the sketch. There were tears in his eyes as he contemplated it.

Lenin turned to me, a look of myopic joy suddenly suffusing his face. 'She is beautiful, isn't she?' he said. 'Just like you are. You know how much I've always cared for you, Priya, and how close we have been in the past. I want to tell you that I have always respected your simplicity and your honesty, and these are all shining through in your face even now. You still look beautiful, Priya.'

At a certain age of wrinkles and hot flushes, a solitary compliment is sometimes enough to spark a complete turnaround in attitude. Suddenly, in that narrow gallery, surrounded by acrylic forests and trees and hunters, Lenin's words made me feel beautiful. Strong and beautiful, at least for a while. After all, Lenin is always truthful—at least in what he thinks he's thinking :)

I searched for Luv, but he had made one of his elusive exits. Paromita had disappeared too. Had they left together? I certainly hoped so.

—

Kush was returning soon. He called with a volley of instructions about getting his car serviced, his air conditioner repaired, his kurtas starched.

'I'm not your PS or your PA,' I protested.

'But you are my mother!' he replied.

—

Luv helped me get on Facebook. 'Time to get connected, Mata ji,' he said, 'to join the dots with the rest of the world.' He posted a nice profile picture of me, sitting in the swing in our lawn. He put up photos of himself as well, and of Kush and Suresh. 'Your happy family,' he declared.

He led me to his homepage to explain what it's all about. There they were, his friends, all the young people to whom the world belongs. 'Who's that?' I asked, my eyes riveted by the snapshot of an exceptionally pretty girl.

'That's Ranu,' he replied. 'She's a huntress.'

'A huntress!' I echoed his words, smiling, containing my surprise.

'Think Warrior Princess. Think the Queen of Sheba. I'm in love with Ranu, maybe. She's from a royal family, and spends her time chasing Nilgai and wild boar. She's fantastic. Why don't you look pleased?'

'Hunting is banned,' I snapped. 'And royals—ex-royals—are an endangered species as well.' I didn't like the sound of this hunter-wali.

'It's just the thrill of the chase,' he replied. 'Ranu's planning to turn to wildlife photography instead.'

A reformed huntress. Marriage and adjustment are part of the same process. My maternal instincts calibrated the matrimonial prospects. I could see myself draped in a fine French chiffon sari, with a gota border, looking aristocratically motherly, as the shehnai players belted out weepy 'bidai' music . . .

Of course her parents might consider us commoners—but then, politicos are the new royalty, aren't they?

But what of Monalisa? And Lenin's daughter Paromita?

'I thought you liked Paromita,' I blurted out.

Bad move. Luv's eyes turned opaque, and he looked suddenly, startlingly, like Kush. 'There's enough love in my heart to go around, mother,' he replied warily. 'Enough and more.'

Will I ever understand my sons?

Luv was staring distractedly at his mobile phone. 'I have to rush to meet Monalisa,' he said. 'There's been a problem! And Ranu's waiting for me too!' And he dashed out of the room.

Suresh entered, as if on cue. 'Who is Monalisa? And Ranu?' he demanded petulantly. 'Nobody ever tells me anything.'

'Ranu's a huntress,' I explained helpfully. 'And Monalisa . . . you don't want to know who *she* is!'

'We need to spend quality time together,' Suresh said. Mr Cliche. And with whom were you spending quality time in Chennai? I thought to myself. My husband was looking more flushed than usual. I examined him closely. There was a mark on his cheek; it looked like lipstick. And on his collar too.

I couldn't control myself. 'Lipstick on your collar . . .' I shrieked, in a high-pitched voice that sounded crazy even to my own ears. Suresh looked at me worriedly.

'I was just feeling light-hearted and young,' I continued lamely. This was not the time for confrontation. Maybe it wasn't lipstick, but an ink stain. Or a paan stain. 'Let's go out for dinner, just the two of us? Quality time?'

We decided on 'Delhi Durbar', on the topmost floor of the Intercontinental. It was quite romantic, a dark, velvety alcove with the city spread out far below us. Suresh talked to me about his work, his career, about political factions and manipulated misunderstandings. 'There is a camp of party men who don't appreciate me, who are working against me,' he confided. 'It's the Rajya Sabha–Lok Sabha divide. Because I'm a professional, because I'm not a populist, they think I don't understand core issues.' Then he started off on the Finance Minister, and the Home Minister, and the HM's coteries and the FM's lobbyists, and although I didn't understand quite who was for or against whom I squeezed my husband's hand and looked sympathetic.

'They are just jealous of you,' I said. 'Because you have a mind of your own . . .'

Suresh looked pleased. He stared at me earnestly for a long time. 'Whatever people may say, I want you to know, Priya, that I love you with all my heart,' he declared solemnly. 'And I always shall.'

I was disarmed. I believed him—and besides, I had no choice. Forget about the lipstick. And the phone call. I hadn't dared dwell on it anyway. We looked into each other's eyes like teenagers, except, of course, that neither of us had looked much into anybody's eyes when we were teenagers. We had gone to the cinema, sometimes, boys with boys, girls with girls. Suresh had probably lusted after Sharmila Tagore, possibly Jaya Bhaduri. And me, I had worked in a swank office in South Bombay and worshipped my boss.

We looked out at the lights, at the city glittering and shimmering in the night. 'Ae Roshniyon Ke Shahar . . .' I murmured. This city of lights—everything had changed. Jaya Bhaduri was Jaya Bachchan now, Aishwarya Rai's mother-in-law. Rekha was still beautiful and enigmatic, but a ghost, really. And Sharmila with the overlined eyes was Begum Pataudi, mother of the new stars Saif and Soha . . . And her husband was a hunter too, I thought, quite irrelevantly.

Suresh reached out to hold my hand. 'Life has treated us well, Priya,' he said. 'Look at where we are today'—and his hand spread over the expanse of distant city lights—'quite literally, it's at our feet. Hard work has brought us here, and dedication!'

I wasn't listening to him, my mind was wandering still. I had forgotten Suresh, so solid, so serious, sitting there before me. I was thinking of BR, of his hypnotic eyes the night when he had first undressed me. When I was young. There had been music playing in the background. 'Stravinsky. The Rites of Spring.' I had not forgotten.

My husband was talking to me. I switched my attention back to the present. 'It's all karma, fate, destiny, kismet . . . Call it what you will,' Suresh was expounding, with almost mystical intensity. 'Que Sera Sera—whatever will be will be!'

He was humming aloud now, with ringtone veracity. 'Que Sera Sera . . .' Mood swings? He was beginning to sound a little strange to me. 'The future's not our..rrss to see . . . ee . . . But it is! I visited this numerologist today. Or rather, she came to see me. She feels extremely disturbed by the vibrations emanating from the sound of my name. It appears the numbers of my Given Name, that is to say my Destiny Numbers, and the numeric strength of my Birth and Fate Numbers are completely out of sync. It's all quite scientific, really, something to do with the DNA. I think that's what she said.'

I listened carefully, clouds of suspicion gathering in my head. The chicken lababdar was forgotten, the rumali roti turning to leather.

'She is amazing—no other word for it—a-ma-azing! Her name is Nnutasha—with two enns. She suggested I change the spelling of my name to Cowshall. C for Canada, O for Owl, W for Winnipeg, S for Simla, H for Holiday, A for Africa, and Double L, both for London.' He spelt it out very slowly, stressing each letter with a wave of his podgy fingers.

As they would say in Hindi, my mercury was rising. Mera paara chadh raha tha.

'NO.' I said very firmly. 'N for Nigeria, O for Orangutan. No cow in my name for me. I don't believe in all this luck by chance nonsense.'

My husband Suresh, Minister of State for this and that, was staring at me in genuine surprise.

'When I married you, Suresh, I was Priya Sharma. I then became Priya Kaushal. Your surname belongs to me, half and half. I am not a cow, and I shall not change my surname, even if some nutty numerologist or sexy arms-dealer's girlfriend with too many Os in her name can persuade you to change yours!'

With that, I rushed to the toilet and burst into tears. I feel safe in ladies washrooms, they are a sanctuary from social disasters, a place to retreat to and to mend and contemplate. I refastened my bra-strap, readjusted the pleats of my sari. A gaggle of happy, laughing girls burst in, like birds flying in formation. They had incredibly slim figures, and were moving restlessly from leg to leg as they revelled in what was clearly the scandal of the moment. There was much 'he said' and 'then she said' exchanged between them, punctuated by floods of helpless giggles. I felt a sharp, bitter stab of envy. I envied their youth, their certainty, their belief in themselves and the world.

This sounds stupid, but suddenly I saw my face looking back at me from the mirror, reassuring me. 'You are Priya Kaushal, not Cowshall,' I told the face in the mirror 'and you must remain her.'

I hovered by the lift for a while, wondering whether to stage a walkout and go home, or turn back to the restaurant and Suresh. Finally, I decided not to, and retraced my way to the Delhi Durbar. He was talking on two phones at the same time. 'She said,' he said, then abruptly cut the conversation short when he saw me. Who was he talking to?

The bill arrived, Suresh searched through his pockets but couldn't find any cash or cards. Finally I had to dig out my credit card and pay for dinner. We made our way home, our brief love-amnesty turned to a watchful truce.

When I returned to the bungalow there was an envelope waiting for me. It was from Paromita, Lenin's daughter. The envelope said just that: 'From Paromita—Lenin's daughter.'

There was a CD inside, labelled 'Hon'ble Shri Suresh Kaushal, TV Interview'. It had her visiting card taped to it. The card had a funky pink-and-blue design with a smiling tree with stretching branches drawn in a tribal sort of style. 'LET IT GROW' it said, in a speech bubble spouting from the friendly mouth drawn on the tree bark. It puzzled me, but not to the point of interrogation. The world is full of puzzling young people and Paromita was no different, I decided.

Luv was not at home, which was not unusual. His mobile had been left behind in his room, to charge. I justified the temptation to snoop as a mother's prerogative. Six missed calls from Paromita, and two messages: 'Call me back please.'

No mystery to it now. Lenin's daughter had succumbed to Luv's charms. She was appealing to his mother for help. And help I would. A mother's instincts are never wrong, and I knew that Paromita and Luv were meant for each other. For an Indian mother, her daughters-in-law-to-be hold the key to the future. Her sons, the chief capital, purpose and gratification of her life, will remain or retract according to the nature of her bahus-to-be. Luv was hovering on the brink of that precipice. It was my duty as his mother to oversee a smooth transfer of power.

—

In just one day, I received four offers of marriage for the twins. The first proposal arrived via my sister-in-law Dolly. 'Dearest Bhabhi,' she wrote, 'hereby forwarding an offer for dearest cutest Luv and Kush's hands in marriage. Netanjali and Getanjali, very suitable girls, are my neighbour's daughters in Mumbai. Mrs Chaturvedi is a homely lady with excellent disposition. They are well-off upper middle-class Brahmin UP peoples with middle-class values. It was striking to me about the pretty sisters that both have milk-white complexion. They are ideal life partner for some lucky guy, and so thought came to mind of your esteemed twin sons . . .' and so on. Although I am a snob, her presumption, more than her bad English, staggered me. Surely she must understand the middle-class dictum of 'arranged match in equal-status bracket only'?

I slipped into a rage, as I sometimes do when confronted by Dolly's tactlessness. I tore up her letter and hurled it into the artistic bamboo dustbin which had been gifted to Suresh during a recent visit to the North East. ('A dustbin?' I had wondered then. 'What sort of a gift is a dustbin?')

On second thoughts, I retrieved the shreds of Dolly's proposal and gathered them into a brown envelope, which I sealed and neatly labelled 'Dolly's Proposal'.

Then I set off to the ladies tailor in Khan Market. About time I changed my style. The old-fashioned katori-cut sari blouses are just too frumpy and day-before-yesterday. Backless, strapless blouses are in, very different from the drab, predictable half-sleeved poplin ones that I'd loyally stuck to, ever since my Bombay days.

Did I dare? I ordered a low-backed sari blouse in crinkled white chiffon with sequins worked in. I still have the figure for it and courage would surely follow. I returned home in time to view the matinee episode of a new horror serial on television—it kept the adrenalin in motion. I checked my weight, as I do every fortnight. It stood steady at 62 kilos. I wondered whether to call BR in Bombay. There is an etiquette to these things. Had he already forgotten our Night of Love?

A phone call from Pooonam UmaChand. She sounded as friendly and enthusiastic as ever. 'I have a proposal for you, Priya,' she said. 'Can I come over and discuss it with you? Pleeze pleeze!'

We housewives are not as stupid as we may appear. Pooonam and her astrologer friend Nnutasha were on the other side of the divide—the Righteous Indian Women team versus the Predatory Other Women brigade. Bhartiya Nari vs Husband Snatchers. In marriage, constant vigilance is the price of bondage. I was on my guard. Yet I invited her over.

My new friend staggered in wearing the most absurdly high heels I have ever seen. 'Jimmy Choo,' she announced, as she walked in. 'Only eight hundred dollars!'

I converted that into rupees, and gasped. My sandals, the kolhapuri with kitten heels style that I always wear, cost not more than eight hundred rupees. That converted to twenty dollars. And eight hundred dollars converted to? My mind boggled and my eyebrows went up like car wipers on a trial run.

'I love my feet,' Pooonam murmured, sinking into the sofa with a blissful expression on her pert, animated face. 'What I wear on my feet is as important to me as sex. I have a Jean Paul Gaultier, and an Alberta Ferretti, and a Valentino,' she confided. 'And of course some Manolo Blahnik and Ferragamo shoes. And Prada, for daily wear.'

'That's quite a lot of lovers,' I replied. I thought that was quite funny but she took no notice of my friendly joke. Instead, she continued massaging her absurdly tiny feet, a sensuous expression flooding her face as she stroked them.

'But Jimmy Choo is on top of my must-lust obsessions.'

I didn't know quite what to say to that.

'In the end it all boils down to accessories,' she went on, 'shoes and bags and glasses. Ideally I suppose one mustn't mix brands, but I'm quite adventurous on that front. Handbags and heels! That's what life's all about!'

I was listening bemused. My poplin sari-blouse with its elbow-length sleeves pricked at my skin, my comfortable kolhapuri chappals shrivelled up in shame.

'How do you manage it, Pooonam?' I asked abjectly. 'How do you manage to float around in such high heels?'

She looked philosophical. 'There's a trick to it,' she replied. 'The way to wear Very Very High Heels lies in disconnecting your feet from your head. Deny the pain. Refuse to feel the hurt. And, above all, don't teeter or totter. Learn to levitate six inches above the ground. Like a hovercraft.'

With her glowing skin and her seductive confiding voice, and her languorous reclining pose, Pooonam seemed to be slowly expanding and filling up the room. 'I ordered a Mondrian-inspired organza dress from Bhootika and Bhayanika today,' she said, changing the subject. 'Somehow, it's so very me. It has an empire cut, and the high-waisted bit really does things for my oomph!'

There was a wild look in her eyes now. 'It really turns the men on,' she murmured reminiscently. 'An empire waist and a bit of frilly-front boob show and poof!—the man is mine!'

I was mesmerized, like a rabbit on the road hit by a hunter's blinding headlights. 'Just like that?' I asked weakly. 'That sounds great! I mean, wow, really great!'

Pooonam stared at me consideringly, sizing up my boob size, my waist. 'You could do it too, yaar!' she exclaimed. 'You could go for an empire cut. A classic empire style—that's the story this year, in New Delhi.'

She fell into a fit of giggles, soft wiggly squeals that were accompanied by a sinuous laughter-dance. Then she extended a long, curved, red fingernail towards my shoulder, and stroked my spine softly. 'It turns them on,' she whispered. '*I* turn them on!'

It almost turned me on too, her slithery fingers creeping over my back. Could husband and wife be turned on by the same woman? No, I decided firmly.

'Like it?' she said, shaping her mouth into a seductive pout. I wondered worriedly if Pooonam was on something, but she didn't do it again. Instead, she suddenly sat up straight and looked normal once more. By her standards, that is. 'Only joking, my darling!' she said. 'I have a proposal for you, Priya—a serious proposal. For your twins. Luv and Kush. Such cute boys, such sweet names. How old? Twenty-five?'

I nodded, still speechless and a little shaken from her earlier performance.

'Two two boys—you are really lucky yaar. I hope you realize how lucky! You just must listen carefully to me pleeze. Quietly! Bilkul chup! My partner—my biz partner Manoviraj Sethia—has a bee-ooo-ti ful daughter. Suzi's sister, Suki . . . you saw her at the wedding. Now my Manoviraj wants his daughter Suki to settle down in a decent cultured family. Like Suzi did. And he is ready to pay for it. Dowry is a dirty word—bada ganda lagta hai. We are not talking dowry here. We are talking about a settling-down sum. A settlement. A flat in Golf Links—or Jorbagh. And six crores in cash. Totally, it's several million dollars plus. Negotiable on the table. Besides that, all the shaadi vaadi ka tamasha, fancy five-star wedding, VIPs, Cabinet ministers, industrialists, all that lot. A beach reception in Bali for everyone. Not Amrana fort again. And Bangkok is so vulgar, you know.' She had begun to squirm around on the cushions, like a beached mermaid.

Luv? or Kush? Which of them had a beautiful heiress in their destiny?

'But they don't know each other,' I said, breaking in nervously as she stopped to take a deep breath. 'And they may not like each other!'

'Like-shike nothing!' Pooonam replied firmly. 'None of that matters. Love is a lottery. Besides, marriage is not forever.'

Junior's sister-in-law Suki. The girl in the golden lehnga. The wannabe Bollywood babe. Might she make one of my sons happy?

'Think about it again,' Pooonam said gaily. 'It's value for money. Cash and kind and a bee-ooo-tiful girl. Take it or leave it!'

She stroked my back again, with her long nails, and pursed her plum-shaded lips into a tight rosebud. Struggling to get up from the sofa, she re-hoisted and balanced herself into her eight-hundred-dollar Jimmy Choo footwear. 'These shoes are killing me,' she winced. 'I wish I was tall enough to wear flats.' She thrust a gift-wrapped perfume into my hands and teetered out into the late-afternoon heat, scattering air kisses in my direction as she left.

I unwrapped the bottle of 'Sublime' and sprayed it on my wrists. Nothing. I could smell nothing. It's a frustrating experience not to be able to smell perfume. I poked a finger into my armpit and put it to my nose. No whiff of sweat. Nothing. No smell. I felt desperate. And disoriented. It was like losing one's instinct.

That evening, I sat in my bedroom, wearing my oldest Janpath batik kaftan, sipping a lime-soda, and surveying the rack of soft well-worn Kolhpuri chappals and modest out-of-style high-heeled sandals. What was wrong with me? Was something wrong with me? Was I losing my senses, to consider selling one of my twins to an eager family of arms-dealers? I had an arranged marriage myself, but this was different somehow.

I broached the subject with Suresh over a simple meal of dal, bhindi fry, potatoes and cucumber raita. (Pooonam was doubtless nibbling on foie gras or asparagus spears or ricotta cheese in her corner of the universe.) 'Pooonam discussed a marriage proposal with me today,' I said tentatively.

'Oh, so she brought it up, did she?' Suresh responded, digging intently around the potatoes as though excavating, and expecting something different to appear.

'The girl seems to be from such a super-rich family. I'm not sure . . .' I said.

'Oh Priya! What's wrong with that? Let's be practical for a change!' he snapped, giving up in disgust on the potatoes.

I sat back, rebuked, stricken by shame and doubt. Had he already discussed this with Pooonam UmaChand? Or with Nnutasha?

'*You* never asked my family for a cowry. When we got married, you told my mother you expected nothing. "Dulhan hi dahej hai," you had said. I remember that still. But you seem to have forgotten, Suresh!' I couldn't keep the hurt out of my voice .

'Priya my rani. Those were different days. We must move with the times, with our status. After all, we don't need to make the same mistake twice. Do we?'

'I was a mistake?' I asked, tears stinging my eyes.

'Don't be silly, Priya, you know exactly what I mean. It's a good family—good enough for Bucky Bhandpur, good enough for

Paro's son. It could settle Kush forever. Or Luv. Cash and kind never hurt anyone! And darling, can't we please move on from this boring dal and potatoes menu sometimes? It's loaded with carbohydrates and so very predictable.'

We had been eating dal bhindi aloo all our married life. And now he wanted to move on.

The third proposal came from my old office friend Mary Gonsalves, who had caught up with me on Facebook. 'Remember vada pao and aamchi Mumbai and your old friends Ivy and Mary?' she wrote on my wall to announce herself.

Mary and I used to work together at the head office of Sita Sewing Machines. Her husband Robert was currently Special Secretary to a Gujarati billionaire—one of the 'Big Five', she told me. 'Mr Melwani's eklauti daughter Ina is sterling swayamvar candidate for one of your handsome sons,' she wrote. 'Look her up on FB for details.'

I summoned up Ina Melwani but there was only a picture of her pet poodle on view.

The last proposal. It came from Paromita herself. 'Cn I c u tonite, Priya aunty?' she asked, in an urgent, cryptic sms message. '10 pm plz if not 2 late?'

Our dismal dinner over, Suresh had settled himself in his study, where he was poring over a stack of files. 'Pls cm' I messaged back to Paromita, and waited in my room, watching a mindless Saas Bahu soap on television.

Paromita rushed in wearing a vermilion crinkled cotton skirt with gold khari work motifs, and a white cotton man's shirt with rolled-up sleeves. Her lovely hair was open, fanning out around her tiny waist. She was wearing gold jhumkas in her ears, silver payals on her feet. Kohl-lined eyes, glass bangles and a man's watch completed the strange but charming ensemble.

'I don't know how to say this, Priya aunty,' she began, without any preliminaries. 'I want to make a proposal. I want to marry your son. Luv. Do you think he would agree?'

Was she crazy? What was wrong with her?

'I know you must think I'm crazy, aunty Priya, but the world has changed, and then it hasn't. My parents won't arrange a marriage for me, they are much too preoccupied with their own lives. There aren't that many suitable boys around in Delhi. And all the nicest ones are gay so that counts them out.'

She took a long deep breath. 'I must tell you this too. I was in a relationship but it didn't work out. And now my biological clock is ticking away.'

Paromita was wringing her hands in agitation, and flicking her long hair this way and that as she spoke. 'And then I met your son—and it was as though I had known Luv already for thousands of years. You know what I mean. I think I love him. And so I thought—why not take my own *rishta* to his family? And then, I'm sort of traditional, so I thought why not go about it the old fashioned way?'

I was staring at her, flabbergasted. She reached for her bag and took out a red cloth-bound booklet.

'I brought my horoscope along,' she explained, 'just in case you needed to see it. And you already know my family—I mean I'm your friend's daughter, you know my parents already—I think.'

I took her in my arms and hugged her, 'You sweet silly girl,' I said. 'You are Lenin's daughter—and it shows! I would love you to be my daughter-in-law, but . . .' Even as I spoke, an army of tanks rolled over my imagination, all labelled CAUTION! 'But we have to ask Luv first. And his father.'

'Well, then, I'll leave this with you,' Paromita said, handing me her horoscope. 'And yes, I can cook and I'm well trained in housework by a very strict mother!' An unexpected dimple appeared on her cheek and a mischievous look lit up her eyes. 'The world has changed, you know, aunty Priya, since you were young. One has to be proactive, and ask for what one wants, or else someone else will grab it.' And she matkoed out.

An sms message flicked on my screen minutes after she had left. 'DNT TLL PPA PLZ' it urged.

I didn't mention Paromita's proposal to Suresh or to Luv. My artist son seems to be caught up with all sorts of things. He's busy contemplating his future. He's occupied designing a range of male fashion accessories for a new luxury outlet in Mumbai. He's obsessed with luring the huntress Ranu out for dinner. He's constructing a mixed-media memoryscape dedicated to Monalisa Das Mann. It's titled 'Tryptich of RegretS' and has torn-up pictures of her stuck around three fanned-out boards covered with laminated egg-trays. I hope that is a negative signal.

—

Luv displayed 'RegretS' to his father with trusting enthusiasm. The egg-tray tryptich had Suresh flummoxed. He scratched his head, then pulled at his ear, trying to conceal his puzzlement. 'Very nice, very nice,' he murmured. 'Really quite original work.'

'Have you ever considered studying law, Luv?' Suresh ventured a little later, at breakfast. My husband was working through a bowl of fluorescent-orange seedless disco-papaya, and a bit of it had attached to his chin. Otherwise he was the very portrait of paternal concern. 'All this art shart—I wouldn't depend on it, son,' he said. 'Whereas law is a steady and stable profession.'

Luv looked alarmed, then betrayed. 'Really papa, what are you suggesting?' he said, after chewing on the idea for a minute. 'Do you really expect me to go waddling around, dressed like some wacky penguin, pimping for weird criminals and cheats, M'Lording judges with exaggerated opinions about themselves? Let me concentrate on correcting the aesthetic aberrations and design catastrophes in our culture!'

What long words he uses, I thought. Like Paromita, really. Are they soulmates?

Suresh reacted to this rambling retort by ignoring it altogether. 'And what about marriage, son?' he continued, wiping the papaya off his chin. A confiding man-to-man note had entered his voice. 'Have you thought about getting married? Finding a life partner?'

Luv looked embarrassed and tugged awkwardly at the safety pin on his lip. 'Actually, there are a lot of babes who seem to be on your wavelength too, but count me out of the action, Pitaji.'

Suresh sent me a secret, conspiratorial look. 'There is a young lady we would like you to meet,' he said, 'the daughter of a dear friend. If you married her, you could continue painting shainting without any financial worries.'

'I'm still young, pops!' Luv protested, 'Give me a break. One day I'll walk in here with the devi of my dreams—until then, be patient please.'

Luv and Suki? they belonged to different worlds. I thought of Paromita, with her long hair and crinkled skirt, and her determined proactive proposal. I could see Paromita as his wife. But I said nothing.

Suresh was by now distracted by two simultaneous phone calls and some breaking news on television. Luv slid off on one of his mysterious errands and I settled into a cane chair in the verandah and surveyed my bungalow-kingdom over a cup of coffee.

It was the prettiest sight in the world. Parrots cavorted about the mango trees. Crows cawed wisely as they dunked their scavenged snacks into the terracotta bird bath I had artistically placed in the centre of the lawn. Doves cooed among the cornices of the pillars in the verandah. Bees buzzed about the flowerbeds, while birds twittered and waited patiently for their turn in the birdbath after the crows had left. This idyllic calm was broken as a ginger cat leapt from a tree and caught a dove in mid-flight. Suddenly there was a fluttering and flapping around me—panic in the avian world—and I was left reflecting on the vulnerability of all happiness.

I got on with my day, my life. I checked the dust-levels in neglected corners of the bungalow to ensure the peon on duty had reached out with his blue checked duster for eye-level dirt and above. It's anyway perplexing for a 1BHK-born girl to supervise the upkeep of a 4-bedroom-2-pantry-3-living rooms-twelve staff-quarters-plus annexe two-and-a-half-acre bungalow. And 18 Darah Shikoh Marg is in constant need of first aid and emergency repairs. The plumbing in the spare bathroom had returned to nature. I got the office to request the CPWD to send someone to tackle it. But the Central Power and Works Department dedicates itself to the whims of the high and mighty and, as a junior minister's wife, they never pay much attention to my complaints. I will tell Suresh to tell his PA to tell the PA of the Urban Housing minister. There is no other way.

Mayaram, the washerman from the staff quarters, came to see me about a new electrical point for his heavy iron. Coal was becoming unaffordable, he lamented, and the electric iron just didn't have the same weight and pressure. Then there was the matter of my new spaghetti-strap sequinned blouse. The sequins fell out on being ironed, he said. 'No good, no good,' he added, suddenly switching to English. I'd been cheated by some third-rate designer, he commiserated in Hindi. His daughter Dayavati was studying Fashion Technology at the Vocational Studies Polytechnic. 'My daughter Daya, she is making blouse for you Madom,' he said, again in English, although I was speaking to him in Hindi. 'Daya is very latest fashion designer.'

He presented me with a bound portfolio of Daya's designs. They were surprisingly good, very understated and sophisticated. 'Daya designing sari blouse for you Madom,' the dhobi persisted. 'She will make the visit to you tomorrow.'

What was wrong with the man? Had he suddenly forgotten how to speak in Hindi?

'Why do you not speak in Hindi?' I asked, trying to sound puzzled, not irritated. It wasn't as if I believed he had no right to speak to me in English. But a confidently English-speaking dhobi confused me.

'I am doing Rapidex English Course, Madom,' he replied.

'Without the English bhasha, no progress, no aage badhne ka proper chance. You hear of Angrezi Devi? She is goddess of English language. We pray to her. She blesses have-nots to move up. Thanks.'

Just then I received an excited phone call from the impossible Pooonam, begging me to join her for coffee at the Park Inn hotel. 'It's a crisis, my darling,' she wailed, as the dhobi said 'See you, Madom' and left. 'I need your wise advice. Pleeze pleeze pleeze Priya, I need you.'

What was up? I needed to stay in the picture, so I set off with Ghafoor to the Park Inn, thankful that it wasn't a Friday.

The coffee—a Javanese and pure vanilla concoction—seemed priced at a month's wages on the current poverty index. Pooonam began on her woes. 'I'm spoilt for choice, Priya,' she declared. 'There are two offers before me and I have to decide between them. One is to head a big charity—the Hope for the Helpless Trust—to really help the poors This charity-sharity gives a good opening into society, you know. Also to bureaucrats. And of course I am a kind-hearted person.'

I nodded, though I couldn't say I agreed.

'And now Cancelli are entering the Indian market. It's a top-end international brand. They are setting up new shoe-and-bag retail outlets, and they want me to be their brand ambassador!' Pooonam fluffed out a bit while announcing this, like a pouter pigeon.

'Why can't you do both?' I enquired innocently. Pooonam screeched so loudly that the people at the next table turned to stare at us.

'Meri Jaan!' she chided. 'A brand ambassador has to look beautiful *all* the time. It takes a lot of mehnat and very hard work to look beautiful. I need to tone and exercise, groom and accessorize. I have to nurture and exfoliate my skin. Jayanti has to do my hair. I have to have a gorgeous man on call to escort me—or a high-profile woman friend like you. How can I rush around slums in high heels carrying Cancelli bags? Tell me that, my dear Priya, if you are as intelligent as I know you are . . .'

She was cooing at me again. I was mesmerized by her. Pooonam dripped, radiated, glamour. And she seemed to genuinely like and admire me. I wasn't used to that.

'The choice is clear, I suppose,' I pondered. 'Cancelli wins, Lady Brand Ambassador.'

'Then maybe you could take on the Hope for the Hopeless?' she pouted. 'Be the change—it's all about the power of one! Pleeeeze darling, do help me out on that. I will suggest your name to the committee. Say yes, my gulab jamun.'

I have always been touchy about my wheatish complexion. 'What do you mean gulab jamun?' I bristled.

'Oh sorry darling—I meant my rossogolla!' she tinkled, a hint of mischief in her highlighted eyes. Was she laughing at me?

A familiar looking young girl ran into us in the lobby, just as we were about to step out.

'Suki—what a surprise!' Pooonam exclaimed. 'Sukita, meet my bestest friend Priya. Suki is Manoviraj Sethia's younger daughter. And Priya is the mother of the two handsome twins Luv and Kush. Arre look at you . . . you are both wearing blue. Two in blue! Tee hee!! That's a good sign, isn't it?'

I examined Suki with interest. She was wearing solitaire danglers the size of grapes, and the effect was blinding. She held out her hand; her palms were damp and clammy. I had the uneasy feeling of being carefully scrutinized. My sons and our family were on offer.

'Hello, Mrs Kaushal,' she said at last, after a minute or so of intense consideration. 'I've heard so much about you. I'm sure we'll meet again. Soon.'

'I have to leave now; my husband must be waiting,' I said, as I stepped into the shabby government Ambassador car.

'We're planning a Botox brunch next Sunday,' Pooonam called after me. 'Do come, it will be good for your marriage. And learn to keep your husband waiting sometimes.'

I was furious. I would see less of Madame Brand Ambassador in future, I resolved.

We were passing Jantar Mantar to make our way to Janpath, when we were halted by a protest march. A tide of women in red and blue ankle-length ghagras, heads and faces demurely covered, their feet in hardy leather jutis. They carried placards in Hindi and English. 'Hunger is the Oldest Violence' they said, and 'Food Security is Our Birth Right'—'Aahar Hamara Adhikar Hai'. Men in bright turbans were trailing after them, but it was the women who were doing the protesting.

A frail figure was crossing the road, a shabby jhola slung from his shoulders. Suddenly he fell into a faint before us. There was a furore among the women. 'Bhaiya ji gir gaye!' they exclaimed, milling around to attend to him.

I recognized the man. It was Lenin. He was ashen-pale and soaked in sweat. He didn't seem to recognize me. We got him into the car. 'Take us home, quickly,' I told Ghafoor. 'Jaldi ghar chalo!'

In the car, Lenin gave me a sideways look but seemed not to have registered who I was. His head was lolling slightly to one side, and a dribble of spit and froth was settling on the edge of his lip. The lifeless pallor of his face frightened me. His nails were encrusted with dirt. Had he been drinking?

We reached Dara Shikoh Marg. I led Lenin to the living room, and settled him on the sofa, making sure that his filthy jhola stayed on the floor. Ramdhan brought him a glass of chilled water, which I coaxed him to drink.

Just then Suresh entered the room, followed by an entourage of assistants and secretaries. A look of extreme surprise crossed his usually impassive face.

'It's our Lenin—Avinendra Shukul,' I explained, a note of apology creeping into my voice. 'Surely you remember him. Our friend—*Paro*'s friend! Lenin wasn't feeling well, so I brought him home.'

Suresh examined Lenin with astonishment and slight distaste.

Then he turned to his PA. 'Call for a doctor immediately,' he snapped, and left the room again.

Lenin was looking a bit better now. 'I'm sorry, my patient Priya,' he said. 'I've had a bout of tummy troubles after spending a month in Chhattisgarh, in the forests with some hapless tribals. The government, including my respected wife Geeta, calls them M-Maoists and t-t-terrorists but really they are like people everywhere, threatened and trying to s-survive.'

'I met your daughter Paromita again recently,' I told him, 'and she's lovely.'

'Aah, Paromita . . . the poor child. I named her after our Paro, and Geeta after her favourite Buaji, her father's sister. Paromita seems to have taken after me more than her mother. That's a difficult inheritance, as you know, P-Priya, better than anyone else.'

'What complete nonsense, Lenin!' I protested. 'You are one of the nicest people I have ever met. You know exactly how special you are, for all of us.'

Lenin was getting into form again. 'Special!' he scoffed. 'Yes, especially naïve, especially s-stupid, th-that's me. In a world where s-success is all that matters, I'm a s-sentimental failure, a b-blot on s-society. A prodigal father. I hope Paromita keeps away from my example.'

'Don't be silly, Lenin,' I scolded affectionately.

'But I have been a prodigal parent. You know me better than most people, Priya,' he continued. He was talking very slowly and softly and it was a strain to listen to him 'I have a confession to make, about my d-double life. About ten years ago, when Paromita was thirteen, I ran away. I couldn't cope any more with the cruelty and complacency of India Shining, and with Geeta, who was on the success curve, climbing up. I opted out, left home and moved to a village in Bastar where some friends ran an NGO. I didn't do anything there, just smoked a lot of hash and beedis and lay in the grass looking up at the blue sky, and wrote a diary sometimes.

'I met Banwari there, fell in love with her. Things were already getting difficult then. The Naxals were growing stronger, and the Sulwa Judum was active too. Ideologically, I sided with the Marxists—I m-mean that's clearly where the balance of justice lay—but I was so deeply in love with Banwari that nothing else seemed to matter. I lived in her petticoat, literally, for those years.'

I nodded sympathetically. 'Banwari died last year in an encounter—I'm sure the cops just shot her, because I never saw her with a gun. But she had changed too, you know. She had begun to despise me, thought I was weak and w-worthless. I suppose she was right. It's Paromita who rescued me, got me home, rehabilitated me into the middle classes. It was difficult to return home to Geeta, but Paromita looked after me like a baby. She is a good girl, a good daughter.'

A good daughter makes a good daughter-in-law, I thought to myself.

'Winners and losers, that's what this new world is about,' Lenin went on, unable to stop, as if making a much needed confession. 'It's not poverty that is considered the problem anymore—no, it's the poor themselves! My wife Geeta says I romanticize poverty. You know that's not true. I love the good life, always have. Paromita took me to one of the new malls recently, and I thought I had died and reached heaven. There was a man playing the piano near the elevators, the theme tune from *Dr Zhivago*. We went to an organic ice-cream outlet and had a "Slurpy S-Strawberry Special". It seduced me, that mall, until we stepped out and I saw the steel and glass reflected in the eyes of the b-beggar children outside . . .' I knew Lenin, and his constantly self-questioning honesty.

'So did you enjoy the ice-cream?' I asked, trying to lighten the mood.

Lenin nodded sadly.

'Call me sentimental, or out of tune with the times,' he continued. 'Everybody has a mobile with a jhinchak ringtone and life sounds bhangra pop all the way, but I can't get over the sense of having lost something very precious, something the others haven't yet noticed in the rush of getting on to the success bus, in the f-fear of getting l-left behind.'

His head was beginning to loll, in the alarming way it had earlier. The doctor walked in escorted by Suresh's PA. He checked Lenin's pulse and listened carefully with his stethoscope before prescribing some innocuous placebo. And then Lenin was in a sudden hurry to leave. 'I'm all right, Priya, I really am,' he insisted, as he wobbled out of the room.

I called for Ghafoor, instructed him about the medicines, settled Lenin into the car, and sent him off home. I tried Paromita's number on my phone, but it was switched off.

Lenin has left his jhola behind. I shall return it to him when I see him next. It's filthy; maybe I should wash or dryclean it before that.

—

I emptied out Lenin's cotton jhola and sent it to the dhobi to be washed. There was a notebook in it and two photographs. One of Paro, a publicity still from when she had acted in that dreadful Krishen Narain Singh convent-Hindi production of *Clytemnestra*. The other was of a shy, attractive girl wearing two noserings and a flower in her hair. Banwari. She looked like an ayah, if you know what I mean.

One is taught not to snoop, but I couldn't resist the temptation. I opened the notebook and began reading . . .

There was an entry, with a strange heading. 'A Donkey Factfile' it read.

A beast of burden, a complicit domestic creature, the donkey is the true metaphor of our times. The price of a donkey depends on its height, colour, age and number of teeth. The costliest donkeys in India, from Kathewada in Gujarat, are priced at 10 to 15 thousand rupees each. The work output of an average donkey equals that of seven to ten manual labourers, depending of course on their height, race, age, etc. As migrant labour from Bihar, Andhra, Uttar Pradesh, and Rajasthan demand at least minimum wages, builders and construction companies have turned to donkeys for support.

Lenin's handwriting was getting larger and stragglier and more difficult to read. I struggled to make sense of the words but couldn't, and gave up.

So Lenin had fallen in love again! Lenin the Maoist, the perpetual revolutionary. I knew it was all talk, I couldn't see him hurling bombs and plotting effectively against the state. He didn't have it in him.

I tried to picture him with the girl in the photograph with the flower in her hair. She was completely and absolutely the opposite of Paro, but that didn't surprise me, somehow. Lenin was a romantic, doomed to lose in love. That explained the hurt that had settled over him, the despair that seemed to engulf him.

I looked at Banwari's picture again. She had been very young then, whenever the photograph was taken. Poor Lenin. And, I suppose, poor Banwari.

Bumped into Poonam in Khan Market today. She was walking a tiny Chihuahua pup on a long spangled leash. She let out an excited squeal when she saw me. 'Isn't Lexus chu-weeeet?!!' she asked. 'Manoviraj gave him to me! And he's going to gift me a real Lexus luxury car next . . .'

Well, she certainly does have her boyfriend on a leash, doesn't she?

—

Kush returned from the States looking unusually upbeat. I had to unpack his bags, send his jeans and underwear to the dhobi, make sure that there were enough starched white cotton kurta-pyjamas in stock for his Delhi desi-boy style profile. I found a pack of condoms in his bag. It shocked me, though I do of course realize that my son is a grown-up man with a sexual life and all that.

Suresh discussed the proposal with him. 'Manoviraj Sethia's daughter Suki is a highly suitable marriage prospect,' he said. 'It's a good idea for you to meet her and judge if you are compatible.'

'I'll ask Suki out for dinner,' Kush replied unflinchingly. 'Do you have a number for her? Though I know her on Facebook already.'

Kush took Suki to see a film and for an Italian meal after that. He charged the dinner to his father. He discussed it with us over breakfast the next morning. Luv was still asleep—breakfast isn't his time of day.

'I've assessed the Sethia chick,' Kush announced. 'It's like a merger or an amalgamation. One has to study the fundamentals.'

Kush told Ramdhan to get him a poached egg and a bowl of cereal. I reached out for a chikoo. It was soft and sweet and brown.

'So the money is fine—there's lots of it and I can use it in my political career. And Suki's fine too, she's pretty and fun and practical. But the crucial question remains: Can Sukita be an effective political wife? Can she help me fight an election? Is she the right candidate for that role? Ma, Papa, I'm not convinced about that. But I'll date her again and weigh the options.'

Suresh and I exchanged glances. A practical son and an impractical one. Couldn't God have evened it out a bit?

I hadn't forgotten Suki's clammy handshake and her scrutinizing looks. She was clearly used to getting what she wanted. If she knew what she wanted, that is.

Kush had gone off again, on a mysterious weekend trip to Dubai, where he was to meet with an Islamic banking consultant to discuss some pending deal that didn't seem to be moving. I hoped that he could leverage it so he never had to depend on the Sethias of this world for money. Or on Suki.

THIS MORNING, AS I REACHED BLEARY-EYED FOR MY WAKE-UP CUP OF tea, I saw an arresting photograph on page one of the *Indian Times*. It was of a noble-looking person with a flowing grey beard atop a reluctant donkey. There was something Biblical about his pose, about the tilt of his head. Compassion reflected in his eyes, and a sort of silent sorrow. Behind him, an unshaven young man who looked like an auto-rickshaw driver held up a placard that read: 'I am NOT a Dunkey.' The eyes held me, even though my mobile was buzzing and my morning tea getting cold. It took me some time to make the connection. The man in the 'I am NOT a Dunkey' photograph was my friend Lenin

Lenin had helped organize the 'Donkey March for the Dispossessed'. Coordinated by a consortium of radical NGOs, it got a hundred donkeys plodding from Jantar Mantar all the way to India Gate, defying police restrictions. 'Ham Gadhe Nahi Hain' the placards read. 'We Are Not Donkeys'. 'Give Us Back Our Rights, Give Us Back Our Land.'

The *Clarion* carried a thoughtful editorial piece, written by a JNU professor, about the significance of the Donkey March. It discussed pressure on agrarian resources, the conflict between Bharat and India, and the needs and demands of the two Indias. Lauding 'engaged catalysts' like Lenin, it spoke of 'staying alive at the bottom' and of the 'binary bifurcations' between urban and rural India. It despaired about the haves and the have-nots, even as it summoned the spectre of sub-Saharan Africa. It spoke of labour nomads, marginalized landowners, and the dynamics of poverty. Good stuff, I thought, even if a bit over the top intellectually.

'The rich get richer, while the poor get poorer,' it concluded, 'but the Public must remember that the poor are NOT Dunkeys.'

I had read it carefully. There were lots of words I did not understand. 'What is "immiserization"?' I asked Suresh, who too was pondering the picture of Lenin astride a donkey.

'Immiserization?' he replied. 'I haven't heard that word before. Why don't you ask that joker Lenin? He seems to know all about donkeys and monkeys.'

There was a note in his voice, not just of scorn but of mild envy—jokers who made it to the front pages of newspapers were clearly jokers of a different scale.

—

The Donkey saga hasn't ended. The television channels have lapped up the March of the Dispossessed, they can't seem to have enough of it. 'What precisely are you trying to prove by this march?' glamorous young women anchors ask the protestors, in a range of variously accented voices.

'That we are people too.' 'We are not donkeys.' 'We want our rights.' 'We demand our rights.' 'It's the police who are donkeys . . .' 'It's the government which is full of donkeys . . .'

I surfed the channels searching for a glimpse of Paromita but Lenin's daughter was not to be seen either as an anchor or among the ranks of the demonstrators. There was a short clip of Lenin riding on a donkey. Some trick of the light gave the shot a strange, surreal serenity. Light filtered through the branches of a leafy tree, framing his face in a luminous halo.

'Why are you here, in this donkey march?' The girl who asked Lenin the question had a wide space between her two front teeth, and a visible squint. 'What is the message of this march?'

Then the sounds of birds chirping on the soundtrack. 'I am here,' Lenin replied, 'because I believe in India—in our country, in our future, in our past.' Then he switched to chaste Hindi. 'Vyang mein yeh bhi kaha ja sakta hai ki bechara gadha hamari sabhyata ka prateek hai,' he said. 'The donkey has become a symbol of our culture. It is a patient, noble animal. The donkey serves mankind, it endures insults, it does not rebel. There are strengths in being a donkey, in gadhagiri.'

Lenin smiled, an act of such beatific innocence and compassion that something moved in my heart, like a piece of ice melting. It was enough, in that moment, to know and remember that not everybody had sold out and bought into the current myth of India

Shining. It was good to know that people and donkeys could be stubborn and carry on.

It made me think.

—

Luv came to my room looking unusually pleased with himself. He strolled over to the full-length mirror and preened before it. 'Notice anything new about me, Maa?' he enquired. 'Kuchh adla badla?'

'A new hairstyle?' I hazarded, checking out his slickly-gelled locks. Then it struck me—the safety-pins had disappeared. Why? What was up in his life?

'The safety pins have gone,' he said. 'I've decided to grow up. Finally. It's clean-up time.'

'Are you in love again?' I asked, fear and hope tugging at my heart. My sons, my sons.

'No. I simply decided on a mid-course correction,' Luv replied. 'I sold a painting yesterday, and the gallery is talking of a solo show. But I've been thinking—the arts stream is too subjective, too self-indulgent as a discipline. I felt maybe it's time to go straight.'

My heart stopped. A coming-out-of-the-closet confession? 'Straight?' I blundered. 'You mean you were . . .?' I stopped.

'Gay?' I couldn't say the word, but my lips had spelled it out.

His cheerful smile turned into a ferocious snarl. 'Gay? Gay?' he mimicked viciously. 'It's unbearable. Homophobic Indian mothers are impossible! You need to get a life and let me lead mine. Leave my sex life alone please. Maybe I should just return to the States!' He stormed out from the room, banging the door behind him. I had done it again. Bungled it up.

He was home again by lunchtime, my son Luv, complaining about the food. 'I can't eat these vegetables, Mater,' he said, 'they are all too oily and spicy.'

'What's with the Mater?' I asked suspiciously.

'Sorry, Mataji. You know that I can't eat matar—I hate peas! Also baingan, kaddoo, karela, tori, tinda—all the inedible category vegetation. Could you please instruct your esteemed staff about this? I know you are much too busy and preoccupied to actually step into the kitchen, but I might die of protein deprivation unless I get some chicken-shiken into my diet.'

'Why don't you get married?' I snapped. 'Then your dear wife can make sure you get your fat-free chicken curry exactly the way you want it.'

His eyes gleamed with sudden mischief. 'That's *your* call, Mataji,' he said. 'I'll marry whoever you tell me to. Let's list out the candidates . . .'

'You could marry Paromita, our friend Lenin's daughter!' I exclaimed, jumping the gun in my excitement.

Luv's expression became guarded and inscrutable, but only for a minute. 'Hey, give them all a chance, Mataji,' he said. 'Let's begin the status check with my ex-fiancée Monalisa. She gets full marks for being incredibly brainy and sexy. Loses them all for being unbearably difficult and neurotic.'

'Is that Monalisa Das Mann in Delhi now? Are you in touch with her?' I asked with concern. 'We have nothing against her . . . we'll follow your wishes. But I thought we had explained to her that you were engaged to our friend's daughter, to Paromita.'

'Let's not mix up Bollywood farce and real life all the time. That was just an exit line.'

'But she is our friend's daughter and you like her,' I persisted. I wouldn't let that Monalisa into my family, not ever.

'And the loaded dowry-prospect suspect you and dad have been lining up for us? For me and Kush?'

'Not me, I'm not selling you for dowry,' I declared firmly.

'Luv weds Paromita. Now that sounds nice!' he continued slyly. 'Kush can take the cushy option. Luv will go for love, for the girl next door who has won his mother's heart. A two-generational romance, scripted by Karan Johar. Boy returns home from phoren lands, dumps westernized desi, and embraces True Indian Values.

Ma embraces Bahu. Box office hit. A happy ending with a great soundtrack!'

'There are other proposals too,' I said righteously. 'Atul Bhaiya and Dolly have suggested . . .'

The message tone on my mobile bleated an alert. 'Watch DD news interview,' it said. 'On air now. Suresh.'

'We have to watch your dad on TV,' I said, fumbling with the remote. Suresh filled up the screen, sounding impressively articulate on the issue of base procurement prices and well-rehearsed with quotable quotes on the subject of Foreign Direct Investment in food retailing. 'The Food Sector is the soul of our economy,' he said, wearing a suitably soulful expression to match this noble sentiment. He used the word 'paradigm' more than once, and 'framework' in every sentence.

The interviewer, a sad bald man, announced an 'after the break' halt. Advertisements for underwear, skin whiteners and toilet-bowl cleaners followed. Bucky and Junior Bhandpur were endorsing the toilet bowl cleaner. What the world will do for money. My husband reappeared to continue with his solemn pronouncements on matters of Vital National Interest. He talked of the 'structural framework', and 'the new nutrition paradigm', whatever that was. I listened dutifully, but Luv was getting impatient.

'How can a government television channel subsidize government propaganda, Maa?' he demanded. 'It's we taxpayers who subsidize Doordarshan.'

I reminded Luv he didn't pay taxes. At last, mercifully, the programme was over. I sent Suresh a prompt and dutiful sms: 'Simply brilliant, darling.'

'Tks' Suresh texted back.

Luv took the mobile phone from me and switched it off. Then he took my hands in his. 'I meant what I said, Maa,' he said earnestly. 'I'll marry whoever you tell me to. Honest. I trust your instincts.'

I was flabbergasted. What exactly was he trying to say? Hope and caution jostled in my heart. In this state of nervous excitement, I turned to the television for reassurance, for a sign or an omen.

Ranjit Verma, the oiliest anchor in India, leered at me from the screen. 'Shocking Startling Breaking News!' he declared. 'Human Race Under Attack. Scientific Tests have Proved that Aliens have been sending Radio Messages announcing they will Attack India Next Year!' All this with backdrop pictures of cute aliens atop UFOs readying to attack.

That decided me. 'I shall get him married before the year is over,' I resolved. 'Before the aliens destroy us.'

Young people should settle down early. Luv will marry Paromita, he must. It was a considered decision, a time-bound plan. I would go about it scientifically. First I should check if the stars were ripe—astrologers do somehow manage to put things in comforting cosmic perspective.

I searched for Luv's horoscope among the transparent green plastic folders in my steel cupboard. All sorts of forgotten milestones popped up to distract me. My mother's death certificate, Kush's birth certificate, the twins' class reports from Grades I to XII and a folio of sketches by Luv while he was still in school.

The two natal charts lay nestled together in a swathe of red mulmul cloth. Luv and Kush, born just six minutes apart, but destined for such different lives. An artist and a determined political heir. My boys.

There's an astrologer I know. He has a consulting room the size of an open suitcase, sandwiched between a butcher's shop and a jalebi stall. It's in the DDA market in Zamroodpur, a boutique slum in the heart of poshest Delhi. I had been to him twice when we still lived in upmarket, overrated GK, and I went to him again. He's no celebrity astrologer, but I trust him.

The sign outside read: 'G.D. Goria. Astro-Lodger'. Goria ji was listening wearily to a YouTube presentation of a jaded Bollywood number.

'Kanya Rashi,' he said to me, looking up from the screen. 'Moon in Virgo. You want to ask about the marriage of your sons?'

Right as usual. 'TOB and DOB please?' I gave him the horoscopes I had brought along, and filled in the Time of Birth and Date of Birth for the twins in a photocopied form he handed me. His hands were trembling, and he had grown very much older since I had seen him last.

He studied the natal charts, with the planets playing hopscotch across the different houses.

'Saturn,' Goria ji grimaced. 'Saturn is the ruling planet of Kalyug. This is the last of the Four Cycles of Mankind: this age of evil and confusion that we live in. The sages had predicted that in the time of Kalyug, women and low castes shall rule. That is modern democracy for you.'

I hadn't asked him about Saturn and Kalyug and all that. He examined the horoscopes again, in a distracted way. 'Your son Luv—and this kanya named Paromita. Their signs and chinhas match like Shiva and Parvati! Like Rama and Sita! Like Aishwarya Rai and Abhishek Bachchan!'

Rama and Sita? Abhishek and Aishwarya Rai Bachchan!

'They will be married within one year. Two babies in four years. Boys only. Jai ho.'

That seemed to settle it. But Goria ji hadn't finished with Kush's horoscope yet. 'Your older son—there is suspense like in Hindi film. And surprise ending. Jai Ho.'

I stepped out of the kiosk, worrying about Kalyug and what surprises Kush might have in store for us. In the shop next door, a batch of freshly fried jalebis was resting on the slotted steel karchi, waiting to be dunked into the treacly chashni. I gave in to temptation and bought half a kilo, delivered in a sticky plastic bag leaking syrup.

The jalebis were deliciously, sinfully sweet and Suresh and I had them at teatime, with pakoras and hot masala chai. I told Suresh about what the astrologer had said, but not the bit about Kush. No point jumping into the future before it arrived.

—

Later, I cornered Luv in his room 'Let's talk it through,' I said. 'Let's list out the candidates. Are you still seeing that Monalisa?'

'She's over, Mom ji,' he said. 'Miss Das Mann was a phase, a comma. We've both moved on. And her father is a real toenail. Monalisa stands disqualified, you knew that already.'

'When did you see her last?'

'Yesterday,' he admitted, 'but that doesn't mean anything. There are things we appreciate about each other. Besides, she's writing a book, about our relationship.'

'I want her Date of Birth,' I persisted. 'Just in case . . .' On-its-head logic somehow seems to work better than surface reason with my children.

'But I don't require your help in marrying Monalisa, Mom ji,' Luv said, his good humour mysteriously resurfacing. 'I thought you had a line-up of candidates. That's why I've left it to you.'

I decided to call his bluff. 'Have you fallen in love with Paromita, Luv?' I asked. Unblinking. Looking him directly in the eye. 'Tell me if you have, son, let's not waste time beating around the bush.'

He blushed. Maybe he wasn't so different from his father, after all. 'I like her a lot,' he said, 'a lot, and I respect her too. I'd like to get to know her better.'

'Do you want to marry Paromita?' I asked.

Luv squirmed a bit. 'I think so,' he said. 'Perhaps. She's different. Kuchh hat ke . . .'

'Have you proposed to her?' I persisted. 'Have you asked her about marriage?'

'No,' he replied awkwardly. 'That's why I came to you. I've left it for you to set up.' He bent down and touched my feet, with mock humility. 'My life is your hands, Mataji,' And he left the room. Dramey-baaz.

Does art imitate life? Does life imitate art? Are Indian marriages made in Bollywood? I tried to work it out. If Paromita and Luv were in love, as they clearly were, why didn't they settle it between themselves? Why follow the 'arranged love' formula?

How very odd. In my time the rebellious young—the impractical artists, anyway—they ran away, they broke the rules, they wanted to change the world. I was a little in awe of them. What had happened to the young of new India? What, for all the safety pins on the face and carrying condoms where a mother would find them?

Would I have it any other way? Of course not. It is good to have sensible sons.

—

A phone call from Kush, from Dubai. 'I need a dozen starched kurta pyjamas on standby, Mom,' he instructed. 'And make sure you check the drawstrings too. Last time the nadas had slipped in and it was a real nuisance.'

'Yes, son,' I replied dutifully.

'And see that my white Nike shoes are cleaned and the small bag is empty. There is a SEZ tour lined up and I can't carry a large bag in the copter.' No hello, no goodbye. Just those instructions. He needed a wife too—though somehow I didn't see Suki laying out his starched kurtas and checking the drawstrings.

Suresh strode in, looking self-important and a little bad-tempered. 'What's wrong with you these days?' he said accusingly. 'You are beginning to neglect me!'

'Not at all, darling!' I smiled. 'Is there a problem?'

'That careless dhobi has over-starched my kurtas,' he complained. 'Kush and I are going for a site inspection for a new food processing park, and I need wearable clothes. Fire the dhobi if you have to—he has begun to think too much of himself. Or use a proper dry-cleaner, the one in Khan Market!'

'Don't worry, my darling,' I soothed.

'Not too much—' Suresh continued—'and not too little. I need a light crisp starch on the kurtas. Of course we will be in airconditioning most of the time . . .'

'I'll see that the dhobi gets the starch off your kurtas straight away,' I said, and gave him my most patient private-valet-service smirk.

It's practical. These projects spell big bucks. A single sensible deal could keep us in clover. After all, money doesn't grow on trees. Kush will need cash if he has to contest an election—politics is an expensive business. It needs capital. Even a Rajya Sabha seat costs money. A lot of money.

The clothes are important. White kurtas are to politicians what six-pack abs are to film stars. The Indian political establishment survives on the strength of its dhobis, hereditary starchers and bleachers of the crisp, dazzling robes that are our swadeshi uniform and badge of office. The dry-cleaners can never get it right.

I sent for the dhobi but his daughter Dayavati came instead. She came in looking as chirpy and glamorous as ever. She assessed the starch on Suresh's kurtas with her long pink-frosted nails, and agreed with expert judgement that it was slightly overdone. Ramdhan brought out Kush's khadi kurtas as well, and I explained to Dayavati that she wasn't to get the two piles mixed up, but keep Suresh's and Kush's kurtas in separate sets.

'Dont worry, aunty ji!' she replied. 'We are three generations of dhobi family living in this banglow ka quarter only. My grandpa was dhobi to first Law Minister—then many more ministers, they come and go from this banglow, but our family, we are permanent. So we are knowing very well how to starch khadi for big people and neta-log!'

A dhobi dynasty! We would have our own mini-dynasty too, and soon, if Kush had his way. I would have to be vigilant in searching out the right sort of wife for him.

Suddenly, I had one of those illuminated moments when everything seems full of lucid clarity. I remembered the day when mother first showed me the photograph of Suresh, plump and intensely serious, leaning against a Standard Herald car. A black-and-white photograph, now grown grainy in memory.

It was his car that had decided me. I married Suresh, and we held together through the struggles of middle-class life. We were making our way up when Paro came into our lives, opening up a new world whose margins moved with every unsure success. Fear and insecurity had dogged me along the dizzy ascent up the political ladder. And this was why it had all happened—why we were fated to have met Lenin, to have known Paro, to have shared those youthful times together. That farishta Lenin, with his angelic and infuriating innocence, was meant in the scheme of things to marry a control-freak like Geeta: the dance of their DNA to produce Paromita, whose auspicious signs matched those on my son's natal chart and horoscope. They would marry within a year and have two babies. Sons only. Tathastu!

Paromita rushed into the room. She was looking breathtakingly pretty. Her soft skin was glowing, and her smile had a knowing, mischievous edge to it.

'Well, Paromita,' I said. 'Well, well, well.'

She threw me a naughty look.

'Will you be my daughter-in-law, Paromita?' I asked. 'And should I speak to your father about it—or to your mother?'

She rushed to give me a hug, then bent down to touch my feet. 'I want your aashirwad, Ma,' she said.

My eyes misted over. 'Beti . . .' I said, stroking her cheek. Then I decided to stop. It was all getting too sentimental, a Bollywood tear-jerker. Before one knew it, I would be starring in my very own fantasy *Hum Aapke Hain Kaun* home video production.

Luv was nowhere in sight. He had no lines; the script seemed reserved for the saas–bahu duo.

'Give me your mother's number, Paromita,' I commanded. The ringtone belted out 'Hum Honge Kamyab' for the longest possible time. 'Ek din! Ek din!! Ek din!!!' it rang. But Paromita's mother Geeta didn't take the call.

'Don't worry, Ma, I'll tell mummy,' Paromita said, 'and then you can tell papa.' She had called me Ma. My mother died a long time ago, I never had a sister. It would feel good to have another woman in the family.

At this point, Luv materialized out of nowhere. Had he been hiding behind the curtains? He was smiling from ear to ear, looking sheepish but ecstatically happy.

I summoned the rest of my family. Suresh was in a late parliamentary sub-committee meeting, and Kush's phone was switched off. I called Ghafoor and sent him off to buy ten kilos of sweets in half-kilo boxes. 'Twenty boxes of mithai,' I explained, 'in half-kilo boxes of mixed pista, kaju and badam barfi.'

'We should be buying laddoos, mom,' Luv said, 'I don't much like pistachio barfi.'

'Shadi ka laddoo,' I told him. 'Marriage is like a laddoo. You have to taste it before you can understand it.' An absurd euphoria had overtaken me. Sweets were distributed to all the staff at 18 Dara Shikoh Marg. To the row of vacant-eyed chaprasis who sat outside the house—Mange Ram, Bhure Lal and Dinesh Jadhav. To the typist, PA, PS, the drivers, security guards, one and a half malis, to the dhobi and his family, Ghafoor and his clan, the sweeperess and the cook and the helper.

Kush returned too, asking about his kurtas and if I had remembered to pack his Nike shoes.

'Your twin brother is getting married,' I said, 'and Paromita will soon take charge of his life. It's time you got married too, son. I have a line-up of candidates for you.'

'All women are the same,' he replied, before bursting into an energetic and enthusiastic bhangra, and getting Luv and Paromita to dance in step with him. He lit up the leftover crackers from last Diwali, and they were all going 'Balle Balle' as I clicked the picture on my mobile and saved the moment for eternity. A family moment.

When at last Suresh arrived I greeted him in theatrical congratulatory mode—covering my head with my sari pallav, like a Rajmata, and delicately popping a large piece of pista burfi into his astonished mouth.

'Congratulations! Our Luv has proposed to Paromita—and she has accepted!' I said, twisting the sequence a bit. The truth has to be colour coordinated when it comes to sons and husbands.

Suresh choked and his face went purple. 'That's wonderful,' he said. 'Have you spoken to her parents?'

'Geeta isn't answering my calls,' I replied.

'Give me her number,' he said. 'I should speak to her.' But Geeta wasn't picking up her phone, still.

Suresh called for his PA. 'Get me the number of Mrs Geeta Devi, Minister for Coal, Mining and Industrial Production in Chhattisgarh,' he said. In less than seven minutes, the PA was holding the cordless and smoothly addressing the PA on the other end. 'I am calling from New Delhi,' he said. 'Mr Suresh Kaushal, the honourable Minister himself, wishes to speak to Geeta Devi ji, Saar.'

The PA handed the phone to Suresh. 'Geeta ji, ek khush khabari hai,' Suresh said, in his lawyer's voice. 'We haven't met for many years—but we were all friends of Paro, me, my wife Priya, and your husband Lenin. And now our children—your daughter Paromita and our older son Luv—have decided to get married. By God's grace.'

He gave it a precise, eloquent dramatic pause, before switching over to an asking-for-votes voice. 'We trust—we know—they have your blessings. When will you be in Delhi next, Geeta ji? We should fix a date for the wedding soon. Of course it must be when Parliament is in session.'

She didn't ask to speak to me. Suresh said she was planning to be in Delhi soon, to discuss the marriage, and I left it at that.

'There's a lot of money in Eastern UP, Chhattisgarh and Jharkhand,' Kush remarked thoughtfully. 'Poor states but rich in resources. There's a lot of action there . . .' Then he went off to pack his suitcase for the SEZ site visit.

As for Lenin, he had simply disappeared from the radar.

Everyone, including Geeta, her staff, and even Paromita, seemed vague about his whereabouts. I'd given up on locating him; I'd tried my best and failed. It seemed odd not to have spoken to our future daughter-in-law's father, especially when he was our oldest friend. Knowing Lenin, he would surface in good time, and we would share our joy and celebrate together then.

ALL KINDS OF STRESS. POLITICAL TENSIONS AND PERSONAL CONFUSION. 'The Left is blackmailing the Nation,' Suresh declares, with monotonous predictability, over breakfast, lunch and dinner. He's looking gloomy these days and tense and his eyebrows, never his best feature anyway, are all knotted up. The distinguished Cabinet Minister for Agriculture is giving him grief as well, encroaching on his portfolio and being rude about it in the process.

Paromita's mother, Geeta Devi, is expected in Delhi over the weekend, but we have only managed an inaudible attempted conversation with Lenin. He's in Chhattisgarh, fasting for the release of Dr Binayak Sen, whom the government had branded a Maoist and put in jail. I spent half the morning trying to inform Lenin of the engagement, but the line would crackle or go dead every time our conversation reached the crucial point. Finally I gave up and sent him an SMS.

'Our older twin Luv and your daughter Paromita decided to marry. All delighted. Love, Priya.'

Another round of frustrating, inaudible calls from his mobile, and a half-message that read 'Delig'.

Geeta Devi arrived in a cavalcade of white Ambassador cars with blue and red pilot lights whirling on the top. The security had alerted me about her arrival, as instructed, and Kush and I were in the porch to receive her as she dismounted from her official car, with assistants and minions from the other vehicles scurrying to open the door for her. It was over two decades since I had last seen her, and she had weathered the years well, she seemed to have somehow grown taller, even after I had surreptitiously assessed the height of her heels. It wasn't her slightly archaic bouffant either—she just stood tall, in every sense.

Geeta gave me a regal nod with a hint of a smile. She was wearing a tassar handloom sari with a deep green border, and a set of flawless pearls choked against her throat. She bent down to embrace me, and simultaneously lifted a stern eyebrow at one of her attendants. Suddenly I was surrounded by sixteen baskets of fruit, all covered up in orange cellophane paper, and no less than forty kilo-boxes of sweets. I looked around me in a wave of sudden panic—at the bananas, pineapples, guavas, custard-apples and the piled up mithai-boxes. Geeta regarded me impassively. 'Badhai ho, Priya ji,' she said, or rather, intoned. 'And where is Suresh Bhai?' This was said with rather more animation.

Kush bent down low and touched her feet and she gave him a gracious aashirvad.

'This is Kush. It's his twin brother Luv who is marrying Paromita,' I explained.

'Luv and Kush—what blessed names! We will have Ram-Rajya in our family now,' she said, only half jokingly.

How times change, how life changes, how people change. I could never have imagined the Geeta of yore, the subjugated small-town bride of my friend and rakhi brother Lenin, would transmute into this power-savvy politico. Of course she had a determined chin even then, but the cast of a jaw is not enough to propel someone into the political stratosphere. Her father had been an ex-chief minister, I recalled. But it had been a long journey, a bloody battle, any which way you looked at it.

I led her into the living room. Suresh was waiting for us. 'Where's Luv?' I asked worriedly. 'And Paromita? Wherever are the kids?'

'I told them that I wanted to see you alone,' Geeta said, with the firm, effortless authority she seemed to have acquired. 'There are many things young people don't need to know about. Beta Kush, why don't you go join your brother and bhabhi for a while?'

That should have alerted me, but of course it didn't. Ramdhan brought in a tray with Darjeeling tea, laddoos and freshly fried pakodas. Geeta whipped out an oblong velvet box from her large Shantiniketan leather handbag as he exited.

'For you, Priya didi,' she said, bending down to notionally touch my feet, then depositing her gift in my lap, along with a dried coconut.

I opened it apprehensively. A diamond necklace glittered against the deep blue velvet, finely-crafted swirls of light clustering into a breathtaking garland.

'I can't possibly accept this!' I protested, but she had already extracted another smaller velvet case from her handbag and opened it with a sharp click. A pair of cufflinks twinkled next to Suresh's cup of tea. I was awestruck by their size and quality, and, to my embarrassment, an audible, appreciative gasp escaped me.

Geeta adjusted her own modest pearl ear-studs and threw me a winsome smile. 'I am giving you the most precious gift of my only daughter,' she said softly, 'these diamond-shaimonds are nothing before that.'

It was time for Suresh to take over. 'We belong to one-and-the same family now, Geeta ji,' he said heartily. 'Blood is always thicker than water, even if we belong to opposing political parties! Congress-BJP-BJO-LJD—what is the difference, I say? Only alphabets. After all, in the end we are all working together towards the task of nation building. Except the Left parties—they are all too busy blackmailing the nation!'

Geeta heard him out with an appreciative smile. 'That's absolutely true, Suresh Bhaisaab!' she exclaimed emphatically. 'You are completely right. Parties—ideologies—kya farak padta hai? In the end we are all the same. Country before self, I always say . . .'

A sly, cautious look crept into her face. 'And then we must remember, one family, two parties is always the winning formula. A foot in both boats works in all seasons.'

'Absolutely!' Suresh endorsed. 'We are one happy family now. Family ties are the backbone of our nation. Even our other son, Kush—you met him—has joined politics. For the task of nation building. Our two families are now one, with a common manifesto. It is time we discussed the marriage date with all details. When is your husband, our friend Lenin—I mean, Avinendra—when is he going to be here? Or we can come to Chhattisgarh, of course, whenever you say, to discuss.'

I watched Geeta's face change colour. It grew mottled and dark before my eyes. Her breathing changed too. She was no longer in control, I could see that. 'Oh, our dear Lenin ji,' she said, attempting to sound matter-of-fact. 'My dear husband is on a fast-unto-death for Dr Binayak Sen's release. And I honour his point of view.' A pious tone entered her voice. 'After all, we are a democracy.'

'Yes, yes, yes—the Argumentative Indian,' Suresh said, hastily and a little inconsequentially.

Geeta Devi seemed to have recovered from her rage. Blotches began to clear. 'But I have spoken to my husband about this,' she said, evenly. 'I have spoken to my husband, and he agrees that our Paromita must be married before the end of the year. No delays and absolutely no postponements. Our family Guru, a famous astrologer from Gorakhpur, has specifically advised us on that. No postponement.'

She was playing nervously with her ring now, a large block of sapphire set in silver, obviously prescribed by the abovementioned astrologer. 'Everybody in UP, MP and Chhattisgarh goes to our Guru ji for advice,' she continued. 'Politicians, Industrialists, Film Stars.'

'No postponements.' I seconded. 'We want Luv and Paromita to be married as soon as possible. But where *are* they?'

And the young couple, who had been waiting in Luv's bedroom, arrived as though on cue, looking suspiciously flushed. What had they been up to? They appeared so deliriously in love that all the obscure shadows of our conversation, the awkward edges between us, lifted before their simple joy.

Kush seemed really impressed by Geeta Devi. 'I am your political disciple,' he declared. 'Your chela will learn at your feet. You shall be my political guru.' You had to give it to him—he knows how to grovel. It's an essential skill in party politcs.

Later, I put away the diamonds safely in the locker of my steel cupboard. 'I shall keep these for Paromita,' I resolved. But I knew that somewhere their glitter had seduced me, and that Geeta had won an important advantage in an undefined battle.

—

Winter is creeping in and the nights are getting colder. It's in November that Delhi transforms. Clear skies, the garden in bloom and the social season in full swing. I've had my silk saris ironed and dry-cleaned, and aired my shawls, all the pashminas and jamavars and jamdanis I've collected over the years.

It's unbelievable how things proceed at such a slow and stifling pace, and then suddenly they take a jump and everything is turned upside down and on its head. Life has changed forever. Soon, I shall hand the baton over to my daughter-in-law. Somehow, the thought makes me feel not older, but younger. The fifties are the new forties and all that. It's to be a new phase in my life, I've decided that and I'm ready for it.

Daya came to measure me for a blouse. It is to be in the latest fashion, cut low, with a saucy pussy-cat bow at the back. I'm determined to change my style, somehow—if only I can find it!

—

Poonam called again. She was utterly distraught. Her chihuahua, Lexus, has been bitten by a street dog and developed respiratory problems from the shock.

'Have you taken him to the vet?' I asked.

'The vet came to Lexus,' she replied, her tone changing. 'My poor little prince has been admitted to the Canine Elite Medical

Centre in Mehrauli. I tell you, Priya . . . these street dogs should all be shot dead. Bang! Bang! Bang!'

'Bow wow wow!' I replied. Street dogs had the right to live, didn't they?

'What was that?' Poonam asked suspiciously.

'Nothing' I responded. 'Nothing at all. Just a bad line.'

Suresh met Manoviraj Sethia yesterday, at a lunch hosted by the World Economic Forum. 'He hugged me,' Suresh reported, 'that Sethia fellow hugged me so hard that I thought my ribs would crack! Then he gave me a chummi on my cheek and said "Let the Sethia and Kaushal clans unite. You have two sons and I have two daughters. You give me one son and I give you one daughter and then we can be one family!"'

'What did you say to that?' I asked, in a cautious, official sort of voice.

'I said Kush and Suki should meet up again,' Suresh replied. 'I am going to have a discussion about it with Kush—he is coming with me to Bangalore this weekend. I will discuss the pros and cons with him, man to man. Don't worry, Priya darling.' Then he winked at me and did a thumbs up!

Something has happened to Suresh. Yesterday, he gave me an enormous bunch of silver-sprayed red roses. I looked at them with suspicion. All the women s magazines have red-alert warnings about cover-ups and guilt gifts. Then I realized that the flowers had been presented to him at an official function; a tell-tale card—'To the Hon'ble Minister'—was hidden in the wilting foliage. Today, Suresh presented me with an expensive embroidered pashmina shawl. 'I feel closer to you, Priya, than I ever have before,' he said, 'and with Luv soon to be married, and then Kush, we will be left with just each other.'

I wrapped the shawl around me. It felt soft and luxurious, like an embrace. I'm looking forward to wearing it this winter.

The red roses began to droop overnight. That's the problem with these hybrid Tata roses and perhaps with late romance as well.

The silver spray couldn't have helped either. I tried to revive them, with a fizzy Disprin pill, but it didn't work.

THE RED ROSES SHOULD HAVE WARNED ME, AND THE EXPENSIVE SHAWL. Well, the women's magazines are quite right about guilt gifts. Suresh has been having an affair. This new development has come as a total shock, though I should have known it all along. Or perhaps I did know, from that phone call to the hotel bedroom, but I wouldn't admit it to myself. I was simply in denial.

We had gone for dinner to the Ashoka hotel, where The National Association of Tinned Fruits and Canneries gave me a huge gift-wrapped 'presentation' hamper. We walked out in step, the distinguished politician and his dutiful wife, and Suresh gave me a hug, right there on the porch in front of everybody. 'Lets stop for a coffee on our way home, Priya,' he said.

The coffee shop at the Ashoka is really run down and decrepit, and full of Russian hookers. Or so I'm told. 'Let's go to the Oberoi,' I suggested. 'It's classier.'

In the car, Suresh was unusually reflective. 'There's something I have been wanting to discuss with you for a long time, Priya,' he said, with the practised sincerity that has cloaked him ever since he turned full-time politician.

Alarm bells were already sounding in my head. 'We've been neglecting each other, Suresh,' I said. 'A quiet cup of coffee together is just the thing.'

So there we were, in the elegant lobby of the hotel. Suresh marched in with the slow, deliberate strut of a grade one VIP, and I trailed behind him in reflected glory as he was accosted by the movers and shakers of the capital. This continued in the coffee shop, until we were at last left alone with a cappuccino for me and a latte for Suresh and an over-obsequious waiter listening in to every clink of our coffee spoons.

'I want your advice,' Suresh began, 'and your cooperation as well, Priya. I have been consulting this astrologer—through some well wishers' (he blushed slightly at this point) 'and a group of friends who have formed a discussion group.'

I was suddenly furious. I had been quiet too long. 'A discussion or group to consult an astrologer?' I exclaimed. 'Not Nnutasha again? No cows in my name—don't waste your time, buddy.'

Was I crossing the Laxman Rekha? I had never called him 'buddy' before. But here I was, about to become a mother-in-law soon. Time for me to assert myself. And for him to grow up.

Suresh reproached me gently, even cautiously. 'What's happened to you, Priya? You have changed. You have become so aggressive lately!'

'There is something the matter with you, Mr Suresh Kaushal, not with me,' I replied, as calmly as I could. 'You who have always been so rational. An intelligent lawyer, a thinking man—a true intellectual—and here you are, downgrading yourself before my eyes, succumbing to superstition. Can the spelling of your name change anything? Do you really believe that?'

'Nnutasha is simply a member of this group,' Suresh replied, appealing rather than arguing his case. 'There are some businessmen and lawyers and some media persons who meet once a month, on the first Monday of the month. They seek harmony—harmony between litigants and lawyers, lawyers and judges, bureaucrats and industrialists, politicians and the media. It's a noble cause . . .'

'And this Nnutasha—what does she do there?'

'Oh, she does chakra-healing and Reiki and numerology,' he said defensively. 'She's Pooonam's friend. Your friend Pooonam.' He looked me straight in the eye as he said this. 'Pooonam has been co-ordinating the group—its called INSPIRE. She said she had mentioned it to you . . .'

I looked at him carefully. Was this leading to a confession?

'Wake up and smell the coffee, Priya Kaushal,' I told myself. I sniffed at the cappuccino, hopefully, out of habit. Nothing. I couldn't. Smell the coffee. I can't smell anything since I returned from Mumbai with a cold. It's disorienting, and confusing.

'What is the subject of this conversation?' I asked Suresh, very slowly, but with an edge of menace that had never entered my voice before in three decades of marriage. It surprised even me, that tone. 'Why are we discussing these pushy political groupies?'

The coffee was cold. The waiter wasn't budging from earshot. 'Madam, can I do anything for you?' he said ingratiatingly, zooming into close-up range again.

'You could leave us alone for a start,' I retorted sharply.

Suresh was staring at me with cautious fascination.

'What's wrong with you?' he asked again, after a moment's deliberation. 'Pooonam is your friend—but you don't seem to be able to accept that. Pooonam and Nnutasha are *both* your well-wishers!'

'Don't dare to bring up that Cowshall business again,' I said implacably. 'Nothing, but nothing, is going to persuade me to change the spelling of my surname, do you get that? Buddy?'

'We've moved on from that page,' he explained patiently. 'You must understand that INSPIRE isn't about mere individuals, its about national harmony—international harmony, cosmic harmony!'

I stared at him open-mouthed, but he was in full spate. 'It's about India . . . You see, the numbers just don't add up. We can't have harmony and growth and prosperity as long as we are called India. The numerology doesn't work. So Nnutasha, who is a very highly evolved soul, has suggested that we start a movement to change the name. It should be called Indyaa—with a 'y' two 'a's—and then the aggregates will add up at last.'

'What on earth are you talking about, Suresh?' I demanded grimly. It was a serious matter. My husband was losing his mind. We would have to consult a psychiatrist.

'Yes for Indyaa!' he continued wildly. 'Look at the world around us. It's self-destructing. Look at the Sensex—it's falling exponentially. There are cyclones in Chennai. Drought in Vidarbha. It's all the fault of the British! It's they who named this country India. But if we were to become Indyaa, no one in the world could compete with us. We would become a real superpower—

the biggest and the strongest superpower in the world! It's all quite scientific, if you approach it in the right way.'

There is no known history of insanity in his family. Had he been drinking? Was he on drugs? The victim of black magic?

Reinforcing mutual self-esteem. That's supposed to be the rule in marriage.

'It's a very good idea, Suresh,' I said, reaching out for his podgy hand and stroking it supportively, with all the love I could commandeer.

'Numerology works, you know,' he said confidingly. 'Let me explain.' Suresh was blowing on his coffee now.

'But your coffee's already cold, Suresh,' I chided, to distract him.

'It doesn't matter, it is important to start the right vibrations, even in a cup of coffee,' he replied. 'The universe is composed of energy, and all energy has vibrations. These vibrational patterns are coded with numbers.'

I nodded encouragingly. No negative signals.

'Pythagoras understood the truth of numerology—he invented it! And Einstein was a believer too. American presidents have followed it. Ronald Reagan did. Spanish dictators have survived because of it. Why not Indyaa?'

'Why not, indeed?' I echoed, stirring the tepid coffee with icy matrimonial resolution.

'Think of Pooonam,' he continued. 'She was plain old Punam earlier, with a single 'u'. She worked with an events management company then, and sold Tupperware in her spare time. Three moons was all it needed to change her destiny. And look at her now—one of the richest women in India. And possibly one of the most beautiful . . .'

Things were getting out of hand. 'Are you in love with Pooonam?' I asked firmly. 'We have been married for over thirty years now. You can tell me the truth. You *must* tell me the truth.'

I held his hand as I said this, gently at first. Then harder as the tension mounted within me. He winced and pulled his hand away.

'I love you, Priya,' he said despondently. 'You know I do. You do. Know that I do.'

And I did know. He was not lying. He did love me. And (this came as a surprise to me) I sort of loved him too. From duty, in default, from habit, but I did. I do.

'And Pooonam? Have you slept with her?'

I had to ask, I couldn't contain myself. I was burning with proprietary outrage. Suresh is my husband, he belongs to me. Pooonam can't have him, ever, however many extra moons she might add to her name. I began stroking his knee, but the waiter was hovering around us again. 'Tea, ma'am?' he asked, smiling to display teeth the size of an Arctic ledge.

'We have just had coffee, why would we order tea after that? Get us a bottle of wine. The house red, please,' I said to him. Then, I turned to Suresh again.

'So have you slept with her or haven't you?' I asked adamantly. I was tired of pussyfooting around the truth. 'Make up your mind and tell me. Quickly. Now.'

My husband's face crumpled. He extracted a starched white handkerchief from his pocket and buried his face between its gray borders. He was sobbing helplessly. 'Not Pooonam,' he whimpered. 'It wasn't Pooo. It just happened. She threw herself at me. She seduced me. I was weak, I didn't mean to!'

A hot flush was creeping across my body, like an advancing fire. A blue and purple haze was swimming before my eyes, and on the far shore, my husband Suresh, bathed in a sudden fierce flame of desire. My man.

'Who is she?' I demanded. 'Tell me who she is! It's that Nnutasha!'

'No, not Nnutasha,' he whimpered on. 'And not Pooo either. I confess I was attracted to her, but it remained just that. An attraction . . .'

'Who is this other woman?' I persisted, unbending. It's the sort of dialogue meant for the theatre, or English films. Not for me and Suresh.

'No one you know. She's a divorce lawyer—from Mumbai,' he said wildly. He was still sobbing, his face half hidden by the oversized handkerchief. 'She was blackmailing me! She threatened she would tell you. I have never been unfaithful before . . . and I promise I never will be again. If you forgive me. Darling, I'm so ashamed!'

'What's her name?' I continued uncompromisingly.

As a lawyer, Suresh is a master cross-examiner; he knows all the tricks of partial admission.

'Her name? Does it matter? She's in the past, let her remain there. Let's look at the future, Priya. Together.' He finally looked up at me. He had really been crying.

My resolve melted. She was in the past. The future was in my own hands.

'Lets forget about her—and Pooonam and Nnutasha and all those wicked chudails!' I whispered. 'It's time we returned home. Let's go now.' I deposited a thousand-rupee note on the table and ignored the waiter as he approached busily with the wine.

What is it about men? Jealousy can be a turn-on, sometimes. That's why women forgive men when they are bad, and hold on to them.

In the car Suresh blabbered a little more, about how sorry he was, how afraid he had been that he might lose me. Then we were back in Dara Shikoh Marg, in his bedroom, and it was as though we were on our honeymoon again—except that we had never been on a honeymoon then.

Late at night, when his rhythmic breathing had broken into a contented snore, I crawled out of bed and sneaked into the bathroom with his cellphones to scroll through the messages. There were none, Suresh had deleted them all. Relieved rather than disappointed, I rearranged the phones beside his bed, with his watch and the glass of water and the pills he had forgotten to take.

A single determined fly was buzzing around my face. It didn't disturb Suresh, but woke me up everytime I lulled myself to sleep. Unbearable—and when I reached for the fly-swatter to whack it by the light of the dim blue nightlamp, it would settle on the surface and start buzzing again. An infallible strategy, I noted mentally—the fly on the fly-swatter.

POOONAM IS REALLY THE MOST INSISTENT, PUSHY PERSON I HAVE EVER met. She called again today. Her voice sounded more cautious than usual, or perhaps it was my suspicion at work, projecting things.

'Hello Priya, my dear,' she cooed. 'And how are we this lovely morning?'

'I'm well, Pooonam, though I wouldn't know about you,' I responded, trying to sound as normal as possible. I couldn't let my suspicions show through.

'This is about the Botox brunch we had planned. Let's do it next week my darling,' she continued. 'My hairdresser is helping organize things. Idli and sambhar and scrambled eggs and croissants—the Intercontinental could do the catering. There's this team from Thailand, they do a massage and makeover at the same time, and a Thai girl who strums the lyre to relax the facial muscles.' I listened carefully; I had to keep track of her movements. She was not to know that I knew. Not that there was anything to know.

'Your face doesn't need any Botox, Pooo,' I said, soaking my words in sugar. 'You have such naturally lovely skin!' I could play the game too.

'Pooo?' she asked suspiciously. 'You've never called me that before, Priya . . .'

'But your close friends do,' I said. 'I've overheard them.'

Pooonam let that pass. 'Actually, I'm getting my derriere done,' she said.

'Your what?' I exclaimed. 'The line is cracking up!'

'My derriere—as in my bum, my bottom. It's begun to age. Time to enhance it, just a bit. And smoothen out the sag. Maybe we could *both* get it done. On discount.'

All sorts of unwelcome thoughts and images began to crowd into my imagination. 'Count me in for lunch, Pooo my dear,' I said, crooning out the words with venom in my heart. The fly on the fly-swatter, that was my new approach. I'd watch out for the predators that way.

I took a deep breath, looked up towards the high ceiling and recomposed myself. There was a trail of dangling cobwebs I hadn't noticed before.

'See you—oo . . .' Pooonam warbled.

A pigeon sat on the ledge of the skylight, its beak bent attentively, as though in conversation with its mates. The straggly nest was silhouetted against the dusty glass. Wasn't there a season in which pigeons build their nests?

'Oh, another thing,' said Poonam just as I was about to end the call. 'It's the mating season. The birds and the bees are at it. Time to get your twins married. Have you thought of introducing them to Suki?'

'Keep your beak out of my nest,' I replied, calmly, still considering the pigeon.

'What was that again?' she asked.

'Keep your beak out of my nest, Pooo,' I repeated.

'What?!' she asked again. Couldn't she hear me?

'I'll discuss it with Suresh,' I said, and disconnected the line.

As I walked out into the back verandah, the spring on the wire-mesh door caught on my chiffon dupatta, leaving a long tear in the fabric. I'd cut it out and stitch it up again where the tear had been. That was the way to deal with these things.

Kush and Suki? Would she be any good as a budding politician's wife? Her money might be useful, though; politicians need lots of money. Not like artists.

No, not Suki. But we had to find a suitable wife for Kush. I wished he would help out in the process, like Luv did.

I'd be a mother-in-law soon. My husband was having an affair. It was all too confusing, and disturbing.

'Take a long hard look at yourself, Priya Kaushal.' I said the words out loud. There was nobody to hear them, except perhaps the pigeon in its nest.

The mirror in the verandah is the truest one in this house. It's more flattering in the afternoons, but the harsh morning light is always faithful. I looked at my face, but was distracted by the white rattan chairs reflected in the glass. One of them had a dirty hand towel draped over it. I smiled at the reflection of the neem trees that skirted the back garden, swaying slightly in the breeze. And at the clear blue sky, which seemed to press across the mirror in which I stood reflected.

'You will be a mother-in-law soon, Priya Kaushal,' I said to myself. 'You're getting older but no wiser.' The face, the features that have announced me all these years, seemed a bit startled by my scrutiny. My skin still firm, though etched with new lines around the eyes—two delicate creased fans. And a ravine between the nostrils and lips, quite elegant really, I decided. It disappeared as I tested out my smile.

'Smile more often,' I instructed myself. 'That's the way to remain happy. And to keep your family happy.'

I don't usually to talk myself. I save my confidences for these silent pages. But today, I needed to speak out, to sort things out with that mirror. The dhobi's daughter, Daya, was gliding in from the servant quarters. A model's gait, as though she were on the ramp in a fashion show. A stack of freshly ironed clothes was balanced carefully on her bangled arms. Had she heard me muttering to myself? She placed the laundry on the white rattan chair, very carefully, and flashed me a smile. A confident young smile, no fears or wrinkles or shadows in it. 'Wait a minute, aunty,' she said, to my relief, in Hindi. 'My Papa has told me to offer you sweets. We are celebrating today! But I wasn't sure if you were at home.'

She was back in a minute with a sticky kilo-box of Agra ka Petha. 'We are very happy to be distributing sweets today,' she explained. 'My father's brother, my Tauji, has won the by-election in Agra—he has become an MLA!'

I was suitably impressed. A Member of the Legislative Assembly! 'Badhai ho beta,' I said, congratulating her, already modulating my voice. 'And where is your father?'

'Papa is in Agra organizing the victory rally.' I had a moment of social dislocation. She was our washerman's daughter, now the niece of an MLA. 'Which party?' I asked cautiously, though I knew already what the answer would be.

'Of course Didi ji ki party,' she replied. 'The party of social change. We all voted for the chariot. Though my mother's family—they are still loyal to the Congress party. Purane Congresswale hain!'

The times they are a'changing. People who reach the top of the heap find it is only until the next general election. Even as people like us get used to the comforts of our colonial bungalows, everybody in the real India is pushing and pulling to get in. What if . . . I wondered. What if Kush were to fall in love with Daya?

What if Daya's uncle became a minister? Or a chief minister? 'Perfectly acceptable,' I reassured myself. India is a fair and free democracy.

But still.

So far, Suresh has managed to sidestep general elections and remain in power through the Rajya Sabha route. He's been lucky, I think. But he will have to face up to the public some day. And so will Kush. Would our dhobi vote for them? Would Daya?

POOR SURESH HAD A BAD MORNING. HE WAS ALL SHAKEN UP WHEN HE returned from North Block, where he had been summoned for discussions with the Finance Minister. This always depresses him, as he compares the viceregal grandeur of North Block with the filthy, shabby environs of Shastri Bhavan, where his office is located. The marblex tiled floors they are laying on his floor in SB might make it look less drab than before, but it still has no style (but then, does he?!). When he had finished with his meeting, as he waited outside the pillared gates for his car to drive up, one of the rampaging monkeys that flock around the Fin Min, intent on creating havoc in the very heart of the Indian administrative empire, jumped on him from behind and decamped with his spectacles.

It was a half-blinded husband who staggered home, very nervous and upset. 'Everybody began laughing at me,' he said aggrievedly. 'All the drivers and peons and chaprasis, and some babus who were hanging around. I just hope that the FM doesn't hear about it, or the whole cabinet will be mocking me next.'

I soothed him, found him another pair of spectacles, made him a cup of masala tea. 'Of course nobody will laugh at you,' I said. 'It could happen to anybody, this monkey business.'

We watched television together, after lunch, and there was Paromita conducting a spirited interview with the new Magsaysay award winner. 'She will be an asset to our family . . .' Suresh said fondly, 'just as you are!'

'Oh, me . . . I'm just a housewife!' I protested. But it feels good to be appreciated.

Later, I decided to tidy our bedroom. I marched ahead, flourishing a cotton jhadan, with Ramdhan following in my wake, waving a feather duster. We discovered dhool and grime in all the expected places, on the windowsill, on the bookshelf, behind the giant TV screen.

A red leather suitcase was stowed under the bed. I checked it for dust, before unzipping it. Inside it was stacked with pale-orange thousand-rupee gaddis, neat piles of freshly minted currency notes bound together with black rubberbands. I shut the bag, and hastily dismissed Ramdhan before opening it again.

Those cheerful piles of cash, stacked with clinical precision. I went into a little rhapsody. I could still remember the first suitcase I had encountered, a few years after my marriage to Suresh. It had belonged to a trusting property dealer client who was about to be raided. A Samsonite bag piled with hundred-rupee notes had been left for safekeeping in our flat. The rupee notes looked thumbed and dirty, and a stale smell rose from them and wafted and settled around the room. It was a smell of sweat and stagnant water. For many years after that I associated that precise odour with the scent of money, the fragrance of hard cash.

In the days of hundred-rupee notes, ten lakhs could fill up a small suitcase. I never thought of it as 'black money'—that's such an ugly phrase. Money is money, and it was hard-earned. As Suresh's legal practice grew, it was a part of my housewifely duty to store his non-cheque income, keep it under lock and key. The cash—it gave me a sense of power, to know of those notes that nestled behind the rustle of my silk saris, in the locker of the steel Godrej cupboard in my bedroom. The musical clink of the bunched keys hanging from my waist, safe in the folds of my sari pleats. Home is where the Godrej cupboards are.

When the Reserve Bank began issuing five-hundred-rupee currency, it smelt only of paper, never of sweat and human greed, at least for the first year or so. And the thousand-rupee notes, when they entered our lives and lockers, had the impersonal feel of plastic credit cards. I took a wad of notes from the red leather bag and sniffed it. With my vanished sense of smell, even the fragrance of new paper eluded me. I locked the suitcase, and gave the key to Suresh when he came home for lunch. 'You shouldn't keep cash lying under your bed like that,' I said righteously, 'it's an unfair temptation to the staff!'

'I'm sorry Priya,' he replied contritely, 'but I have to pass it on anyway.'

We didn't discuss it any further, and the next day, the red suitcase was no longer under the bed when I checked. Was Kush handling it? Why hadn't I been told? Was I being dismissed from my custodianship and sacred steel-cupboard duties?

—

A spate of calls and urgent sms messages from Pooonam. I gave in to the relentless pressure and called her back.

She was sobbing on the phone. 'Darling, darling Priya . . . I need you! We women have to stick together. Men are such bastards. And such liars . . . Never, never, but never believe *anything* a man tells you!'

'Or some women!' I thought to myself.

Another cloudburst of tears. 'I need to see you, Priya . . . you are one of the few people I can really trust and respect. The only person I can count upon.'

On the wall before me, a fleshy lizard appeared from behind the curtain and spat out its long tongue to devour an insect, fly or mosquito, all in a flash. The sight jolted me into reality.

'I really find it difficult to believe you, Pooonam,' I said firmly. 'Cut out the hysterics, please. And yes—I need to speak to you, too.'

Something in my tone shook her up. 'Ooohh—now *you* are upset with me as well!' she whined. 'Please, Priya—we are friends. I need your support.'

I hung up on her and contemplated the lizard. They usually disappear in winter—what was it doing here? It stared back at me with beady, contemptuous eyes. Of course the phone rang again and Pooonam, at her most persuasive, had me promising to meet her at the coffee shop in the Park Intercontinental.

I know I should hate her. But she can be charming, and even vulnerable, sometimes. I am drawn to Pooonam by conflicting layers of emotion. Caution and envy compounded by a grudging admiration—for getting what she wants, from men, from women, from shopkeepers, from the whole great marketplace of life. And then, a curiosity, both abstract and practical, about how it is that she manages to fit in boyfriends, lovers, arms dealers, ministers, minister's wives, into a whirlpool of mutual accommodation.

How does she have the gall to be that way? Damn Pooonam, I thought, a fresh wave of bile rising within me. But then I told myself: She doesn't have what I have. A husband, a family, respectability. She can't ever steal these from me. Can she?!

Pooonam was sitting by the corner of the crowded coffee shop, wearing an expression that a B-grade actress would emote as 'sad/

repentant'. On closer examination I could see that she had been weeping. Mascara from her right eye was running in a smudged line parallel to her nose, and Pooonam certainly wasn't perfectionist enough to have faked that.

'Life sucks,' she said, as I settled down on the chair opposite her. The French window opened onto an enclosed garden with exotic green foliage. Pooonam was staring at it with exaggerated interest. A stork emerged from behind the plastic palms, and then another. They strutted past us with studied theatrical indifference. Pooonam turned to me, and gave me a forced all-teeth-bared smile. She was wearing enormous diamond-studded hoops in her ears. There was a slash of lipstick on her front teeth.

I was moved by her sadness. I had never thought of Pooonam as an ordinary being. Glamazon, glamiken, whatever it was that she paraded as, she kept her human frailties to herself. Who was she inside?

'Tell me about yourself, Pooonam,' I said gently. 'Your parents, your family . . . where are they?'

'A brief biodata?' she joked, in a voice that was meant to be funny but was full of rage instead. 'Well-to-do Gujarati man gets married to Punjabi loiness. Two daughters, the younger one being me. The elder was a real Sati Savitri, and good at studies too. Me—I had a hard time at school. I was always looking at movie magazines and pictures of flim stars instead of studying. My parents, they split up, got divorced. My elder sister was engaged to a nice Guju boy. Is it my fault that he fell in love with the younger sister? Harendra dumped my sister and married me. We moved to London. My parents never spoke to me again after that, although my elder sister still writes to me sometimes.' She snivelled again, then composed her face into a bright smile.

'But Harendra was rich—I proved my teachers wrong! It's *Stardust*, *Flim Fare* and *Cosmo* that made me who I am.'

She called it 'Flim Fare', not 'Film Fare', but I didn't comment on that.

'His mom—my ex-sasubai—is the Laddoo Queen of Leicester.

Honestly! She sells twenty thousand laddoos every Diwali. She caters for all the desi weddings. But I wasn't cut out to be a Laddoo Queen's daughter-in-law. Besides, Harendra had a roving eye. He cheated on me. We got a divorce and I returned home to India. My mom-in-law was loaded. She gave me a golden handshake. I join an events company in Delhi. Then I join Manoviraj Sethia's company. And then, a repeat of the earlier script . . . As I said before, life is a bitch!'

She looked as though she were hurting a lot, as though it had cost her something to say this. I squeezed her hand across the table. 'Life changes,' I said sympathetically. 'It gets better.'

'Or worse!' she replied. 'But friends get us through. Friends and flim magazines!'

And it's true. It's other people who help us carry on. Women need to hold on to each other, together through the tough times. Pooonam seemed a bit discomfited by her bare-all confessional. She sat up and determinedly rearranged her features. This was the old Ms UmaChand again, the Exocet, ready to aim and shoot.

'Thank God for women friends!' she declared, with such studied delivery that I suspected she had rehearsed the line. 'I have a present for you, Priya my darling!' She scooped the gift out of a swanky bag from under the table and there it sat before me, an utterly elegant white bag. Four letters clinked charmingly from a ring attached to the strap of the bag. They spelt 'Dior'.

'Women friends, handbags and lipstick—that's all life's about, ultimately, Priya!' she said, her smile coming undone at the corners again. 'That's what it boils down to. And yes, there's diamonds, even if they come attached to the wrong men.'

I hadn't rehearsed my lines and didn't know how to respond. A young, attractive waiter was hovering around us. He gave me an attentive look, and threw an appreciative one at Pooonam. She waved him away with a dismissive gesture. She may be hyper, she may be manic, but Pooonam spells glamour and bling. She's got what it takes.

'Let me tell it as it is,' she said. 'I have to confide in someone

. . . and I trust you more than anyone I know! You are sincere and you are kind and you are straightforward.'

That sounded like me. Her sincere appreciation of my sincerity did it. I felt my heart melt, my resistance falter, even as my mind was telling me sternly to watch out.

'That bastard Manoviraj Sethia has taken up with another woman,' Pooonam hissed, in a sudden change of mood. 'First he started off about his ex-wife—that cow Sunita—how he still loved her, wanted to give it another chance, things like that. I told him, No!' She banged on the glass-topped table with a fork for further emphasis. 'NO! NO! NO!'

'NO!' I repeated after her, as though hypnotized.

'You can't keep switching life-partners without good reason! There's such a thing as loyalty! That's what I told the bastard.'

The storks had begun their parade again.

'Loyalty,' she stressed. 'Don't you agree, Priya?'

How could I not?

'And then that bastard forgets about his wife and about me and falls in love with a mere hairdresser!'

'*Your* hairdresser?' I asked, examining her low-lighted locks with curiosity.

'Yes,' Pooonam replied, '*my* hairdresser, Jayanti!'

'You mean *the* Jayanti? *The* Jayanti is your Jayanti?' I exclaimed, impressed in spite of myself. Jayanti is a legend, not a hairdresser.

'*That* Jayanti,' Pooonam replied, a flash of fire in her eyes. 'I was a regular in the salon—even loaned her money to set it up. I would sit there with all that goo in my hair—serum, henna, conditioner, colour, vitalizer, revitalizer, whatever whatever. I paid through my nose for those treatments, Priya. I used to pour my heart out to her. I told her about my problems with Manoviraj, how he wanted to return to his wife again. I told Jayanti about how he went for women who dressed in white, how he liked women with eyeliner over the lid but never under. I told her of how he got turned on by dirty Hindi swear-words. And then this floozy, this whore—she MC-BC'd her way into his heart! Never trust an arms-dealer, Priya. That's all I can tell you . . .'

Her fleshy fingers were playing agitatedly with a softly glowing diamond and with an emerald as large as a knuckleduster. She took off one of the rings and held it before me.

'Manoviraj gave this to me just last week. It's a pink diamond, set in gold and platinum.' A look of lustful joy spread for a second, like a false dawn, across her tragedy-ravaged face.

I sat there wondering what to say. This was clearly not the moment to confront Pooonam with my own suspicions and jealousies. I decided to play it silent: to watch, listen and observe.

'And then he says—I need to get it re-set, there's a problem with the setting.' She was wearing a ferocious snarl now. I could see the lipstick on her teeth.

'There's a problem with *your* setting, you SOB! That's what I told Mr Manoviraj Sethia.'

'When did you find out about Jayanti?' I asked. 'Wasn't she supposed to organize your Botox brunch?'

'Today! I found out today,' Pooonam replied crisply. 'But I've had my suspicions for some time.' Her hurt and rage seemed to have subsided; she was examining her pink diamond with the quiet satisfaction of one who has weathered the storm and arrived at a hard-won calm.

'I was going through Manoviraj's papers—as I always do before he comes into office. Anyway, he's a really late riser, because of all that partying! I have a right to look—after all, I'm a director of Universal Tools and Weapons, not a hairdresser! And I saw that he had invested in her company. 'Hair, Cair and Fair. Big bucks in hope of big bangs. The SOB!'

She looked out of the window again, at the storks; and they looked back, incuriously, at us.

'I asked him if he was screwing her, and he said it was more than that, he loved her. She wears white saris and thick eye-liner like Meena Kumari used to, and has worked on all that filthy mother-fucking language that turns him on. Men are such fools.'

We both shook our heads in commiseration. For a moment our pain and anger merged, before I shook myself out of it. I remembered the lizard and how it had looped out its tongue to swallow the helpless insect on the wall. Pooonam is not my friend, I reminded myself. She is manipulative and predatory, and it's only right and fitting that she has at last got what she so richly deserved.

'What goes around comes around, Pooonam,' I said coldly. 'Remember well the rule of three: what you do comes back to thee.'

Some more coffee had arrived, and so I decided to drink it, rather than flounce off and make a scene. Tears were pouring down Pooonam's cheeks, denting her foundation. Her upper lip was straining to reach down, quivering with an almost frightening intensity. I began feeling sorry for her again.

'I don't know why you are being so cold with me, P . . . P . . . Priya,' she stuttered, the runny mascara now smudging both her eyes. She looked like a Chinese panda bear. 'Nnutasha had warned me that it's a bad month for Scorpios, and she was right.'

That got me worked up again. 'I'm sick of all this superstitious astrology nonsense!' I said. 'Why don't you, for once, take responsibility for yourself? Changing the spelling of your name doesn't change your actions, Pooonam!' Uncharacteristically, I had at last recaptured the high moral ground, and it made me feel incredibly better.

As I got up to leave, Pooonam grabbed the bag and pushed it into my arms. 'You've got to take this with you, Priya . . .' she sobbed. 'It's a symbol of our friendship—even if it's destroyed.'

I looked covetously at the white handbag, at its flawless lines and smooth leather and discreet label. In that moment, in the coffee shop, with the storks watching us through the glass, I knew I wanted that bag. I picked it up, held it tentatively.

'Ok, then, Pooonam. I'll take it—for your sake,' I said, even as another voice inside was urging me not to. Greed triumphed, appallingly, and I left carrying the Dior bag with me.

It's important to be truthful, at least in these pages. To say it like it is, even if somebody were to read this, someday. A handbag is not just a handbag. When, in the time of hunter-gatherers, the female of the family went to the forest to find nuts and pick berries, I'm sure she longed for the most beautiful, best-woven basket of all the women in the cave. No, I'm not ashamed of taking that bag from Pooonam.

BANO WAS HERE, TO GIVE ME A MANICURE AND PEDICURE AND FLOWER facial, and to update me on Delhi gossip. She opened with the slightly stale scandal of the Ludhiana businessman's daughter who had a sex change so she could inherit from the boys-only will. Everybody knows about Vimal/Vimla Puneeet Singh, even I. She/he has been talking about it to the press everywhere. But Bano continued with graphic details of Vimal/Vimla's body waxing routine, until the gory details piled up to an unbearable visual overload under my rose-water-anointed eyes and I begged her to stop.

The Sheherzade of Facepacks then embarked on the tale of the Star-TV-crossed lovers and the jealous politician. This story, featuring a famous TV anchor and an unhappy menage a trois, got my ratings if not my eyeballs (which were covered by cucumber slices now) but Bano stopped short of the climax. 'Arre, Priya didi, you surely know what happened after that,' she said, with a fine sense of suspense. 'The whole world knows!'

She started off next about the income-tax raid on a powerful arms dealer. 'Model Suji's father,' she announced, with proprietary pride. 'My client since childhood. I was doing her waxing–shaxing . . . now my cousin sister is her full-time beautician. And for her sister Suki also!'

I grunted encouragingly from under the piled-up face mask to indicate my curiousity and interest. Bano continued on cue. 'Some staff informer gave a tip off. Income-tax people found diamonds and rubies, and one pooja room full of cash. Even a statue of goddess Lakshmi made of pure platinum—but they cannot take that away.' A note of righteous censure entered Bano's voice. 'We poor people who work hard for a living cannot even imagine how much money they found there—how much gold and jewels!'

So Manoviraj Sethia had been raided. The news left me unmoved. It is an arms dealer's karma to be in trouble, and the Russian submarine deal stinks, or so I am told. Her time up, Bano moved from disseminating gossip to showering practised compliments. 'O Priya didi—you look like a teenager! Kasam se, how your skin is shining!' and so on.

I gave her a larger-than-usual tip, and she left in a good mood.

—

I daydream and panic, alternately, about becoming a mother-in-law. These last few days have passed in a haze—shopping for Paromita's trousseau, planning in my mind for the big day. Whenever that is, for we haven't fixed a date or anything like that yet. I've bought some traditional Kanjeevaram saris, with broad borders, and some Ikat silks and Benarasi tissues. I'll ask Paromita to come with me one of these days, to look at lehngas.

Outside the calm sanctuary of our bungalow, the world is going mad. Important things, big things, are happening. Oil prices are on the rise, as are inflation and anti-government feelings. Bombs keep going off, expectedly, unexpectedly, across the map of India. Detonators, gelatine sticks, RDX, are a part of our daily vocabulary now. But there is something about the heart of Delhi, the wide roads, the gracious trees, the sprawling bungalows, that makes the rest of India and its troubles seem very far away.

Pooonam phoned several times today, a rising tide of hysteria in her voice. 'I have to share this with you,' she said, when at last I took her call. 'My business partner Manoviraj Sethia is in deep shit.' (She always evaded describing him as her boyfriend) 'The papers don't seem to have picked it up yet, but I wanted you to know.'

'Oh that's awful! Unbelievable!' I replied, although of course Bano the beauty lady had informed me already.

Sethia had been raided on a tip from a business rival, Pooonam continued. 'Probably the Khoslas,' she speculated. 'They were being a little too friendly recently. That's always suspicious! Isn't it?'

'It is indeed,' I said, 'one has to be careful with so-called Delhi friends.'

'That's it! Exactly what I meant,' she replied darkly. 'But I'm not talking on the mobile. I'm sure these bastards have it tapped. I'll call from the landline.'

I didn't take the call, and specifically informed the office staff to tell Pooonam UmaChand that I wasn't at home if she telephoned. It's a tested New Delhi dictum that bad luck is contagious, and I didn't want to put our good luck under scrutiny. I didn't tell her about the engagement, either. I'm not crazy, inviting trouble into my life when everything is going so well.

Suresh is leaving for Bhopal to lay the foundation stone for GEECC, a Green Energy Efficient Cold Chain Infrastructure. And Kush is accompanying him. I packed vests and underwear and handkerchiefs for my husband, and two sets of freshly dry-cleaned cream safari suits. His cupboard was a complete mess, the shirts and kurta-pyjamas mixed up, the Jawahar jackets lying crumpled in a corner. I resolved to clean it after I returned from my walk.

It's a new routine I've begun. I intend to look good for the wedding. Chugging along the crowded walking track at Lodi gardens, with the tombs to my left, a vista of palm trees to my right, I was just beginning to get into stride when a familiar figure came into view. It was Pooonam, dressed in a glamorous military jacket, narrow-leg trousers and studded high-heeled boots.

Here she was again, the stealth missile! 'Why are you dressed like that?' I asked.

'It's called military chic,' Pooonam cooed. 'It's all about attitude.' She held me in a detention clinch and awarded me a red lipstick smear on my cheek. I'm sure she was reeking of perfume, but thankfully I couldn't smell it.

'What a surprise!' she exclaimed. 'Let's walk together. Pleeze?'

'Somebody could name a glue after you,' I remarked acidly. 'Or you could be a brand ambassador for an adhesive company!'

'Very funn-eee. Let me give you an update on my life, Priya,' she said firmly. 'Now that Mr Sethia has been raided, the ball is back in my court. The CBI is bad enough but it's always the DEO that's the real killer.'

'What's the DEO?'I asked.

'Don't you know?' she replied, genuinely shocked by my ignorance. 'The DEO are the Big Boyz! The Department of Economic Offences, of course! And that means the Finance Ministry which means Mr So-and-So is paying the high-ups to get at Manoviraj!' Pooonam sounded unduly upbeat about the prospect.

'They are on Mr Manoviraj Sethia's case,' she continued smugly. 'The DEO want to play fill-in-the-blanks on Mr Sweetheart Submarine Deal. And they want to play footsie with Pooonam Umachand. For I, and only I, know the details of Mr Manoviraj Sethia's numbered accounts. I know about the hanky-panky he has done with the high-ups in the Defence Ministry. I have taped his conversations, I have photocopies of files, I have saved every SMS he ever sent me.' Her lips locked into a determined pout: 'Pooonam UmaChand will go for the jugular.'

'What will you do?' I asked, wonderstruck by her balls, her sheer gall.

'Well, Pooonam UmaChand has two choices,' she said, continuing to speak about herself in the third person. A thoughtful note had entered her voice. 'First choice is to turn approver; after all, I have all the dope. Or . . .' and here her voice turned dreamy, even romantic, as she kicked at a stone that lay on our path. 'Or else, Option Two. Pooonam UmaChand might decide to marry Manoviraj Sethia. The time is ripe!'

'What!' I exclaimed, genuinely shocked by this brazen declaration.

'It's known as the Moll-Girls Choice,' she responded deadpan. Just like that. 'Mrs Pooonam Manoviraj Sethia. PMS. How does that sound, Priya?'

'It sounds wonderful,' I said, 'and very appropriate. But I'd really much rather walk alone. You slow me down and I have to do another round. I have to be back soon. I have things to do.'

'What sort of things?' Pooonam persisted. It was futile. She just never gives up.

'I need to sort out Suresh's cupboards.'

'Oh goodie,' Pooonam exclaimed. 'Can I come back with you? I want to see Suresh. I need his advice on this. Suresh is such an absolute darling—always so helpful!'

Suresh. Something snapped inside me when Pooonam mentioned him. Suresh was my territory. He belonged to me.

'Such a darling . . . always so helpful!' I mimicked. Then I took a deep breath. 'Please keep away from my husband, Madame Slut!' I heard myself say. 'And I mean that. Now listen—this park is large enough for both of us to walk here at the same time. In two different directions. And it's chock full of important politicians and bureaucrats. Why don't you bump into them instead, and chipko there, like a cheap adhesive, and leave my husband and family alone!'

Pooonam didn't miss a beat.

'All right then, Mrs Menopause,' she replied briskly. 'I've done my best to be nice to you, but I guess some people never learn.' She executed a little pirouette as she said this, and stuck her tongue out in a schoolgirl gesture of defiance. Then she stepped off the walking track onto the grass, and prettily stomped her way out of my life. Or so I hoped.

'Remember this, Priya,' she said, turning her head back for one last barb. 'We all get the best friends we deserve.'

—

It's becoming a struggle to read the morning papers, and even the computer has begun to strain my eyes. I stopped at the opticians in Khan Market to get my eyes tested. Peering through the double lenses on a steel frame, I watched the letters on the screen change from sharp to fuzzy to sharp again.

DENHFB

PTEFLAU

UNHCADT

. . . Or some such cryptic sequence of letters. My distant vision hasn't changed, but my near sight seems to be worsening. I struggled with the small print on the lit-up rectangle that the optician handed me.

'Beauty is in the eyes of the beholder,' it said. 'What is beautiful to me may not be beautiful to you and what is'—(the print got bigger at this point)—'What is beautiful to your neighbour may not be so to you . . .'

And then everything became clearer, if only for a moment. It's all in the lens, and the focus, and how you view the world.

'New frames!' I told myself. 'Nothing but the best!' I ordered an elegant rimless style, and it's true, the world does look different, without my usual elongated schoolmarmish frames.

MUMBAI AGAIN. SURESH RETURNED FROM BHOPAL BY THE MORNING flight, and we crossed each other at the airport. Dolly has been calling for days now, and I've been evading her. Finally she managed to get across, and informed me that my nephew Tanmay was getting engaged the following evening. That's today. The words spilled out of her like a suburban train speeding on sarcasm. 'You are my sister-in-law, Priya didi, and my husband's only living relative. As blood is thicker than water, I thought it was my duty to inform you. I know we are not VIP's but mere commoners. Still, I must do my duty and invite my royal sister-in-law.' The bitch—trying to put me on a guilt trip. Why does she hate me when I've always been nice to her?

There was no option but to leave for Mumbai post haste. I still haven't told my brother's family about Luv getting engaged. Not yet. I'm superstitious about these things. It would have been nice, though, to have Paromita accompany me. That would make Dolly burn.

I booked a room in the Taj, to establish a clear social and geographical distance between south Bombay and my suburban sister-in-law. With hours of solid traffic between us, I intended to turn up at the engagement dinner, which was in some remote marriage hall in the boondocks, for the briefest possible time. I'd resolved to teach her a thing or two about family duty, and about VIPs.

I sat in my room in the old Taj, luxuriating in the carpeted quiet. Outside, the Arabian sea lapped at the rocks, and gaily decked boats bobbed in the water. Buggys and Victorias laden with happy tourists passed by under my window, the faint clip-clop of the trotting horses climbing up through the double-glazed windows into my room. I felt nostalgic and happy at the same time. I smiled down at the balloon sellers and the bhelpuri-wallahs. Life was good.

On an impulse I telephoned BR. His number was in the tiny diary I carry in my purse, although it is prudently deleted from my phone memory.

'My one and only Priya!' BR exclaimed. 'What a pleasure and privilege to know that you are here in Mumbai, breathing the same air as us mortals!' I was, as always, left speechless by his charm. BR continues to have that effect on me. I gulped and wondered what to say next.

'I am coming over this very minute to pick you up, my love,' he continued. 'I shall see you in the lobby in precisely forty minutes.'

I watched the sun plop into the Arabian Sea. The lights in the boats flickered on, one by one. The sky was dark, but a wisp of pink cloud continued to float on the horizon. Then I realized with a start that BR would be waiting in the lobby. There was no time to fuss—a smear of lipstick, a whoosh of perfume, and I was in the lift, heading down.

He walked into the lobby just as I did. He was limping slightly, but otherwise he looked like the BR I remembered—dapper, debonair, handsome.

'Ah my sweet!' he murmured, lifting one eyebrow in a well remembered gesture as he examined me appreciatively. 'Let us have a drink together and hold hands again.' And then we were in the rooftop bar, doing precisely that. A bottle of Merlot, the sea, the flares from Bombay High—it was as though I was in a dream, in a film script, in a bubble of ageless romance.

'A penny for your thoughts,' he said, in a gentle teasing voice.

A series of inconsequential images passed through my mind. 'Oh, I was thinking of Marine Drive, and the Queen's Necklace, and the traffic lights glittering like diamonds, and a diamond necklace somebody gave me,' I confessed. That sounded quite poetic.

'Well, after all, girls will be girls, Priya,' BR responded, clutching my hand even harder. His fingers felt ancient and clawlike, and I recoiled ever so slightly.

'If you were my wife I would load you with diamonds. I hope that fellow Suresh is doing his duty in that department,' he continued.

'Suresh,' I said, playing with my gold bangles as I spoke, and wishing I had the courage to say 'yes please!' to his diamonds. 'Suresh is an extremely honest politician.'

'Only joking, my sweetheart, only joking!' he replied, squeezing my hand again. We quaffed the wine at a good speed. BR also ate a surprising quantity of crisps and roasted peanuts. I observed him with concern. It didn't seem right, at his age.

'I grow old, I grow old . . .' he recited, in a dramatic stage whisper that was quite effective really.

'. . . I shall wear the bottoms of my trousers rolled.' He looked out at the sea with a melancholy look, then turned to me.

'Who said that, Priya?' he asked. 'I mean, who wrote that?'

'I don't know,' I confessed.

'T.S. Eliot,' he declared gravely. 'A great poet but forgotten. Nobody reads T.S. Eliot anymore. Like me, he too has been discredited and shorn of his greatness.'

I didn't know what to say to that, and so we went back to drinking the wine. BR sent for the bill and signed it with a flourish.

'And now I shall take you for a drive through my city,' he said, and led me, down the lift and through the crowded lobby, into the car. It was an old Mercedes, but not old enough to be vintage. The driver was decrepit and unshaven, perhaps even a little drunk. Something was wrong with the air conditioning, it wasn't cooling properly. I could feel a hot flush coming on. 'Mrs Menopause', Pooonam had called me. I found an elaichi in my handbag and chewed on it. The cardamom made me feel better, at least for a bit.

The familiar streets of South Mumbai. Marine Drive, the Queen's Necklace, Peddar Road, the road to Haji Ali—we drove through restless crowds and fierce traffic, past jogging millionaires sweating on the streets, past silent, joyless prostitutes, past limbless beggars and homeless vagrants. BR was holding my hand again, his fingers were cold and his nails were biting into my flesh. At the traffic lights before Haji Ali, an emaciated woman tried to sell us her last string of wasted jasmine and mogra buds. From the other window, a beautiful young boy with an intense stare held out a bunch of withered red roses. I avoided eye contact with both.

BR had been silent all this while. Suddenly he began talking to me, in a confiding voice, about the Bombay club, and the importance of a level playing field. 'Nobody buys sewing machines any more,' he mused. 'The FMCG market is doing fine, and so is the Milan Mixies segment, but housewives don't stitch their own clothes nowadays. Silly fag fashion designers do the job for them. And the small tailor is a dying breed too—we are witnessing the death of the darzi! Sita Sewing Machines has to concentrate on industrial machines now, for the garment industry, and for exports. That's saturated too. China's done us in! There's just no place left in your modern world for the housewife's friend.'

He fell quiet for a while again, and then he turned to me with a sharp look. 'That fellow you married—what's his name?—Suresh. He's done rather well for himself, hasn't he? You must be proud of him.' I don't think he expected an answer to that, and I didn't give him any.

The driver seemed to know the route he was expected to take. We passed Mahalaxmi, and Parel. The beloved city of my youth. There were people everywhere, spilling out of restaurants, stepping into dark buildings; and suddenly there were patches of empty silent road, alternating once again with the same frenetic pattern of activity.

BR was dozing now, in the seat beside me. His breath fell out in short unexpected bursts. He had let go of my hand, and his head lolled back, as though he were examining the roof of the car with his eyes closed. A sliver of spit glistened at the edge of his mouth.

Then he was awake and all charm again. 'I was dreaming, not sleeping,' he said. 'Now we must return you to your hotel. Pawar, turn the car back to the Taj. And some music, please.'

Farida Khanum's liquid, ageless voice rose like a slow wave around us. 'Aaj jaane ki zid na karo . . .' I was surprised. In the old days, when he was my boss, BR had scorned 'local' music and scrupulously adhered to western classical.

When we reached the hotel, Farida Khanum was still singing. 'Turn this bloody racket off, Pawar,' he shouted to his driver. In the sudden silence, he recited a line of poetry.

'I have heard the mermaids singing, each to each,' he whispered. 'I do not think that they shall sing to me.' And he was gone.

—

Back in the hotel, I ordered a bitter chocolate ice-cream from room service and ruminated on love. Or was it just lust and loneliness? Would I ever see BR again, hobbling into the Taj to hold my hand in the rooftop bar? Do we ever grow wiser as we grow older?

Lately, I've been brooding about love. What is it, what does it do to us? I think of me and BR. Of BR and Paro, and Paro and Lenin. Of Luv and Paromita. Kush and himself. Me and Suresh. I think of Pooonam and Manoviraj Sethia. I try not to think of Pooonam and Suresh. And why should I? There's nothing to think about!

There must be some rules to love, surely. Something that makes the world go round. I thought about it all through that night, even after the clip clop of the horses had stopped and the moon had set somewhere behind the Gateway of India. I thought of this game called love.

Dear diary, I can share this only with you. If anyone were ever to read it, they would split their sides laughing. They would think I was completely crazy, and I'm not. I've tried to be a decent human being and to hold on to my marriage and my duty and my family, whatever happens. So I'm not crazy. But love is. Crazy. I thought about it and came to some conclusions.

The fundas of love are as follows:

Rule # 1: Love Is Not Room Service.

This came to me when the waiter knocked and I answered the door. This ancient Angrezon ke Zamaane ka Taj waiter swept in holding the scoop of bitter chocolate ice-cream with a wafer sticking out of it as if the tray held the crown jewels. Or the Kohinoor. I know I'm rambling, but what I mean is this: Love Is NOT Room Service. It's never delivered on demand. There's no price, no menu, no tip we can pay. No final bill of settlement either, when we check out of the hotel.

Rule # 2: If it hurts, it's probably love. Or if it makes your heart go thump, or gets you smiling for no reason at all.

Rule # 3: It comes and goes. If love stops hurting, it's gone (like any other disease). Or it has become a chronic case and you've got used to the pain.

IF ONLY WE COULD CHOOSE OUR FAMILIES. ATUL BHAIYYA IS OKAY, BUT I find Dolly profoundly depressing. The engagement was a nightmare. It was hot, with the feeblest air-conditioning in the Sabhaghar hall hired for the trans-continental occasion, and some shaky pedestal fans wheezing away. The bridegroom, my nephew Tanmay, appeared annoyingly pleased with himself. Dressed in a dark blue lounge suit, with a yellow silk handkerchief peeping from the front pocket, he paraded importantly among the guests, pausing every now and then to strike a pose for the video cameras which were avidly recording his every move.

As the Most Important Relative, I was given the full nine yards. Mrs Suresh Kaushal was proudly introduced to a medley of curious neighbours and inquisitive colleagues, all of whom rolled out a gratifying display of the middle-class respect for political clout. The larger half of Atul's boss posed for the cameras with me. She searched for her husband to join in the picture, but he was not to be found.

Dolly produced a machine-made gold necklace, which she draped around my neck in full public view. 'Can you wave to the camera please, Priya didi?' she requested ingratiatingly, as she moved my sari pallav around to better display her expensive gift to one and all.

'But where is your daughter-in-law to be?' I asked. I had brought a tanchoi sari for the unfortunate girl, and an embroidered pashmina shawl for my sister-in-law, to atone for what might seem like arrogance (but is actually a biological irritation, like an allergy).

'Oh, Tanya is on the screen—theer before you,' Dolly said brightly. 'Perfect astro- match for our Tanmay. She is NRI, you know. Full green card holder Non Resident Indian.' I could see the dollar signs gleaming in Dolly's eyes. 'Our Tanya she works in Communications Technology company and so her friendly colleagues they set it up for us. Look—she is smiling at us now!'

And so she was, all her teeth on display, beaming through the giant LCD screen. Tanya and her mother and her brother and her uncle, all in faraway Philadelphia, partying across the globe in tandem with us, enjoying a vegetarian engagement brunch. Though it would be dinner time there, or even later. I waved at them, while Dolly continued to fuss around the gold necklace she had given me.

'We thought, why to waste money flying her down here—unnecessary expense-shexpense,' Dolly explained. 'Besides, Tanya's father he is ill, admitted in hospital in ICU theer, so she couldn't come. But he inseested they have a celebration party.' As usual, Dolly was pronouncing 'there' to rhyme with 'here'. I tried very hard not to sneer, but Dolly's failed pretensions, rather more gross than mine, have put me off ever since I've known her. And nothing has changed.

'Here's a shawl for you, Dolly Bhabhi,' I said, as affectionately as I could. (Of course it's always too warm to wear a shawl in Mumbai, but so what?) 'And a sari for Tanya when you see her off screen.' The sari was displayed through the camera to Tanya in Philadelphia, and I was rewarded with a flying kiss. I spent time with my niece, Neha (who looks disconcertingly like her mother) and with my favourite nephew, Prem, the youngest of them all. Successfully evading the attention of Atul's boss, Mr Mittal of the Rani Sati Sewa Samaj Samiti, I rewarded my brother with a quick hug before I left. Then, my duty done, I fled back to the Capital city where I belong. Away from the tacky middle-class enthusiasms of my brother's family. It's not that I'm a snob, and it was nice of Dolly to gift me the expensive gold jewellery, but Delhi does insulate one from the rest of India.

The chaotic under-reconstruction airport in Delhi revealed Lenin, searching for his luggage and looking extremely harassed. The assistant protocol officer from the ministry had been sent to receive me. He saw me watching Lenin. He sized up this oddly helpless-looking man. And with the unerring clerical instinct of the Indian babu to recognize the ruling classes, he homed in immediately. 'I'll get the luggage for you, saar,' he said deferentially to the ragged Lenin, taking charge of the baggage tags.

Lenin hugged me like a lost child. Tears were streaming down his eyes. 'These are tears of joy, Priya,' he explained. He searched for a handkerchief in his kurta pocket and extracted a freshly laundered napkin with an airline logo embroidered on it. Had he been travelling business class? 'I have been trying to call you, every day,' he said. 'But I never seem to get across. I sent you an inland letter, from Chhattisgarh . . . have you received it yet?'

'I'll check with the office, Lenin,' I said, 'maybe it's still in the mail.' I hadn't received an inland letter in years, only chit funds and pesticide advertisements and things like that are communicated through inland letters these days.

'I wrote to tell you how happy I am about the marriage. My bitiya, my little Paromita—she is yours now! Take good care of her, Priya. I know you will.'

'Little Paromita?' I joked. 'Your daughter is a big girl now, Lenin!'

He looked confused. 'She will always be a little girl for me . . .' he said. 'Although it's really me who hasn't managed to grow up.'

Lenin was looking visibly tired. 'When did you break your fast?' I asked concernedly. He had lost so much weight, he looked almost transparent, as though the slightest breeze might blow him away.

'Yes, I did give up on my fast,' Lenin replied indifferently. 'I realized that the denial of nutrition to a dying body was a meaningless act of ego. Or of penitence. In any case, the powerful of this country don't care about whether I, or anyone else, has food going down their gullets!'

'Can I force-feed you at home, please, to celebrate the children's engagement?' I cajoled. I wanted him to be like the light-hearted Lenin I had known all those years ago.

'Of course, Priya, we'll drink and dance like we used to . . .' He smiled the old, familiar smile that I remembered so well. We fixed up lunch for the very next day. The protocol officer had located Lenin's moth-eaten khaki bag. We left the airport together, to go our separate ways. Through the horrors of the under-construction flyover, across dust and disorder and the chaos of traffic finding its own level, I returned to the order and beauty of Lutyens' Delhi, to 18 Dara Shikoh Marg.

I sat with my laptop in the garden, contentedly observing the trees, the neat flowerbeds, the vistas of bougainvillea, the fragrant roses, the sturdy bushes of mogra, the champa-chameli in the hedges. There was a tea tray on the cane table, with a pot of first flush Darjeeling, and a bowl of low-fat puffed-rice *muri*.

Only junk and 'forwards' in my inbox. 'FW: To all my lady friends . . .' the first one read. 'Flour and Water—when you mix the two together you get glue . . . And then you mix eggs and sugar, and you get cake . . . Where did the glue go? NEED AN ANSWER? That's what makes the cake stick to your BUTT. Spread the message, send this to a friend you care about.'

Everything about this pointless forward infuriated me. Why did I need to spread the message? Why were women supposed to constantly obsess about their weight? And which friends could I spread the message to? How many? Why didn't I have more friends? I remembered my lonely childhood. In my schooldays, I had been almost invisible in the classroom, in the playground. My widowed mother had never allowed me to even have a birthday party, although Atul Bhaiyya's *janamdin* celebrations always deserved laddoos, once even a cake. I snapped out of my self-pity. Look where I am now! And Atul is, face it, a nobody. I was pacing around the garden, worrying about my weight, wondering whether I needed to tone up my butt, when the crows descended on me, like an inexplicable premonition.

It was still light, although the shadows were setting in. Suddenly a flapping of wings and a battalion of crows converged like a looming nucleur cloud. They cawed and squawked above my head, engrossed in some compelling crow-conversation. A grey-black underfeather floated slowly down and settled on the hand-embroidered traycloth.

The crows made a beautiful picture: the dusky texture of a Delhi evening, the calm lawn, the still trees, dark forms darting against the unhurried sky. Were they trying to say something, convey their crow-wisdom?

But I was just a blot on the grass; a blob of maroon Ikat sari against the green lawn and white cane chairs. Two circling crows swooped down in a whirr of black feathers. As they pecked at the puffed rice in the bowl, their unblinking eyes met mine. They manouvered once more around the tray, unconcerned by my presence, and flew off.

The phone rang, and of course it was Pooonam. 'I have been trying to find you for days, dearest,' she said plaintively. 'I thought you were my friend.' No mention of the circumstances in which we had last parted.

Resignedly, I opened the hatch and let her into my life once again. 'I'm busy for the next few days. Let's meet again after that, Pooo,' I said. Habit is a powerful force, in friendship, marriage, or even hatred.

'I'm sending you a photograph of myself,' she replied. 'Open it, and you'll understand why I need to see you.'

'Okay, I'll wait,' I said resignedly. There's no one to beat Pooonam when it comes to getting her foot into the door. She is like the glue in the forward.

A blip on my laptop announced a new message, from <pooo@pooonam.com>: 'FW: LOOK AT ME NOW' it said. I scrolled down to the main text. 'I am a victim of sexual harassment, physical abuse and social cruelty. My "friend" has done this to me. The police don't care; they are always on the side of the rich and the powerful. But you are human—if you want to raise your voice against violence to women, phone, mail or message your protest. <manoviraj@hotmail.com> <mv.s@sethia.com>, text 981093 . . . Or sms NO to womenscell 5656 to register your protest. Thank you for your sensitivity and support!'

The attachment opened up to a passport-style picture of Pooonam, with a black eye the size of a fist. I didn't know how to react. Was this hysteria or courage? I called her back, but the line was busy.

'Disgusting!' I spelled out on the keyboard. 'You should be ashamed of yourself, you animal!' and I sent it off to Manoviraj Sethia, on his email id, and his mobile too, with my new Blackberry. We women need to show solidarity with each other.

LENIN CAME FOR LUNCH. HE ARRIVED HALF AN HOUR EARLY, LOOKING extremely tired. He was wearing broken kolhapuri chappals, with the toe straps missing, which necessitated his walking with a quick shuffle. His long grey hair was tied back with a clasp; it looked extremely odd. Hair and beard both seemed unwashed. He was not, in short, easy on the eye.

I had planned an elaborate lunch. Lenin loved aubergines, I remembered that, and got our dour Garhwali cook to prepare some baghera baingan, Hyderabadi style. The paneer and butter chicken was for Suresh, and mutton stew for Luv. Salad and dahi for Kush, who is on a diet again. Some beans and dal to round it off and later, rassogollas and rasmalai for dessert.

We sat together in affectionate silence, though I was a bit alarmed by Lenin's appearance. 'Who would have ever thought . . .' he murmured, 'whoever would have thought . . .' then left the sentence hanging, unfinished. I got the drift of it, and nodded my head in agreement.

Suresh was busy with some important visitors, and took his time to join us. Paromita and Luv were reluctantly persuaded to exit from his bedroom, and we made our way to the dining table. Kush made a late entrance too. Lenin had launched into a rather pointless tirade.

'Urban excess' was the phrase he used. 'Priya, my dear respected

Priya, I sincerely hope that I have not been the provocation for this urban excess. I simply need dal and two rotis, that's enough for me and for all of you too.'

I was offended by his tone and stupidly took issue with him. 'Really Lenin,' I chided, 'we are here to celebrate our children's engagement, and all you can do is take off at a tangent. I thought the farmers that you go on and on about might get more money if I bought more vegetables! And a dead goat means less grass being eaten up, less carbon emissions! So what are you grumbling about?' I looked to my husband, the Minister of State for Food Processing, for support.

Paromita was sitting very still, wearing an inscrutable expression. She adored Lenin, and I was worried that I had hurt her feelings. Luv changed the subject with lightning tact. He told us of the exhibition his friend was putting up. 'This new show is all about the food chain,' Luv explained. 'Very witty, very graphic, radical figurative work. After all, there's always somebody eating something, or something eating somebody! Isn't there?'

Kush was muttering something about the market economy. This might have been the cue for further provocation, but it was Suresh who bailed us out now, embarking on a long explication on processed foods and NGOs and rural women's co-operatives and pickles and mango-crops and social capital. This dull and boring monologue managed to soothe everyone, allowed us to eat and digest lunch in peace.

Lenin didn't eat much, he stuck to dal and two rotis, and a small helping of aubergines. After we were through with the khana, Lenin looked at the rossogolla and mithai with mild disappointment. 'Don't you have any strawberry ice-cream?' he asked plaintively. 'I like strawberry ice-cream!'

'Not today,' I said, 'but the next time you are here. And I promise to serve gallons of it at Paromita's wedding!'

Suresh had to rush back to work, as usual, but I sat with Lenin and the children over a cup of coffee. My samdhi-to-be extracted two betel nuts from his pocket. They were wrapped in tiny scraps of newspaper.

'This is an engagement gift for you,' he declared. 'It was sent by a starving family near Chhattisgarh.' With that, he ceremoniously presented the betel nuts to Paromita and to Luv. The young people accepted the gifts with very good grace, going on about what a wonderful idea it was. Lenin retrieved the scraps of newspaper and put them back into his pocket.

Kush was staring at Lenin in wonderment, as though he were from another planet. He shook his head in disbelief, then left the room.

What an odd set of bipolar parents poor Paromita is burdened with. No wonder she had chosen to approach me herself with her innocent wedding proposal. Well, she would have a normal family now.

Then Lenin began on Dr Binayak Sen. 'Dr Sen is a humanitarian revolutionary. The Sulwa Judum militia movement against Maoists is simply and totally inhuman!' he said, in a soft voice that was almost a whisper. 'A bullet cannot always be tackled by a bullet. The detention of Dr Sen is the grossest and most blatant injustice this country has ever witnessed.' His voice rose, 'We will all pay for it. You'—(pointing at me)—'and you'—(pointing at the children)—'and all of us. Sooner than later, I suspect!'

I wondered what his wife thought of all this. Geeta was after all a minister in the same state government that was arming the Sulwa Judum. But of course I refrained from being provocative. After all, civilized society is about accepting each other's hypocrisies, isn't it?

Lenin wasn't finished with his harangue. He started off again, rather incoherently, about 'class enemies', wagging his finger at us as he spoke. Then he sat up, determinedly; his head wasn't lolling to one side any more. His voice returned to normal, and he seemed more focussed, suddenly. 'The seizure of power by force, and the settlement of the issue by war, is the highest form of revolution,' he declared, quite collectedly. Naturally, none of us knew quite how to react to that.

Paromita stepped in to take charge of her father and wind up what had become an awkward afternoon. She persuaded Lenin to get back to the guest-house where he was staying, to get some rest.

'I want to go for a walk after that,' Lenin insisted, in a feeble, strangely childish voice. 'I want to go for a walk. I must go for a walk today.'

Paromita soothed him some more. 'Of course you will, Papa,' she said. 'I'll make sure the driver and car Mummy has organized will stay on till later. And I'll get you some strawberry ice-cream as well. Mummy rang up this morning to check up on your health. She is really very worried about you.'

Lenin looked at his daughter with something resembling a smile. 'Your mother, Paromita, is a unique person. She is a Stalinist without being a communist.' And with that, he loped out, leaving behind some of the hurt and pain of that other India in my well-appointed drawing room.

I had forgotten to return his jhola, with the photographs and that rambling notebook. I thought again of Banwari, and his double life. Lenin wasn't looking at all well. I was worried about him.

—

Resting comfortably in Suresh's bedroom after dinner (mostly left-overs from the disastrous lunch), I felt an unusual sense of contentment. This, ultimately, was the joy of marriage—watching over each other, watching over our children.

'I feel very sorry for Geeta ji,' Suresh observed, in his most serious lawyer's voice. 'I feel your Lenin has seriously lost his balance and his bearings.'

'He's not *my* Lenin,' I protested, then stopped myself. He *was* my Lenin, and I would stand by him. 'And perhaps he's right. There is something to what he's saying.'

Suresh was diligently checking through his phone messages.

'Have you seen this forward from poor Pooonam?' he exclaimed, genuine horror and consternation in his voice. 'I don't respect men who beat up women. It's the lowest form of aggression! I'm inclined to go give that Manoviraj a punch in the eye!'

Men. Men are like that. I remembered, suddenly, that night when Suresh had hit me. He had punched out at my face, at my breasts, he had shown his male strength. 'I have never hit a woman in my life,' Suresh continued. I said nothing. It had been a long time ago. Suresh and I, we have marked and measured the distance between us. And now, after all these years, I'm discovering that I do care. Belated lovaria. It's nothing new, I told myself philosophically. That's the way things are in arranged marriages.

—

It was six in the morning when I was awakened by a sharp knock on my bedroom door. I opened the door sleepily, rubbing my eyes. There was Luv, in a pink candy-striped nightsuit. 'Paromita's father has died,' he said. 'They found him in the park this morning. Some early morning joggers called the police. My father-in-law. He's dead.'

That was that. I'm practical when it comes to death. Not that I've seen much of it; but we all have to die, I know that, I'm aware of it. You could say that there was a stone in my heart, or that an iron gate clanked shut, closing up my feelings and emotions. I took charge, as though it were a military operation.

Luv left for the guesthouse. The police had arrived there already, they had been alerted by the joggers. Paromita's number had been in Lenin's pocket. With the scraps of newspaper that had held the betel nuts, maybe.

The police were suggesting a post-mortem, so Suresh was put in charge of handling that. We didn't want Lenin's body taken to a mortuary and people messing around with it.

Geeta Devi hadn't been informed. Paromita didn't want to be the one to tell her. She answered the phone on the first ring when

I called. 'This is Priya Kaushal, from Delhi. Your husband Lenin, Avinendra, is dead. He died sometime last night.' It was a bad line, but across the static I could hear the sound of her life shattering, like glass breaking. 'I'm sorry to be the person to tell you this. Paromita is all right, don't worry about her.' I handed the phone over to Suresh, who spoke to Geeta in hushed whispers for a very long time.

Then Suresh and I got dressed and went to the guesthouse. Lenin was lying in bed, as though asleep. His face was peaceful, the lines and wrinkles all seemed to have disappeared. He looked once more like the young, carefree Lenin, who had loved Paro, who had declared himself my rakhi brother.

The staff in the guesthouse, two young Assamese bearers, were in a state of nervous shock. 'But he was okay in the afternoon,' they kept repeating. I got them into the kitchen to make some tea for all of us.

Then it hit me, all of a sudden: Lenin is dead, life has defeated him and dragged him away. It's all been a blur after that. I can't control my tears, but these are on the surface, splashing on this notebook. The real grief is deeper inside, and it's for so many things, not only Lenin's departure.

I remember that Luv and Suresh sat in vigil, and later, Geeta, who had arrived in the chief minister's plane. Somebody must indeed have taken charge of the flowers, of the bier, of moving Lenin to the floor and bathing him. I was breaking down, cracking up, and I came home and took a sedative and tried to sleep. I didn't go for the funeral. Women didn't go to the cremation grounds when I was young. Suresh and the twins handled that. As Lenin didn't have a son, Geeta and Paromita attended to the last rites, and Paromita lit her father's pyre. They returned, drained and exhausted, but with a sort of exalted nervous energy surrounding them.

The sedatives didn't help; I couldn't sleep. I had to say my personal farewell to Lenin. Ghafoor drove me to Nigambodh ghat. We lost our way, at first. Ghafoor stopped to ask cyclists, autorickshaw wallahs, motorists, but all in vain. They pointed out Rajghat, and Vijayghat, and all the rest, but nobody seemed to know or care where the burning ghat was. At last an ancient paan and beedi seller with long matted hair, who looked like an out-of-work ascetic, guided us to the funeral ground. 'Past Inter State Bus Terminus, after U-turn, beneath Peepal-tree,' he explained.

I walked amid the burning fires, searching. There were six pyres alight in a row, some in first flame, others reduced to ash and embers. Luv was seated on a collapsed concrete bench, staring at the river. He led me to Lenin's pyre. The smouldering fire had already eaten away the piled-up wood. I sat with Luv on the broken bench, as the dirty waters of the Yamuna flowed swiftly, silently, by. A light breeze ruffled my son's hair. I could feel my blood, my flesh, in him. It's not so easy to die; we live on in others, in those around us. And so it would be with Lenin and his daughter Paromita, my daughter-in-law-to-be, and the grandchildren she would bear. I thought again of Paro and all that she had meant to me. I had come here with Lenin the night that Paro died. A spark from an unknown pyre had burnt a hole in my sari pallav. It was that night that the twins were conceived. She had lived on in my mind, all these years, her spirit and her fierce, spiteful will. Even in death, I had defined myself by her absence. With Lenin gone, I felt a sense of the gates closing. Paro's ghost was finally laid to rest.

Across the river, a boat halted before a small shrine by the waters. I could hear the bells tolling, and the sharp hoot of a train, as it crossed the bridge across the river. Generations on the move.

LENIN'S GONE. I CAN'T COME TO TERMS WITH HIS DEATH. IT'S ROBBED me of my personal history, of the past we shared, of our youth, all the good and the bad times. With his departure I am older, nearer my own end. Today, Paromita came to see me. She's been weeping, her eyes are red and swollen with tears, but she tries hard to stay in control, even managing a heart-wrenching smile.

'Can we sit in the garden?' she asked. 'Under the sky. I have something to give you.'

So we sat in the lawn, with the black crows and green parrots and the enormous drooping roses. Paromita handed me a transparent cellophane bag. 'Some books . . .' she explained. 'And some photographs. I don't want my mother to have them. They don't belong to her. He would have wanted you to keep them. They are safe with you.'

Lenin's notebook. He had left it behind, that day, with his jhola. I understand how it is with diaries, with old letters and photographs. Why we keep them, why we lock them up from the world—and why we leave them behind where someone will find them after us.

'I really miss him,' Paromita said, hot tears dropping from her eyes. 'I don't think I want to live any more.' She sobbed for a bit. Then she reached for her capacious pink handbag and fished out a bottle of bright red nailpolish. Bending over, she began painting her toenails. 'I have to go with Luv to an art show,' she explained.

What do the young know of death? There were still some tears clinging to her long lashes. I cried too, and my tears had an edge of sweetness to them. We had a nimbu-soda each, with salt and sugar and chaat masala in it. We talked of other things, pointless conversation that cheered us up. Then she left in search of Luv.

I sat in the garden, leafing through the sheaf of photographs, mostly of a young woman. In one, Banwari wore a flower in her hair. Another had her sitting on a rock beneath a tree, smiling broadly. She was posing in a khaki uniform in the next one, but there was no gun. The pictures had been laminated, but were grubby under the coating. A photograph of Paro, a seductive studio portrait with pouty lips and a knowing smile. And another blurred, faded Polaroid picture of her getting into a car, a blue Fiat.

There was a copy of the Bhagavad Gita, dog-eared and heavily underlined. A book of poems without a cover on it. And a little red book.

I squinted at the poems, which were printed in exceptionally small type on yellowed decaying paper. It was 'Leaves of Grass' by Walt Whitman.

Agonies are one of my changes of garments.
I do not ask the wounded person how he feels
I myself become the wounded person . . .

The little red book was just that—the *Little Red Book*. It was the size of my palm, and had a mottled red plastic cover with 'The quotations of Chairman Mao Tse Tung' imprinted on it, and some squiggles of Chinese calligraphy. It was published by the Peking Foreign Languages Press, I couldn't tell in what year. I flipped it open randomly: *On the Correct Handling of Contradictions Among the People: Two types of social contradictions, those between ourselves and the enemy and those among the people themselves, confront us. The two are totally different in their nature.*

Lenin's other life. Or maybe what we saw had been the other one. I thought of Banwari. And Paro. *Agonies are one of my changes of garments.* I liked that. Lenin was like that.

I continued to sit, brooding, in the darkening garden. Ramdhan, the Bihari help, brought me a pot of tea and some hot samosas. There is a kindness about Ramdhan that expreses itself in unsaid ways. The samosas were his way of expressing affection. 'Madame, Ghafoor driver is needing to speak to you,' he said. In English.

I am used to Ramdhan's sing-song Bhojpuri accented Hindi. 'Hindi bhool gaye kya?' I asked sharply. What would happen if every Bihari in Delhi were to begin babbling away in English?

'Dhobiji and I are doing Guruji Rapidest English Course together,' he replied sheepishly. 'But why you are not liking?

'I am liking . . .' I replied, sounding a little apologetic. 'And please to bring Ghafoorji here.'

Ghafoor was in tears. He stood before me, hunched and very still. A line of black kohl had crawled down his cheeks, from his lined eyes. 'They have taken him away,' he said. 'The police have taken my son away. You have to do something, Madam ji.'

'Police! Oh shit!' Ramdhan exclaimed.

'Please speak to me only in Hindi, in future,' I said. 'No more shit.' Then I turned my attention to Ghafoor.

It was the same old story, encountered in the papers every morning. Ghafoor's son Afzal grew up with his grandparents, his nana and nani, in Ahmednagar. He studied for B.Com in Pune, and had a job there, working as an animator in a software firm. He had a group of Muslim friends, whom he met at a biryani lunch home every day. One of the friends, who was from Azamgarh, had borrowed Afzal's phone one afternoon and disappeared with it. The friend was detained, for questioning, after a bomb blast in Satara. And now Ghafoor's son was in custody too.

Ghafoor has five sons. One is in Dubai, and one in Batla, with his in-laws. Two live in the staff quarters here with Ghafoor. Afzal is the oldest from his first wife. Ghafoor handed me a piece of paper with Afzal's full name and date of birth, and the address and phone number of the police chowki where he had been detained. What are called the 'particulars'.

'It's all in Allah's hands,' he said, 'but I know that you will help me.' He spoke with such simplicity and with so much dignity that I was shamed.

'Of course I will,' I reassured Ghafoor. 'I promise I will help you. Whatever Sahib and I can do, will be done.' But it wasn't going to be so easy. I knew that. Wrong religion, wrong time.

When I told Suresh about what had happened he got extremely agitated. 'Terrorism is terrorism, Priya,' he said. 'It's not for me to interfere in these matters. What do you expect me to do? Call up the Home Minister?'

'Ghafoor's son is not a terrorist,' I said stubbornly. 'We'll find him a civil-rights lawyer. I'm sure there is a way out.'

'I'll try,' Suresh said resignedly. I could see that the prospect made him uncomfortable.

Kush reacted differently. He got really upset. 'It's not right,' he insisted, 'it's simply not right. I'm going to make sure something is done.' There was anger in his voice, a quiet anger that surprised me.

I hadn't realized this about Kush—he isn't a coward, like his father. There is a sense of justice hidden away somewhere behind that load of ambition. And I was puzzled and a little hurt again by how much of my sons' lives were a mystery to me. We lose our children in many ways. I understood some of Ghafoor's pain.

—

After Lenin's death, the process of winding up. All the things that need to be done: the half-page advertisements in Hindi and English papers, the crowded prayer meeting, the daily ritual prayers by their family priests. Geeta and her large and resilient family are firmly in charge, on top of things.

My heart goes out to Geeta. It couldn't have been easy to be married to Lenin, however adorable he was from a distance. I'm sure she had loved him too, in her way. As much as Banwari. She looks sadly fetching as a widow, white suits her, and she has lost weight. There are slight shadows around her eyes, but sorrow has pushed her into beauty. She wears no jewellery except for yellow sapphire pendants in her ears, and a man's Rolex watch on her wrist.

'It used to be Lenin's,' she said, holding out her slim wrist to show the watch to me. 'My father gave him this watch when we got married. So it has memories of both of them . . .'

Loyal at last! I've begun to respect Geeta, even more than I did before. Behind her deceptive Indian-woman persona, she has lived on her own terms in what is still a man's world. She has handled her life well; better than Paro. I've been thinking about Paro a lot, she's been on my mind after Lenin's death. I even dreamt of her last night. She had been stepping into a car, as in the blurred snapshot in Lenin's notebook. What would Paro be like if she were alive today? She would have rebranded herself, that's for sure. The new India may even have suited her, but I couldn't help feeling she wouldn't have dazzled us as much now as she did then. Maybe she was lucky, dying young, and living on as a legend in the minds of her friends

Paro and Pooonam: so different from each other, like nylon and silk. Where I was obsessed by Paro, Pooonam is in insistent pursuit of me. Paro was beautiful, always. Pooonam is merely pretty, a glam-sham construct. Unfazed by the world, our Paro had cared for nobody and nothing except herself—or perhaps not even for herself. Pooo is the very opposite, needy, seeking approval. They are completely different, I've decided. Paro had been a triumphant original; Pooonam UmaChand a clever wannabe.

But she's unstoppable. She's been ceaselessly phoning, texting, emailing me, hounding me on Facebook. Finally, I relented and returned her call this morning. 'Darling—I can't live another moment without seeing you!' she declared, moving straight away to the next level of encroachment. 'I must meet you. Straight away. Khan Market in half an hour? Choko-la? Ple-eeze?'

I agreed, partly out of curiosity. I want to check out her black eye, witness her humiliation first hand. A base sentiment and one I wasn't proud of.

Pooonam was dressed, predictably, in pastels—a flimsy chiffon creation accessorized by long strings of pearls and outsize dark glasses. How fortunate for her that big shades were in, I thought to myself.

'You awright?' Pooonam said, looking at me perceptively. 'You look sorta saddened. Your eyes look sad.'

'I lost a dear and old friend,' I replied sombrely.

'Who? Somebody I knew? No time to check the obits recently.'

Pooonam hadn't met Lenin, or Geeta. I hadn't told her about the engagement, even though she had gone off her 'Marry Suki' campaign. 'You didn't know him,' I said. 'My son Luv is engaged to his daughter.'

'Oh rreallly?!!!' she exclaimed, in a sort of horsey little-girl neigh that startled the waiter who was approaching us with a carefully balanced tray. He almost dropped it.

I stared at her in surprise. I had resolved to be kind and sympathetic, but Pooonam's behaviour left no scope for my well-meaning interventions.

'What fun!' she tinkled. 'What fun! Two weddings in a row. We can do all our shopping together!'

'And how's your eye, Pooonam?' I asked, my curiosity rising again. 'What bastards these men can be.' I don't usually feel comfortable using swear words, but I felt the circumstances allowed for strong language.

'My eye?' she replied, sounding surprised. 'My eye is fine—there's nothing wrong with it. I went to the surgeon to have my eyelid fixed, and then I got this allergy! My system is so sensitive, you know.' She tilted her head and gave me an inscrutable look from behind her massive Bulgari shades. 'And I wouldn't say all men are bastards! Speak for yourself, if you please, my dear. But I think most men are just little boys. One just has to handle them right.'

Her lips curved into a knowing smile, and she played dreamily with her long strings of pearls, so large and flawless that they couldn't possibly have been real. Or were they?

'I'm getting married next week,' she announced, 'to the man of my dreams—the one and only man I've ever loved!'

'Who's that?' I wondered aloud. The encounter with Pooonam was not turning out to be as satisfying as I had anticipated. She looked much too pleased with herself.

'Manoviraj, of course,' she replied. 'Manoviraj Sethia. Who else?'

My jaw fell open. I stared at her with goggle-eyed surprise. 'He landed you with a black eye!' I exclaimed. 'You despise him, Pooonam! You want to destroy him!'

'Priya, Priya, Priya' she said amiably. 'How can you *say* such things? It's true we had a lovers' tiff. It's true. Then one of his girlfriends—that slut who is after his money—that gold-digger Jayanti—sent out those nasty emails and SMS messages, supposedly from me. So that Manoviraj Sethia and I would break up! As if!!'

'But I got the message from your number! And from your email ID . . . pooo@pooonam.com!'

'Jayanti hacked my email. And she stole my phone.'

'But you called me from that very same number today, Pooonam,' I persisted, sticking to logic and reason.

'I got it back,' she replied dismissively. 'Just why are you getting into pointless details, Priya? Aren't you *excited* about my getting married? We'll do all our shopping together, for our two weddings. You will be the most beautiful mother-in-law in Delhi. What fun it'll all be! And then Kush can marry Suki, afterwards.'

She leaned across the table to give me a kiss on my cheek. I couldn't help but feel happy for her. We women have to stand together. And in love, the end justifies the means. Maybe.

Pooonam was in shopping mode now. 'Life is just a big sale, Priya,' she said, dragging me across the other side of Khan Market to a boutique jeweller on the first floor. She tried on the latest style in outsize diamond danglers, all astronomically priced, completely out of range as far as I am concerned. Her hair got into her eyes, and she had to take off her Bulgari shades to readjust it. There was an ugly swelling on her perfectly made-up face, the blue and black bruises blending in perfectly with her shimmering green shadow. I turned away, pretending not to have noticed.

—

Still no news of Ghafoor's son. He's gone on leave, in search of Afzal. Another driver has been assigned on duty to me. But Ghafoor turns up every evening, grave reproach in his eyes. 'Kuchh pata chala?' he asks, in the same resigned tone. 'Could you find out anything, Madam ji?'

Kush has been working on it overtime. He even visited Pune

last week, on his way back from Mumbai. The police records are a mess, he says, but he'll crack it.

The lawyer friend, now state counsel, whom Suresh had put on the case, has also said there is no such name in the records in the police chowki where Ghafoor's son is supposed to be detained. He's talking about invoking habeas corpus, if need be. Suresh has told him not to take that route, he'll try another channel.

My husband is a lawyer by profession; he believes in the Constitution, and in Civil Rights—unlike some of the other politicians we know. I can see that Afzal's disappearance is bothering him, too. He's trying to do what he can, even though he's under so much pressure.

Suresh is having trouble at work. Food processing is an innocuous portfolio, it keeps my kitchen stocked in huge abundance with sample packs and gift hampers, jams and pickles and squashes, even after distribution through the platoons of peons and chaprasis and PAs and assorted office staff. But the despair on the agricultural front can't really be denied. Drought and debt are driving farmers to suicide. The Minister for Agiculture was asked about this on television today. The script went like this:

> Interviewer: 'Sir, there have been five farmer suicides in the drought-ridden —— district in the last week. What immediate steps is the government contemplating to alleviate this?'
>
> Agriculture Minister (scratching his head): 'Suno ji—Pharmers are human beings only and all are suffering naarmal human problems—love, break up, deepression. They have deadened themselves, which is offence—but government has decided not to take any action against expired farmers. We will provide free pranayam deep breathing course for deepression.'

This guileless reply has upset sensibilities in the Party high command, and outraged the farmers and development agencies.

There was a sensitization meeting today, for bureaucrats and politicians, about development issues. Suresh has fared well at that, but I knew that he doesn't feel on top of things. And then, contentious new issues like Tesco supermarkets and BT crops keep coming up, or old ones such as minimum support prices, and grassroots marketing strategies, continue to stubbornly resurface.

There are rumours of a cabinet reshuffle. Inflation and oil prices and the iffy yes-no nuke deal has the jai-ho 'we Indians will rule the world one day' atmosphere rapidly de-escalating. There's also Climate Change, and the unseasonal rains that have flooded the capital city. Sometimes, when I go through the newspapers, I start wondering about our country, and what an ajeeb society we are. It's all too jagged really; the highs and lows, and the haves and the have-nots, all seeming to live in mutual ignorance of each other. I mean, maybe it's true that there is a trickle-down effect or some such thing, but more people having cellphones cannot possibly make up for people starving and dying of hunger, and the other half not even noticing. Or so it seems to me . . . Maybe it's Lenin's influence. But then I'm not an economist or a politician or even a journalist. I'm just a housewife, even if my husband has gotten to be an important man.

—

The more I think about it, the more I worry about Kush. He doesn't seem to have any obvious friends, and yet he's out all night sometimes, and surfaces with dark shadows under his eyes and a visible hangover. He wants to be a politician, but his lifestyle is more like a young prince. He hasn't met Suki again, after that dinner they had together. What is he up to? What does he want from life?

—

I think of Lenin a lot. What must it have been like, to be an idealist, to want a just society, to have your heart bleed for the poor and helpless and not to be able to do much about it? I've resolved to keep the wedding as simple as possible. No show, no unseemly extravagance.

But Indian marriages have a momentum of their own, as I'm rapidly learning. First, the struggle with the dates. Geeta is determined not to delay the ceremony.

'Lenin wouldn't have wanted us to postpone it,' she insisted. 'Besides, I don't believe in long engagements, they are potentially very dangerous.' Geeta threw me a significant look when she said this, and I gave her a similar meaningful one in return, though I couldn't understand what she was hinting at or why she was getting so agitated.

Their family priest has suggested two possible dates, when the stars are in perfect conjunction. These are supposed to be the luckiest marriage muhurats in decades. Wedding planners and venues across India have been booked months in advance for the auspicious Thursday and Friday. Geeta wants the marriage to be on the Friday.

We have begun preparations for the wedding. I'm drawing up guest lists, to-do lists, shopping lists. Our dhobi's daughter Dayavati has got an internship with Jerbanoo Darzi, the high-profile fashion designer, and she's planning wardrobes for all of us. Jerbanoo is making a full-skirted velvet lehnga for Paromita at a hefty discount. It will be a Mughal ensemble in royal purple zardozi, costing a don's ransom even after the discount. Not that it bothers Geeta.

Silence from Pooonam for a while. The gossip columns and Page 3 paparazzi are treating her wedding plans like breaking news. I'm glad to have her out of my hair—for as long as that lasts.

Suresh brought me a bouquet of silver-sprayed orchids again, with a card that said: 'To the Mother of my Sons, and Mistress of my Life.' Flowers still make me suspicious; they smell of a cover up. Not that I can smell anything these days. And orchids aren't fragrant, anyway.

'I'm your wife, not your mistress,' I said, as I arranged the flowers in a crystal vase on my dressing table.

'My beautiful wife,' he replied. 'You seem to be growing younger every day.'

My new beauty regimen is serious business—the whole eye cream, neck lotion, under-eye unguent, rejuvenating re-invigorating oxygenating de-pigmenting discipline. A woman is as young as she feels; but she feels as young as she looks.

—

Because of the imminent cabinet reshuffle, I'm glued to the television these days. But there's only the usual stuff, about the Sensex, and bird-hit airplanes, and terrorist threats—most recently, an unexploded bomb in a shopping mall. This afternoon there was news that the Maoists had blown up another railway line. I switched to the Ranjit Verma show. 'Breaking News!' the oily anchor announced, a new octave of excitement entering his shrill voice. 'Socialite falls into Man Hole! City sanitation system breaks down with downpour!' And there was Pooonam, being wheeled away into an ambulance as bystanders braved the rain to stare and gape at her and the camera, alternately.

'Drainage disaster!' 'Criminal neglect of the sewage system!' 'Businesswoman Pooonam UmaChand falls into manhole outside Bank!'

Comic justice! The world is a strange place, I decided, but sometimes there is sense to the strangeness. Curiosity disguised as compassion got the better of me. I dialled Pooonam but her phone was switched off. I searched the channels for a repeat of the news headline, but only the sensationalist Ranjit Verma had considered Pooonam's tumble into a manhole worthy of national news coverage.

The morning papers didn't carry anything about Pooonam's fall. There was too much competing for our attention: Sachin Tendulkar and ten other Indian batsmen scoring centuries against

Afghanistan and being felicitated by the President, Prime Minister and Leader of the Opposition. India announcing its own Mission-to-the-Moon. Bomb blasts in yet another State capital. 'India Flaming', a collage of sati memorabilia, including strips of curtains from the burns ward of a Delhi hospital, fetching a million pounds at a London art auction. Two more farmers committing suicide in Maharashtra. The sensex in free fall. Poonam UmaChand falling into a manhole was yesterday's news. Still, I couldn't resist phoning, to see how she was coping. She didn't take my call, and I sent her a sympathetic sms message instead.

—

Ghafoor's son has returned. Kush helped bring him back. He won't say where he's been, or what happened to him in police detention.

'They have broken his leg,' Ghafoor said sorrowfully.

'Who is "they"?' I asked. 'Do you mean the police?'

'It doesn't matter now,' Ghafoor replied. His son stood beside him. Was that anger in Afzal's eyes, or fear? He was walking with a slight limp. It's so difficult, in these situations, to tell what's what.

LUV HAS BEEN DESIGNING THE WEDDING CARD. HE CAME UP WITH AN odd one-eyed Cyclops, inspired, we were told, by Picasso. 'It's to say that Paromita and I shall see things together, with one eye,' he explained. 'It's very symbolic'.

I used my motherhood entitlement to throw a fit. Suresh joined me in discouraging the modernist vision. 'India is a traditional society,' he argued, 'and marriage is a traditional institution. So it's best to have a traditional card.'

Luv agreed, reluctantly and a little sulkily. We've settled now for a square invitation card in expensive recycled handmade paper, with a brocade border, a gold embossed Ganesha, and an appropriate Sanskrit shloka. Luv added a creative touch to it, grains of rice glued on scraps of yellow fabric on the inside fold.

Suresh wanted to insert a 'No Presents Please' line in the invitation, next to the RSVP. I told him no. What's wrong with a young couple receiving gifts when they are starting out in life? Should they be penalized because they are from a political family? I can't see what's wrong with getting presents.

Kush agreed with me. 'I would want to receive wedding gifts if I got married,' he said. 'Luv will set a precedent and then I might be penalized for it.'

'When, not if,' I said firmly.

It was to be what Suresh repeatedly described as a 'sober, simple affair'. His office staff handled all the invitations very effectively. I had a card specially hand-delivered to Bucky Bhandpur, Junior and Suzi. Bucky sent back a scribbled note, expressing their regrets, and a miniature silver cricket bat in a velvet box.

Poonam is getting married on Thursday, the Very Auspicious Date which is the day before Luv's wedding. 'I'm not taking any chances with my luck,' she declared. 'I'm determined to be happy, whatever the cost. Or consequences,' she told me. The two weddings are scheduled back to back. We have planned an ostentatiously simple ceremony, followed by a dinner reception the same day. No such pretensions for Pooo. There's to be a week of hectic festivities for her. The Page 3 media crowd is already jumping with excitement about her elaborate wedding plans.

There's also news that Pooonam has fallen out with her numerologist Nnutasha. The gossip columns say she has begun consulting Mangaul Warsee, who has moved from Mumbai to New Delhi, presumably because politicians have more at stake, and more hard cash, than mere filmstars.

Suzi Bhandpur's father Manoviraj is getting married to Pooonam, but the Bhandpurs aren't planning to attend the ceremony. Suzi can't stand her future stepmother, so they are all going off on a cruise. The family boycott is compounded by Manoviraj Sethia's older brother Rajan being stuck in jail. Rajan Sethia is charged with bribing defence and income tax officials, and his bail application has been rejected. But Pooonam isn't deterred. 'The lesser the merrier,' she asserted emphatically, in an interview to a Saturday supplement. 'That's my rule for family.'

Her wedding planners have come up with a 'fortress' theme. I guess that works for defence agents. The card has crossed swords as an improvised heraldic emblem, with a rising sun in the background. She insists that this is their new 'family logo'.

'Tell your friend that she must have a motto as well,' Luv joked. I told Pooonam this, when she called me next. (The frequency of her calls is decreasing.)

'But we do, already,' she responded. 'Do or Die—that's our motto!'

The card arrived with tri-colored ribbons and the motto embossed in gold. Some of the snooty sophisticates are mocking her over-the-top taste and cracking private jokes about Pooonam's successful guerrilla tactics in becoming Mrs Manoviraj Sethia. The rest, as is usual in Delhi, simply couldn't care less; they are ready, always, to party at someone else's expense.

It's rumoured that she's hired a hundred firangi white men in smart black suits as guests from the UK, through a casting agency, to add international gora glamour to the festivities. The Blue Orchid hotel in Gurgaon has been booked for five days for the celebrations. It's to be dressed up as a fort, with false ramparts, and cannons and elephants at the gate.

Suresh says we should attend only the final wedding reception. 'It's prudent to keep away from these wheeler-dealers. In the end, they spell trouble,' Suresh said philosophically, with what I guess is the wisdom of hindsight. 'Attending one function is quite enough.'

'Can I attend the hen night?' I asked. I'm really looking forward to that, I've never been to one. It sounds like a load of 'girlz will be girlz' fun.

'Hen night will be a ladies function, Priya, not like a stag night. No harm in your going, I'm sure,' said my husband graciously.

—

'Hen night will be a ladies only function, Priya, not like a stag night. No harm in your going . . .' my husband had said. But Pooonam had warned me already.

'It's going to be a daring evening. I'm not afraid of having fun! We have to show these men who's on top, don't we?' she had giggled. I wondered about what to wear. I was determined to shine, to show her that I was somebody too.

The theme for the party, the 'motto' as she called it, was 'Young and Old—Go for Gold'. I arrived at the hotel-that-was-now-a-fortress in a shimmering gold tissue sari, for which Dayavati had assembled an elaborate pleated chiffon blouse. The banquet hall had been given a makeover. It's walls were swathed in embossed gold satin, and the circular tables had tall golden candles piled around with gold-plated coins. Good-looking waiters wearing shiny gold cummerbunds were tripping over themselves to be helpful. There were a lot of bubbly champagne-like women too, all dressed up and raring to go, looking forward to the evening of their lives. Many of them were a bit drunk already.

Each table seated five 'ladies' and a male host. The men had familiar faces, which I could recognize but not identify. They seemed like fringe models, actors and operators. I was seated with Llilly Vaish, the art dealer, and some society types I didn't recognize.

The host at our table was—hold your breath—the film star Rajkumar Khanna! The Prince of Hearts had been the personification of romance. Women across India swooned at just the mention of his name. The love triangle of *Toote Phool* had the whole of Bombay weeping. I had fallen in love with him then, we all had, a generation ago.

Now here he was, sitting before me in a suit one size too large for him. The brown eyes, tinged with sadness, that I remembered from the dark of the cinema hall, stared soulfully at me. 'Welcome, beuteous lady,' he said, in that deep, familiar tone. 'I am Rajkumar'

'I am Priya Kaushal,' I replied, in a faraway voice.

'My favourite leading lady in *Aakhri Shaam* was called Priya too,' he said. Then he took my hand and kissed it. Ooooh!!!

A short, plump stand-up comic came on the ramp, and strolled about, mike in hand, cracking half-hearted jokes, the sort of SMS jokes that Suresh sometimes receives from his lawyer friends. Not very daring, not very funny.

'And now we will raise a toast to our one and only Poooonam!' he announced, rolling out the extra letters in her name even further. 'To Pooonam UmaChand—who is as cool as vodka, as hard as tequila, warm as cognac, exotic as Malibu, mixed up as cocktail, and special as champagne! CHEERS!' I wondered if he meant 'mixed up' as a compliment.

'CHEERS!' the women in the room echoed, raising their glasses. Pooonam was bouncing up and down, as though she was on something. Her breasts were looking larger too, suspiciously so. There was a sudden roll of drums, and a male stripper sashayed hesitantly into the room. I gasped, in horror and disbelief. I'd never seen a nude man in public, ever, except for sadhus and madmen roaming the streets.

This one was naked except for a narrow gold cummerbund wrapped tight around his groin. He walked halfway through the lit-up ramp and stood there, gaping at us.

The women were whistling and cheering. Nobody seemed surprised or shocked. The stripper was a good-looking young man, with a chikna face and a classically sculpted body, and his you-know-what was enormous, the cummerbund barely concealed it. He began a provocative breakdance, but perhaps he hadn't practiced enough He wasn't managing to keep pace with the music, and seemed to be forgetting the steps. Suddenly he stopped, bunched his hands over the bulge in his cummerbund and gave the audience a pleading look. He crouched a little and began to step back slowly. He looked terrified.

The women roared out their disapproval. 'Money back!' one of them jeered. 'Paise vasool karo!' A desi bottle-blonde glamazon from the next table threw a handful of gold coins at him. They hit the boy between his thighs, and he winced. The audience began pelting him with more coins.

The boy turned back and stumbled towards the stage entrance. The cummerbund was tied in a bow at the back, revealing half his bum.

'No show ... no show!' the women screamed. 'Come back, handsome! ... Back here, you chikna launda!' Llilly Vaish was whistling and hooting too. She threw a champagne bottle at him; it hit him on his knee. I couldn't believe my ears. All these respectable wives and mothers had clearly gone mad. What was wrong with the world?

Rajkumar had been downing his whiskies at a furious pace. I was observing him anxiously; there had been rumours about his alcoholic decline. 'This is shameful' he declared suddenly. 'Let's go backstage and rescue the chap. He's an entertainer, not an animal. Come with me, Priya ji!'

Well, I couldn't refuse Rajkumar, could I? We ducked through the velvet curtain to the makeshift green room. The young man had swathed a towel around his crotch. He was weeping. He smelt of sweat, and fear. He was younger than my sons.

'I am from poor but decent family of Ludhiana,' he sobbed, tears streaming down his cheeks. 'I too have a mother and a sister at home. Mein gareeb hoon magar meri bhi izzat hai ... The agent told me this was an important modelling assignment. He never said that ... that ...' The enormity of his humiliation struck him afresh. 'What am I doing here?' he wailed.

Pooonam swayed in. Her perfectly outlined lips were contorted into a snarl. She took the young man by the shoulders and shook him violently. 'Return the money!' she said. 'Cough up the ten-thousand-rupee advance I've paid you, saala! Now, this minute.'

The boy looked trapped and afraid. 'The agent only gave me six thousand rupees,' he replied. 'And I've spent it.' He held on to his towel as he spoke.

Rajkumar Khanna reached for the pocket of his oversized suit, and extracted a faded leather wallet which had seen better days. He counted out ten crisp one-thousand-rupee notes and handed them with a flourish to the astonished Pooonam.

The Prince of Hearts. He was a real-life hero. Filmstars don't fade so easily, the stardust remains in their style.

'No swear words, Madam, sweet words are always better,' he said to Pooonam, with perfect Bollywood delivery. 'Now here's the money, honey—let this bechara boy go home, and we can return to the party.'

'Don't throw your filmi dialogue at me, Mr Phatichar! Do you know who I am, you has-been?' Pooonam frothed. 'You couldn't even manage to rent a suit that fits. I've paid you to attend the party, haven't I? Five lakhs of rupees for a dinner appearance! You can double that up with a nanga naach, if you want—not that anyone would pay to see *you* naked anymore.'

'No refunds on the box office, Madame,' Rajkumar replied. He was still smiling.

Pooonam took a half-drunk glass of champagne from the side table and flung it at my hero. I could smell her heavy perfume, and the stale cigarette smoke, and the sour odour of spilt champagne. I was sickened. 'I'm leaving,' I said quietly, 'and if you have any self-respect, you will too, Mr Khanna.'

So we left Pooonam's hen party together, me and Rajkumar Khanna. I could smell the soothing lavender notes in his cologne when he kissed me good night. On the cheeks. I didn't tell Suresh the whole story. He wouldn't have understood.

'I didn't like what I saw,' I told him. 'I'm not going to attend her wedding, and maybe you shouldn't either.'

'Rajan Sethia hasn't got bail yet . . .' Suresh replied thoughtfully.

And that, finally, was the end of my friendship with Pooonam. I had woken up at last to smell the coffee. It happened that evening: my sense of smell reawakening, with a kiss, though I didn't realize it in that moment. Suddenly my nostrils had come mysteriously alive again, and I have been sniffing at things in delight ever since—the sweet scent of vanilla in my handcream, the woody fragrance of Darjeeling tea, the intoxicating shower of perfume from the jasmine and raat ki rani bushes around the gate at 18 Dara Shikoh Marg. Even the stink of a truck farting diesel leaves me grateful. And yes, the tender, sad caress of the lavender cologne, which has stayed in my memory.

—

Last evening, I was sitting on the swing in the lawn, listening to the wind. It had just rained, and a mischievous breeze was ruffling the neem tree. I had to attend a heavy-duty dinner, but it was a moment of such quiet peace that I didn't want to let go. From the corner of my eye, I noticed the light in Kush's annexe bathroom switching on and off, on and off, like a lighthouse on the blink.

Kush was away on one of his mysterious research trips—why was the light on? I left the evening breeze to its own devices and hurried over to his room. The door wasn't locked, as it should have been; it was slightly ajar. The bathroom light was still blinking. I switched on the light in his bedroom and looked around. There was a faint smell of incense around. A young man emerged from the bathroom, yawning carelessly. He was wearing only a towel. He examined me with polite curiosity, making me feel somehow like an intruder. We looked at each other in silence. He had a very long nose.

'Who are you?' I asked at last, after several moments of cordial if awkward silence.

'A friend of Kush's,' he replied. 'A very good friend . . . And you must be his mother?'

'Yes, I am,' I replied a bit at a loss about what to say next.

The young man in the towel looked amused by the situation. 'You must be wondering what I'm doing here,' he said, 'but I just stopped by to have a shower.'

'How did you get in?' I asked.

'Oh, I have a spare key to the annexe, aunty Priya,' he replied. 'And I shall lock it up again when I leave.'

Kush's subterranean life has always puzzled me. But he is a grown-up now, an adult. Ask no questions, that's the rule with young adults.

'I was just wondering why the light in the bathroom was flickering on and off,' I said lamely, preparing to leave.

'Oh that,' he replied, offering no explanation.

Who was he? Why did he have a key to Kush's bedroom?

I'VE BEEN WATCHING TELEVISION ALL NIGHT. THE DOMES OF THE TAJ hotel are licked by flames, its stonework exterior silhouetted by bayonets and television cameras. The Gateway of India is in the background, lit by weird shadows from the blaze. I used to drink coconut water there, and eat bhelpuri. I would stare wistfully at the Taj Mahal Hotel, its turrets and gables and carved cherubim, trying to peer behind an open window or a fluttering wisp of curtain at the guests inhabiting the magical grace within.

There's an open window on the television screen, the curtains billowing fire as a desperate guest tries to escape the conflagration. I know that window, I have sat by it and watched the sunset. BR has made love to me in that room.

The camera shifts to VT. Victoria Terminus is CST now. Chhatrapati Shivaji Terminus. Commuters, beggars, policemen, mowed down with AK-57s and hand grenades. The terrorists struck here first, before moving to the Taj and the Trident hotels. I would arrive here, every day, and make my way to the head office. Andheri—Vile Parle—Mahim—Dadar—Churchgate—VT, on the clattering suburban train. When I was young.

The gun battles are still on. It's dawn, yet the nightmare continues. This endless siege, with Mumbai hostage to the hatred and desperation these young men carry in their backpacks, with their stocks of RDX and their almonds and energy snacks. They are dressed in Versace t-shirts and cargo pants. They are as young as my sons.

I'm searching behind the murderous newsclips for the city I loved. A ticker scrolls the names of the missing. The death toll is rising, relentless like the high tide from the Arabian Sea. That's where these young men have come from, riding the waves. I've seen a name on the screen. My mind won't accept it and blurs over the alphabets as they spell out his name. But in my heart, I know, and it breaks. Is broken. BR is dead. He has, I discover later, been shot dead, point blank, in the Trident, sitting at a restaurant table.

My favourite author, when I was nineteen, was Daphne du Maurier. My favourite novel was, of course, *Rebecca*. BR's flat lay like a jewel in the palm of Bombay, and in our dreams we would traipse wraithlike through it. *Rebecca* lies on my bookshelf, still. It ends with a fire at Manderley. 'The sky on the horizon was not dark at all. It was shot with crimson, like a splash of blood. And the ashes blew towards us with the salt wind from the sea.'

There is no one with whom I can share this loss. He is gone, this man who was once my boss.

This man that I loved. Once.

—

There's been a cabinet reshuffle. 'The Aftermath of Terror', as the television headlines proclaim. The ageing dandy Home Minister has been dropped, and the FM has become the new HM. Suresh has been moved from Food Processing. He has been given Independent Charge of Micro, Small and Medium Enterprises. It's a real promotion. I should be so proud of him, and of us. But something inside me has gone numb, a bit of me has died with BR.

Rita Ray has managed to manoeuvre her way up. She's got cabinet rank, and they've given her the 'Child and Women Welfare' portfolio. Oh well.

It is a peculiar city; maybe all political capitals are like that. People from Kolkata and Mumbai are always going on about how elitist Delhiwallahs are. We are suddenly being invited out a lot, and whenever people talk to me, there is a deferential edge to their voices. As though my opinion matters. It's a strange feeling, but I'm getting used to it. And to the constant grief, which hides behind a cloud of anasthesia. This is how Lenin must have felt when Banwari died. He tried to carry on; one has to. I'm doing a good job, too. Surviving.

I'VE RECEIVED A HAND-DELIVERED PACKET. IT DOESN'T SAY WHO SENT it. Inside, wrapped up in a crumpled grey-bordered handkerchief, is a Valentine's Day card, with a blotch of bleeding golden hearts and red roses on the cover. I open it to find a poem, written in purple ink, in my husband's familiar handwriting.

'My dear dear Pooonam, I love you dumb
The nice curve of your hips,
The shape of your lips . . .
I love you true,
Without you I'm blue . . .
Your one and only—Suresh.

The rhymester has expressed his sentiments frankly. I am devastated. In all these years together, Suresh never wrote a poem to me. I recognize how he crosses his t and the plump loop of the m. Suresh has written this poem. To Pooonam. And she has sent it to me, to show her power.

I can't pretend any longer. All the evasions and untruths and half-truths that have held up my marriage collapsed with that silly poem. 'My dear dear Pooonam, I love you dumb.' Absurd, really, that it was not a pornographic mms or video clip or any hardcore sexual misdeameanour that spelt out his infidelity, but a sloppy Valentine's Day card.

It's here, in my hands, with their chipped nailpolish and crinkled crepey skin—this love poem by my husband that has not been written for me. I feel faint and dizzy. The pen in my hand is shaking as I write this. But now is not the time to come undone. I must get a hold on myself. There is to be a wedding in the family. The show must go on.

—

I couldn't get Poonam out of my mind. I needed to fix things, to put a band-aid on it. Who what how could help me out? Not my GK astrologer Goria ji—it was all too complicated to explain to him. I needed a life coach, a psychic fixer. And then it struck me, the way out and the way forward. The fly on the flyswatter. I needed Nnutasha. The new-age mystic, Pooonam's discredited numerologist. Nnutasha knew the territory, she would guide me about the way forward.

How to find her? I couldn't ask Suresh or Pooonam, could I? Searching the net, my expert secretarial fingers located her website. 'Nnutasian Phantasian: THE QUEST. THE GRAIL. THE JOURNEY. Click here to proceed'. It listed two mobile numbers and I decided to call rather than register online, it seemed less incriminating somehow.

The gravelly voice on the other end of the line sounded as though she smoked too many cigarettes, and yet it had a husky aftertaste of seduction.

'Who is that?' she quizzed. 'Could you sms me your name please? We don't accept calls from unknown numbers.'

I wondered who the 'we' was, and dutifully smsed my name. Priya. Just that, not Priya Kaushal. Nnutasha called me back that instant, pouncing on me with A-grade charm. 'Priya,' she said, 'I've been expecting your call all day! You appeared in my morning meditations, and I could sense your need to reach out, to share your pain . . .'

'Oh yeah?' I thought, but a bit of me wanted to believe her.

'You were bathed in a misty aura of sky-blue light. But there was a blur of dark negative energy invading it. I see dark forces at work. I can feel bad bad vibes from a bitch bitch woman.'

I nodded my head in agreement, but kept silent.

'You are nodding your head in agreement but remaining silent. You are nodding, I can see that,' she said, in that husky compelling voice. 'Priya, you need to see me.'

Nnutasha works out of a GK flat, just two lanes away from our rented-out kothi. She lives in Gurgaon. I have to admit she's very charming. Grey hair with streaks of red and purple in it, and red and purple flat colour on her lips, red above, purple below.

'Do you know Pooonam?' I asked. 'She used to talk a lot about you!'

'Do I know Poonam?' she replied, arching her eyebrows and flicking cigarette ash off an imaginary cigarette as she spoke. '*Do* I know Pooonam?! Indeed I do—I *created* Pooonam. Sculpted her out of a fat, desperate, deserted housewife, gave her a new name, a new nose, a new butt. I taught her the black arts, and she tried to turn around and use the tricks of the trade on me! The bitch the bitch.'

Nnutasha lit up a real cigarette, a cheroot, in fact, and began a new tirade. 'I introduced Pooonam to Manoviraj but she didn't think twice of cheating on him. A new boyfriend every week—ministers, bureaucrats, film producers, bank loan sharks—anything she could lay her tits on . . . but I guess you know all that already, don't you, Mrs Priya Kaushal?'

This had been a bad idea. I didn't need this Nnutasian Phantasian in my life. But her mood had changed already: she was suddenly poised, melodious and utterly professional. 'I am a spiritual doctor,' she declared, 'a Sufi soul trained in the forty-two Laws of Universal Love. As a renowned tarotist, cabbalist and certified space healer, I offer services in mantra, yantra and tantra, in colour therapy, divination and aura restructuring. In short, botox for the spirit!'

Nnutasha winked, and held my hand ever so lightly. There was a suggestion of seduction in the way her fingers stroked my palm. 'Bespoke Cosmic Karma manipulation . . .'

I noticed that one of her eyelids sagged over, like an old dog's. Her grape-coloured satin kaftan smelt of patchouli and roses and was edged with a twined gold border. It somehow emphasized her taut posterior, which wiggled provocatively as she crossed the room to light up three fragrant purple candles. She lit up again, bending down to draw on the candle flame, then turned back to stare at me squarely in the eye. The room was filling up with smoke. 'Let's not waste time, honey!' she said, 'Life's too short. I have seven years seven months and two weeks left to live. I know, because I know the count of things. And the fact of the matter is, the numbers in your name just don't add up. I already told your husband that. Become Priyaa, with two 'a's not one, and the world is your acorn. Priyaa Cow Shall—that's who you really are. If you dare to become her. No Pooonam can ever aspire to take your husband away from you, then, . . . If! If you gather the courage to take your destiny in your own hands!!'

So she knew already. Everybody knew. More fool me, for coming here. But the smell of roses and patchouli had done something to me, soothed me somehow. It didn't hurt so much, now, to think of Suresh with Pooonam, maybe Suresh with Nnutasha even . . .

'It's all in the numbers,' she continued, her eyes narrowing, looking suddenly out-of-focus, even as the loose flap of eyelid drooped lazily over her eye. 'It all adds up—every single action, every lie, every fraud, every evil intention—the great auditor in the sky adds it all up.'

'But I, Nnutasha, can fool Him with double accounting. I'll sex up the numbers for you. An extra 'a' and a new 'c' in your name, and the karmic balance-sheet changes. The interest rates go down, and you start getting the most incredible deals from destiny. Just plain logical mathematics!'

She stubbed out her cheroot and lit up another one. 'You for instance are ruled by the romantic moon—number two—and creative Neptune—number seven—while Suresh has the moon, Venus and Jupiter lined up to protect him. His political career will only go up and up and up, especially if you change your name to Priyaa. It will lock your fate to his, and then, together, you will change the destiny of this country. Of the beloved nation, our I-N-D-Y-A-A—maathe mein bin-di-ya . . .' she spelt the letters out in a musical rhythm, tapping her golden Swarovski-encrusted clogs in beat.

I came back to my senses. 'No extra anything in my name for me,' I said, smiling sweetly at Nnutasha as I spoke. 'I am Priya Kaushal and I shall remain her. A rose by any other name would smell as sweet. Shakespeare said that. William Shakespeare.'

She was still humming her Indyaa song and tapping her feet as I stepped out into the sanity of noise and pollution.

I mean, the point is that things are what they are. I am Priya and this is India. Bombay to Mumbai, Bangalore to Bengaluru—does it ever change anything? And then perhaps it does. Ms P UmaChand to Mrs Manoviraj Sethia certainly does.

And I was still hurting, not so much from Suresh's infidelity as his writing a stupid poem for someone else, not me.

The truth. It's a funny thing when it lands like an egg in your face, and you can't run away any more. But that's what I did. I ordered a taxi from the local stand, packed a bag with track pants and a salwar kameez, and set off for Rishikesh. I don't know what pushed me to do it. No Ghafoor, no government car, no husband or sons, or daughter-in-law to be. It was good to be alone, without the usual protective bandobast. Just me, in a taxi, and the potholed UP roads. I felt free.

After we were speeding out of Delhi, having crossed the congested Noida traffic, I sent a sms to Suresh. 'Going to seek blessings of Guru.' I didn't know any guru in Rishikesh, but I didn't want to message him about the Valentine card, it would read much too confusedly against a backlit screen.

The taxi driver was the silent type, addicted to a crackling FM channel which belted out seventies Bollywood hits interrupted by the saccharine musings of the radio DJ. I fell asleep, and dreamt of BR. We were in heaven together, holding hands. I was jolted awake as we reached Rishikesh. I could smell incense, and the scent of the river in the evening breeze. I felt a part of the crowd, and yet alone.

Then I saw him, a thin ascetic man with a stoop. He wore a saffron dhoti and held a wooden kamandal in his hand. A luminous light, like a full-body halo, circled him as he walked along the river bank.

I sort of leapt on him and fell at his feet. 'I need your blessings,' I said urgently, 'and your guidance. I need you to explain what I should do.'

My potential guru looked taken aback. 'Please, Guru ji,' I persisted, 'I need your blessings!'

'Come with me,' he said, in the sort of impeccable English accent a university professor might have. I followed him, and in very little time found myself outside a white building with neon tube lights protruding from it like an antler's horns. We were beside the river, and I could hear the waters rushing with quick but measured intent. My heart was beating fast too, as though, at last, some joyous secret was about to be revealed.

The Guru led me swiftly past a lobby full of people who seemed to be waiting for him, as in a dentist's reception. In the middle of the room was a life-sized gold and marble statue (possibly a samadhi) surrounded by offerings of fruit and sandalwood incense. A giant television screen, playing on mute, aired the current IPL cricket match. I followed him into another, smaller room carpeted in orange. It had a large picture window, which opened onto the river. A moist breeze ruffled my hair, and the almanac that hung on the wall began flapping in some kind of agitation.

The Guru settled down gracefully on a low stool, and motioned to me to be seated on the white silk floor cushions by the wall. He was silent, waiting for me to speak. I didn't know what to say, how to begin. The breeze from the river ceased momentarily, then swept through the room again. The waves were beating against the rocks outside. I began in a confused burst about the Valentine's Day card, and Pooonam, and the three 'os in her name, and for some reason about Paro, though clearly she had nothing to do with it at all. 'I can't love him,' I confessed. 'It was an arranged marriage. I've tried my best to be a good wife.' I didn't tell him about BR, even though I meant to. But that story was over now. He was dead and all that had never happened. 'I have always done my duty!' I said wildly.

He was examining his fingernails, a beatific expression on his face. I had no idea if he had made sense of my outpourings, or listened to any of it. A young priest in a white dhoti peered in and pointed urgently at the clock on the wall. It pointed to nine o'clock. My guru continued to smile and stare at his fingernails. Then he turned to me and looked me in the eyes.

Something passed between us in that gaze. It was as though he had stepped inside me and plucked out some hurt. 'I do not know your name,' the Guru said softly, 'but I shall call you Bhavani, because I see the goddess in all women. You too are a goddess, but you have forgotten your beauty, your strength, your spirituality.'

'But what should I do about Pooonam?' I asked, interrupting his mystic flow.

'The world is full of people,' he continued, 'of Bush and Obama, of Modi and Gandhi, of Shahrukh Khan and Salman Khan. The skies are circled by spy satellites, the earth grips nuclear weapons in her bosom. The sea has secret submarines. Everywhere there is anger and aggression. But what can you do about it? What can most of us do about it?'

The young priest was at the door again, pleading for the Guru's attention.

'What can you do about it, Bhavani? Can you change the world?'

No, I nodded. I could not change the world.

'But you can change *your* world,' he continued. 'Your world, your samsara, is about your family and your immediate duties. You have to fight like a mighty warrior to defend your world.'

Yes, I nodded again. He was right. I had to defend my family, my samsara.

'And what is the mantra when things go wrong?' he continued. 'Shall I teach you the mantra?'

I nodded eagerly, consumed by the guru's radiance, enthralled by his gentle, voluptuous voice. I have a thing about voices.

'The mantra is this: there is no mantra. The mantra is silence.The secret is silence. When things go wrong, be silent, look within, and smile. Troubles pass; the world goes on. As long as you protect your samsara, do your duties.'

The lights went off. The light bulb flickered alive for a minute, then the room was dark again. I could hear the generator groaning, and the smell of diesel, but no lights.

The guru was whisked away by the impatient priest. He left a blur of luminous haze behind him. Alone, in that dark room, I looked at the river, at the half moon that hid behind the clouds. The world would go on.

Returning to the taxi I found the driver still listening intently to old film songs on the crackling car radio. I checked my mobile. No message from Suresh, or the twins. Had no one noticed my absence?

'Find me a good hotel,' I said to the taxi driver. 'The very best.'

We drove up the hill to a new yoga spa resort. I watched the half moon that sheltered behind the clouds, and the river that wound like a silver ribbon through the hills. A spartan lobby and a luxurious bedroom, with wooden floors and soft pillows. I slept the sleep of the dead and awoke feeling as though I had just been born. As the morning mist crept through the hills, I paid my bill, declined the offer of a free yoga session, had some toast and jam and coffee, and set back for Delhi.

—

Back in Delhi, I booked myself into an expensive salon for a complete cosmetic makeover. For an Ayurveda facial. An ultra-rejuve hand-and-foot treatment. A haircolour. And a haircut, perhaps.

When I got married, my aunts had given me a ritual milk and turmeric bath. The local hairdresser had fixed a pin-on chignon, and I had a manicure pedicure and bleach, though the henna on my hands and feet had nuetralized that. But that was a long time ago. I deserved the best now, and I would get it.

At the salon, poring over the shade chart, I decided this wasn't the time for surprises. Chestnut 5.5 again. A French manicure, and the same for my feet. 'Why don't you try something new, Madame?' the hairdresser asked me. He's called Daniyal, and has trained under Jayanti. *The* Jayanti. Pooonam's ex-hairdresser. Manoviraj's ex-girlfriend. 'We all need a change, you know.'

Daniyal is plump, broadfaced, with a plume of green in his hair. His words struck a chord. 'We all need a change,' I repeated to myself, like a mantra. 'We all need a change.' It placed things in perspective. I decided to get my hair lowlighted in a glowing blonde-brown, with speckled highlights in the crown.

A sad-looking assistant deposited a pile of magazines on the chair beside me, all the newest women's glossies. I read a short instructive piece on nail care and the dangers of buffing too much, and gave up halfway through a harangue—'Crash-Dieting: Some Basic Cautions'. Adjusting my specs, I picked up a *Femina*. The staid, trusted periodical of my youth had endured a makeover. It carried precise instructions on 'How to seduce your husband—Again!' I flipped through the advertisements for lipsticks and shampoos and haircolour and tampons. Reading the girlie magazines, you would think it's not enough to simply be born female. One has to work at it, ceaselessly refurbishing and reupholstering oneself and using the exact shade of foundation, simply to remain a woman.

I had a haircut as well, a bold departure from my boring pony tail. Daniyal layered it along the lowlights, and feathered the crown highlights, and gave it volume and bounce. He left some straggly curls to peep out here and there.

On another spool, even though the Guru had moved things to a different plane, I couldn't stop thinking about the Valentine card. 'The nice curve of your hips/the shape of your lips'. What sort of man would use the word 'nice' in a poem? 'Nice' hips??

Returning to the pages of *Femina*, I began reading a story titled 'Silence'. It was about an army wife who discovered her out-of-town husband was having an affair. She went to her Ma-in-Law for advice. The canny old woman quoted a Sanskrit shloka to her. 'Maunam Sarvarth Sadhanam,' she told her heartbroken bahu. 'Silence is always the most effective tool.'

The truth revealed twice, first through a Guru and then an epiphany in a women's magazine. 'Maunam Sarvarth Sadhanam.'

An Indian Woman is a goddess with many arms. One arm might wield a battleaxe while the other guilelessly holds a tender lotus bud. Red lacquer for my fingernails, and my toes too. I was a mighty warrior defending my Samsara, my world.

—

Switching on the TV, I found myself watching *Omkara*. It's a Bollywood version of *Othello*, except that it's set in the UP badlands. There's something about Bollywood and the Bard of Avon that always works, maybe it's all the coincidences and melodrama.

I had studied Shakespeare for my Correspondence Course BA degree. '*Othello*, A Quick Guide' by Dr Ramji Lall. I remember this line I read in the kunji version of the play: *That handkerchief did an Egyptian to my mother give*. I felt like Othello, only the opposite, if you know what I mean.

The dhobi presses our clothes in the servant quarters. There is another ironing board in the verandah behind the kitchen. I took the grey-bordered handkerchief there, and ironed it carefully. The steam iron hissed out surrogate tears, but I continued smiling. I returned to our bedroom and placed the handkerchief in the middle drawer of Suresh's wardrobe, along with all the other handkerchiefs.

As for the red-and-gold embossed Valentine's Day card with that pathetic poem about hips and lips, I stored it in the clear plastic folder I keep in my cupboard, along with all the other important and unimportant things that crowd my life.

—

Ghafoor's son has set up a footpath stall in Chandni Chowk, selling bootlaces. He came to see me last evening with his father. They brought me a box of sweets, a kilo box of Habshi Halwa and a steel degchi with kewra-scented sevian ki kheer, to thank me and to celebrate Afzal's new start in life. And the wedding in our family.

'Bootlaces?' I wondered. 'Who buys bootlaces in this day and age? Is that still a good business to get into, Ghafoor bhai?'

He assured me that it is, and that a lot of people buy bootlaces, still.

I wondered about Afzal, and what he was really up to. It's difficult to trust anybody anymore.

TODAY, THE DAY BEFORE THE WEDDING, A SPECKLED SNAKE SLITHERED across the back lawn and settled beside the swing. It was sunning itself sleepily in the grass when the mali discovered it and raised an alarm. Soon, everybody at 18 Dara Shikoh Marg had ventured out to observe it and comment on its species, length and purpose of visit. The secretaries, the PS and the PA, the security guards, the drivers, the dhobi and his family, the malis, the servants and sweepers and chaprasis, all the (human) denizens of the bungalow, hovered and stared from a safe distance at the coiled serpent.

No one knew how to lure it away. Killing it was out of the question. Kush emerged from the annexe and suggested that I locate a snake charmer.

'Snake charmers aren't listed in the yellow pages, son,' I snapped, and returned to the house to telephone Suresh for guidance. Safe in the shabby splendour of Udyog Bhavan, Suresh processed the information about the serpent in our garden. He asked me about its size, colour, and where in the lawn it was sunning itself. Then he fell silent for a while.

'Well, it sounds like a good omen,' he said finally. 'A snake is the symbol of power, of Rajayoga. Place a saucer of milk before it, Priya. Who can tell? Now that I've got Independent Charge . . .'

I married a rational man, but the illusion of power has undone him. I returned to the back lawn, fretting about which saucer to use for the milk to be offered to the snake. The mali had in the meanwhile displayed heroic initiative and persuaded the snake into a jute gunnybag. The security gaurds helped him carry it away, tied up to a pole which they held horizontally between them.

—

The morning of the wedding. I woke up early, and sat on the cane sofa in the verandah nursing my first cup of wake-up tea. There was Kush, in striped blue pyjamas, ambling around the lawn, his tousled uncombed hair like a halo around his face. I hadn't noticed how long it had grown around the edges, though he's balding prematurely over his forehead.

He was looking troubled, I thought, but his face lit up when he saw me.

'Come and sit with your mother, Kush!' I called. 'We found a snake in the garden yesterday. You shouldn't be walking barefoot in the grass.'

He settled himself beside me, stretching out his legs and examining his bare toes as through some deep mystery resided between them. His feet are shaped just like Luv's feet—twin feet, though the resemblance reduces as the gaze wanders up. His toes had bits of damp grass on them.

He looked up, and his brown eyes met mine. It was as though he had let the shutters down.

'I'm not like brother Luv,' Kush said suddenly, in a quiet voice. 'It's time you knew. I'm not straight. I'm made differently. Not that I'm ashamed of it, but I thought you and Papa might be. When I was a boy, I wasn't sure. I liked girls, even fell in love a time or two. Now I know who I am, finally, and I'm not troubled by it. I think I'm in love too, and I'd like you to meet him, Ma. Who knows, we might be getting married next.'

I looked at Kush with a new way of seeing. My son. Was he the man or the woman in the relationship, I wondered. It seemed to matter that I should know. But I didn't ask.

I've spent all the years since their adolescence worrying that one of my sons would tell me just this, that he was my daughter. Another time, another moment, I don't know how I would have handled it. But our eyes had met, and we had looked deep into each other, somewhere. I observed my son's toes with the grass still sticking on them, and his tousled hair, and I wasn't shamed or embarrassed by what he said.

'I'd like you to meet my boyfriend Akshay,' Kush said shyly.

'I'd love to meet him,' I said, 'or perhaps I have, already.'

Kush twiddled his toes some more, trying to shake the grass. 'Don't tell Papa,' he said. 'I don't think I'm ready for that, yet. But you know, and you understand.'

And I do. We are each of us different, and still the same, somehow. Everybody needs to be loved and reassured, and not to be mocked or scoffed at.

'You marry who you want,' I said to Kush. 'I'll stand by you.'

'Don't *you* have any secrets, Mummy?' Kush asked. 'There must be bits of you we don't know about . . .'

I shook my head and smiled. 'No secrets, son,' I said. 'I'm just an ordinary housewife.'

—

The shaadi. Luv weds Paromita. A forest of fairy lights illuminates the garden at 18 Dara Shikoh Marg. There we are, me and Suresh, smiling at our children, at our guests, at each other. A moment in a photograph, to be framed and cherished forever. It all seems very distant, the wrong end of a pair of binoculars.

'I want to tell you something, Priya.' Suresh had said awkwardly while we were getting dressed.

'What?' I asked suspiciously. My feet were hurting already in the bronze high heels with jewelled toes and a serpent's bite which I had rashly undertaken to wear.

'You were the most beautiful bride I had ever seen. And you still are. Beautiful, I mean.'

Bullshit. 'I love you true. Without you I'm blue,' I replied, with a toss of my spunky new haircut. He looked anxious, but let it pass.

The pundits had calculated the exact auspicious muhurat for the wedding ceremony. There was confusion as Geeta's watch was running ten minutes ahead of Suresh's. I fell into a panic, I wanted desperately that the stars be right for Luv and Paromita and all that awaited them. The world was never an easy place, and the way it is changing is absolutely terrifying. My son and his wife and the harsh crowded world which is their inheritance—I want Venus and Mars and all the rest to be in alignment for Luv and Paromita.

At the kanyadaan, Suresh and I sat beside each other while the priest poured ghee into the sacred fire. I could feel the heat of the flames warming my cheeks. The newly weds began the saptapadi, the seven sacred steps. There were tears in my husband's eyes, from the smoke perhaps.

'An Indian marriage is a sacrament, not a contract,' he observed, in his lawyer's voice.

I married Suresh without even knowing him. A stranger descended from a black-and-white photograph and a folded-up sheet of paper with a horoscope scrawled upon it. I thought of all the years that have passed since. It needs grit to hang on to a marriage. Had I lived life, or had life lived me?

—

Clicking through the wedding pics on a digital slideshow. Luv looks like a young royal, wearing the solitaire earstuds which had belonged to Paromita's grandfather. The bride radiant in her purple Jerbanoo Darzi couture lehnga, with multiple strings of pearls and a heavy jadau kundan set that had belonged to her mother. Geeta resplendent in glowing white silk.

The young man in the towel—Akshay—is in the photos too. He's dressed in an elegant shervani and a purple jamavar stole, a hint of kohl around his eyes. Kush introduced us, but I didn't get to talk to him in the middle of all that din. I'll surely meet him again, soon.

The Prime Minister couldn't come, he is on an official tour. But the Speaker was there, and the Leader of the Opposition, and all of Suresh's cabinet colleagues. The new home minister in a spiffy Nehru jacket. Rita Ray draped in an exquisite Dhakai silk hajar-booti sari. Didiji turned up as well, to everybody's surprise, swinging her large trademark handbag. Rajkumar Khanna came too—I had made sure he got a card, and he arrived in a blue pintuck kurta, looking dapper and young. The diplomatic corps were in attendance, including my secret heart-throb, the charming Pakistani High Commissioner. Large tracts of Madhya Pradesh and Chhattisgarh seemed to have descended on Delhi with the baraat. Some businessmen, and yes, a few arms dealers as well. Everybody was there. Except Pooonam, that is.

A troupe of folk artistes from Geeta Devi's constituency performed on a side stage, and their songs could be heard under the noise and the chatter like a soulful undertone.

After the VIPs dispersed the children got busy pulling down the festive marigold strings. Rajkumar sang old filmi songs for us. Jimmy Batata jumped onstage and performed a vigorous

Bollywood-style number, waving his red handkerchief to the beat of a Helen number. Geeta Devi danced too, and Suresh joined in, and Luv and Paromita, Kush and Akshay, and all their friends. The staff were all dancing as well—the dhobi from the quarters, the driver Ghafoor, the warring PA and PS. Also Dolly and Atul, whom I forgot to mention, and their son Tanmay and his American Desi bride Tanya (in the flesh this time).

A remix rhapsody in every sense of the word.

Luv's ex, Monalisa Das Mann, arrived, adding a thirteenth-fairy drama to things. She strode through the crowd, small and proud, escorted by two tall young men with shaven heads. Luv explained to me later that they were not her boyfriends but a steady couple. Monalisa's friends sang a rap number with very strange wordings. This is how it went: 'Me wan' girl like soni koodi/Me wan' girl like sweet jalebee.' Miss Das Mann filmed this on her handycam and Luv tells me it's up on YouTube now.

Shriela Shetty described the wedding as a 'political alliance' in her weekly column. She referred to Geeta Devi as 'the lady politico to watch out for (oh, and man does she wear one!)' This was followed by another item, announcing the 'secret' engagement of Sukita Sethia with the cricketer Gaurav Negi. Well!

One of the local Hindi papers published the iconic photograph of the bride Paromita's father: Lenin atop a donkey, leading the March of the Powerless. The photograph had caught him at an odd angle, and a trick of the flash had given him a halo. That is how I shall always remember him, with a strange light shining behind his long hair and straggly beard and a determined expression on his dreamy face.

And I didn't forget my promise to him, about the strawberry ice-cream, which we served in gallons, along with the laddoos and rasmalai.

—

The night after my son's wedding, I couldn't sleep. The sound of gunshots echoed in my head. I saw fire billowing out of a window near the sky, an overcast sky, and I heard someone speak my name. I woke up, just before dawn, and walked through the garden, examining the remains of the feast. There was an acrid smell, as though of rubber burning. Overturned glasses were strewn about in corners. Two trampled bouquets of flowers—lilies and gladioli—lay in the middle of the lawn. I found a pair of abandoned high-heeled gold sandals, as though somebody had tossed them off and forgotten them, walked home barefoot, perhaps. Separate parties of cats and dogs were attacking the leftovers in the dustbins. Marigold garlands were lying forlornly in the grass, pulled out by children, the petals torn to shreds.

There was a sense of desolation, of things left behind. I sat alone in my suddenly-strange lawn, feeling both happy and unhappy. I thought of BR, without sadness, without regrets. I picked up the trampled bouquets and carried them inside, and put them in a bucket in the kitchen.

—

Scraps of gossip about Pooonam's wedding. Dhruv Desai was at the reception with his Brazilian girlfriend ('Gaurav Negi's marriage has changed his life,' Shriela told me later. 'This is his fourth girlfriend in a row, and his bum is now unmarked, I'm reliably informed . . .' The Brazilian girl was clicking cute tourist snapshots of the elephants that the wedding planners had parked before the fake-fort facade of the Blue Orchid Hotel. One of the tuskers, who didn't like flashlights, picked up Desai's squeeze with its trunk and swung her down again. She wasn't hurt, miraculously. But it's a good story, the sort that amuses Delhi.

Pooonam has the luck of the devil. Spunk too—I'll concede that. She's devoted to her new numerologist, Mangaul Warsee. Together, they are obsessively regrouping the multiple letters in her name. Her new fortune fixer suggested she add yet another 'o' to it, but even Pooonam thought that was too much: she's considering changing it to Pomona instead. Last heard, she had changed the name of Manoviraj Sethia's company—it's called Universalle Hand Tools and Weapons, now.

Perhaps it's working. The Sethias had filed a case against an Indonesian firm about infringement of copyright on its Moulded Teflon bullet-proof apparel. The arbitration went on for ages, and then it went against them. Well, Universalle has won the appeal now, and many millions of dollars in damages. What is it about luck and Pooonam?

—

The young people are off on their honeymoon, they left for Bali yesterday.

Monalisa Das Mann has sent me an advance copy of her novel. It's called *The Unsuitable Bride* and it is about a weak hypocritical young man and his manipulative mother. Sounds familiar?

Her book is being hyped as 'a truthful tell-all on why arranged marriages suck'. Better to read the book than have her as a daughter-in-law, I say. It has a strange cover, with a shiny reflecting mirror on it. The dedication reads, 'To Aunty Priya: The Desi Mom-in-Law from Hell I never had, and the living inspiration for this book.' Maybe I can sue her.

There's a handwritten note inside, and some pressed flowers. 'The nice Indian lady act doesn't fool anyone. Take a long hard look in the mirror. You are not good, only lucky. Respectfully—The Unsuitable Bride.'

I did just that—went to the mirror in the verandah and took a long hard look at myself. The blonde highlights with the creeping white roots. The creases around my eyes, the gently sagging skin. 'Ms Menopause' Pooonam had called me. Well, one can learn to live without tampons. I turned to the mirror again, and flashed myself a determined smile. I might look worse.

Then I took Monalisa's novel and threw it into the dustbin that

Suresh had brought back from Nagaland. We all need to carry on, to defend what's ours.

ONLY A FEW SHEETS LEFT. I'M NEARING THE END OF THIS NOTEBOOK. I've been neglecting these pages, now that I'm getting used to the keyboard, where my legendary secretarial skills have resurfaced. Facebook is beginning to take over too, and I'm thinking of starting a blog.

Even General Pervez Musharraf, the ex-President of Pakistan, is on Facebook. I've asked him to be my friend, but he hasn't responded yet.

—

Luv and Paromita plan to stay at home with us, at least for a while. They will shift 'later' to our old house in GK, where Suresh and I lived before moving here. Jimmy Batata has commissioned twelve paintings on the colour red from Luv. It's to be made into an art calendar, and he's received a mind-boggling advance. I must start painting too, one of these days.

Somehow I feel closer to Kush than ever before. Luv has Paromita, and Suresh has . . . I don't want to think about what or who Suresh has. But my son Kush, he's vulnerable and a bit of him needs me still, I think.

After the wedding, we went together, all of us, Luv and Kush and Paromita, to an orphanage in Chandni Chowk with boxes of sweets and baskets of fruits and packs of crayons. The children smiled and thanked us, and I felt good about that. And I thought of Lenin, and how he would have scoffed at this act of easy feel-good charity. But in the end, every laddoo counts.

I stood there with my sons and daughter-in-law. The girls and boys in the orphanage were lined up before us, subdued, obedient, watchful. Behind them, a portrait of a gleeful, toothless Gandhi. A bunch of kids in the back row began giggling. A scuffle broke out, and the teacher tried ineffectually to discipline them.

Something in that moment suffused me with hope. We will all bungle through somehow, my India and Lenin's India, and Jimmy Batata's. And Nnutasha's Indyaa, too. We'll survive chaos and confusion, ideology, numerology and corruption. Today and the day after. India will carry on.

'It all works out in the end—usually,' I said to myself, loud enough to be heard.

'Mom! You've lost the plot—as usual!' Kush teased.

How do I explain that there is no plot? There never is. The hidden harmony of a housewive's tale is structured, day after day, by simply carrying on. In the storyboard, the drama and heroism lie in the everyday aggravations, the small triumphs of daily life. And the happy endings—they tiptoe in so stealthily that you may already have left the multiplex by the time they show up on the screen.

Acknowledgements

As always, to Ravi Singh, tolerant friend and critical editor. Sarnath Banerjee and Bani Abidi for the wicked lines on the cover and frontispiece, Bena Sareen and Maithili Doshi for their perfect aesthetics.

Gratitude for patient and impatient readings and inputs to Meru Gokhale, Shivani Sibal, Kavita Pande, Sonia Faleiro, Shubhda Khanna, Kanishka Gupta, Bill Haseltine and Marie Brenner.

Anu Kakkar for her excellent editorial suggestions. David Godwin for his enthusiasm and sage advice. John Elliot for the idea of returning to my first novel, *Paro*. To all the readers who kept Paro alive in their hearts and bookshelves. And to Mrs Priya Kaushal, for hanging in there.

Read More in Penguin

PARO

Dreams of Passion

Namita Gokhale

'A watershed in Indian writing in English'
—The Indian Express

'Sexually frank . . . witty and genuinely irreverent'
—The Week

'*Paro* is a magnificent creation'
—London Magazine

First published in 1984, to both notoriety and critical acclaim, *Paro* remains a social comedy without parallel in contemporary Indian writing. Paro, heroic temptress, glides like an exotic bird of prey through the world of privilege and Scotch that the rich of Bombay and Delhi inhabit. She is observed closely by the acid Priya, voyeur and obsessive diarist, who lost her heart to the sewing-machine magnate BR, and then BR to Paro. But he is merely one among a string of admirers. Paro has seduced many: Lenin, the Marxist son of a cabinet minister; the fat and sinister Shambhu Nath Mishra, Congress Party éminence grise; Bucky Bhandpur, test cricketer and scion of a princely family; Loukas Leoras, a homosexual Greek film director; and, very nearly, Suresh, the lawyer on the make whom Priya has married . . .

Read More in Penguin

SHAKUNTALA
The Play of Memory

Namita Gokhale

Namita Gokhale writes grippingly about death, love and lust'

—Khushwant Singh

On the ghats of Kashi, a sightless priest directs a young woman to come to terms with an earlier life that binds her in the eternal cycle of death and rebirth. In the life she recalls, she was Shakuntala—spirited, imaginative and adventurous, but destined, like her legendary namesake, to suffer 'the samskaras of abandonment.'

Original and heart-rending, *Shakuntala* enthralls in its vivid portrayal of the tragic life of a woman whose desire to live on her own terms is thwarted at every turn by circumstance and the age in which she lives. Namita Gokhale combines her extraordinary gift for storytelling with history, religion and philosophy to craft a timeless tale that transcends its ancient setting.

Fiction
Rs 300